Praise for *The Folly of Loving Life*

"You can stop searching for the next brilliant collection of stories because I already found it for you. Monica Drake's *The Folly of Loving Life* is a tour de force... Lovers, lives, relationships, revelations, hilarities and horrors criss-cross in these linked stories, all in Portland. Monica Drake, you've captured my heart again, you've caught the laugh halfway up my throat and suspended it there until it becomes a lump of recognition: our humanity is the thing that nearly kills us while it's saving our lives."

—Lidia Yuknavitch, author of *The Chronology of Water* and *The Small Backs of Children*

"Monica Drake's narrators are like detectives reporting on the weirdness of the world."

—Arthur Bradford, author of *Dogwalker* and *Turtleface and Beyond*

"Like *Red Cavalry* and *Jesus Son,* this is a landscape lit by lightning: a scatter of fragments—stories and vignettes—that comes together in the reader's mind to form a grand whole, in this case a decades-long portrait of a place and a time and a family. This book is correctly pissed off at important things: the failure of those who ought to love you, the disappearance of those who do, the damages of family and war, a girl with "Fry-o-lator" written on her arm in burn scar. Funny and sad, moving and daring, required reading for all of us in the Northwest and well beyond."

—Kevin Canty, author of *Where the Money Went* and *Winslow in Love*

"These are some of my favorite Monica Drake stories. No one else writes as wryly, or close to the bone."

—Chelsea Cain, New York Times best selling author of the novels *One Kick* and *Heartsick*

"I've been waiting for Monica Drake's story collection since 2005 when I discovered her short fiction for the first time. From the opening words of *The Folly of Loving Life*—"You, lamb chop, my sweet, my dearest dear—" I knew I was in good hands. The wait is over and it was worth it."

—Mary Miller, author of *The Last Days of California*

Praise for *The Stud Book*

"*The Stud Book* is a spirited group portrait, full of the messiness of life. In it Drake reminds us, earnestly and poignantly (and in *echt* Portland fashion), of the importance of community: whether you conceive or not, you need a mate, a family, a best friend—or better yet, a gang of them. As Drake notes on the book's very first page, not even an earthworm—or, in her visceral prose, "a hermaphroditic sex organ burrowing through dark earth"—can go it all alone."

—Emily Chenoweth, *Portland Monthly*

Praise for *Clown Girl*

"Riffing on language and revising her jokes in nervous flurries, Nita is the most endearingly teary clown since Smokey Robinson. Grade: A-"

—*Entertainment Weekly*

THE FOLLY OF LOVING LIFE

STORIES

MONICA DRAKE

Direct inquiries to: info@futuretensebooks.com

Future Tense Books
PO Box 42416
Portland, OR 97242
www.futuretensebooks.com

The Folly of Loving Life: Stories
Paperback ISBN 978-1-892061-77-5
Limited Edition Hardcover ISBN 978-1-892061-79-9

Cover design by Bryan Coffelt, photo by Barbara Drake
Interior design by Ryan Brewer

For my parents, Barbara Drake and Albert Drake

CONTENTS

DEAREST DEAR: LETTER IN A CULVERT

You, lamb chop, my sweet, my dearest dear—

I'm sorry I put your good shirt in somebody else's free box. The box is on the corner of NE 13th and Prescott, if that helps. Yes, I tried to throw your shoes over the wire in the middle of the night. They landed in the street, there was a car coming, and I took off.

Here's the thing though—earlier, in the day, I'd hauled our bottles and cans back to recycling. The smell of the recycling corner has an effect. It's horrible, all rancid beer, mold and soggy cigarettes. But you know me, I'm sentimental. That smell reminds me of the day after a good bender, tight friends, house parties, and it makes me want to gag, but I always want to crack a new beer too.

Out of *sentiment.*

It's the way a dumpster on a hot day smells like our vacation in Acapulco. Remember that? I love the smell, because of us. Because of you.

So I was taking cans back, and this woman comes up with a shopping cart full of bottles. We're moving in unison, hands feeding the machines, me all Diet Coke and 7 Up, and her all beer, beer, beer, the sun on our backs. She's got these dyed blue chunks in her pale hair, and she's wearing baggy overall cut-offs. Maybe I was staring. You know how I am—a people person. She looks, and says, "Hey honey, want some extra pots and pans? I'm moving. It's good stuff, I'm trying to get rid of."

I say, "Free?"

We all know what moving is like. So she wants to give things away instead of packing, right? I'm here to help.

She says, "Pretty close by. Walk with me, and I'll hand you this whole set of Revereware. A tortilla maker, too."

We're still feeding the machines, talking over the clank and rattle, that rancid beer party air, and I say, "Sure." Because I'm thinking of you! How you love homemade tortillas.

Then her phone rings. She takes the call, and says, "Dude. Check. Five minutes."

She tells me, "I've got to get back and fix this tattoo."

I say, "You're a tattoo artist?" Her arms are laced with funky drawings of field grass, and briars.

She says, "Not really. Just ink, stick and poke."

I'm crazy about the sound of those words. Why do I like words? I do. Her eyes are pale and kind of nutty, and she's pretty but not perfect, a chipped doll in the wrong clothes, but she's giving off pheromones or something, it makes me dizzy, and right away I like her a lot.

We turn in our receipts, change mountains of bottles into a few bucks, and I follow her down the street, and we stop at a double lot, with a barn that's been made into a house that looks more like a fort. It's cool. There's a giant evergreen kind of tree standing in the middle of the lot. It's just one lone tree, but that's enough to remind me of trees I knew when I was a kid, childhood, and I feel okay about all of this. The door on the barn-fort is open. There's a guy holding his arm like it's in a sling, except it's not, and his arm is patched with dried blood.

She and I, we go in.

She straightens his arm, holds it. His skin is caramel, he's strong, sinewy, and a mess where he's tried to write something on his body. Heathens? Heathers? I can't exactly read it. She smacks his arm, and he pulls it back. She says, "Nothing I can do with it 'til that swelling goes down."

He says, "Who's this?"

Meaning me.

She says, "I'm giving her the pots and pans, right?" Like it's some conversation they've already had, and I want to remind her about the tortilla maker. Because of you, my bonbon, my pumpernickel, my pet. I am thinking of you as I step into their dark, cool cave.

The guy presses his bloody arm against the wall. He's got long, shagged out hair, a narrow nose, and a thin smile, and maybe he's a little high. I could see him as a drummer, behind a drum kit. Maybe he sees himself like that, too. He says, "Can I do you?"

He's got a sewing needle in his hand, with ink-covered thread wrapped around the needle. When he takes his arm away from the wall, a ghost of the word he'd tried to write is left in broken lines on the white paint. *Heathens,* I'm pretty sure now. Definitely Heathens. He's a man willing to live with his mistakes. He says, "I'm good, I just can't do myself."

The woman lifts her patchy blue hair, raises her head to flash the blood-flecked thorns of a rose where they've been outlined in dark ink on the side of her neck, drawn dangerously over those arteries.

I say, "I'm okay."

This guy must be giving off pheromones too though, because I start to like him right away. I like him so much—I kind of want to chew on his split ends, clutch his red, bloody arm. He says, "Starts with an OxyContin." He's plying me. On their cluttered coffee table, there's this mess of pills.

The woman picks one pill up and says, "These are oxycodone."

"Same thing," the man says.

The woman rolls the pill between her fingers. She says, "Not really. One is time released, one isn't. One's long lasting—"

"Don't be a drug nerd," he says and bobs his chiseled, vulture head on a thin neck, smiling.

Maybe I give a come-hither glance at the meds? I don't know, but the guy's inspired enough to say, "I've got Xanax."

A blue pill pulled from his linty pocket says Xanax in all caps, right on it. I'm being careful, reading it first, right? Maybe this is where I go wrong.

I look for a glass of water. He's got a motorcycle, an old BSA, and he's taken it apart on newspaper in the kitchen. I say, "Nice."

He shrugs. "250 cc. Old school."

While that Xanax creeps into my blood, we get into this motorcycle thing. He says, "You look more like you'd handle a 350. Maybe 550." He passes me an open bottle of Maker's Mark, and that's even more of a party than the rancid beer smell. It reminds me of a night, you and me, at the coast, sleeping in our sleeping bags, zipped together, on cold, damp sand, surrounded by sedges, grass and rushes, those evenings of trying to sort out one from another. I have this surge through my veins. The woman crowds beside me, both of us against the fridge, thighs side by side. I'm taller than she is.

I melt into this crazy shy riot of need. To cover what feels like blushing, I say, "Like a fine wine, I'm made to be drunk," and take a swig.

She drinks, too. Turns out the guy has another bike in back, a 350, and offers to let me ride it, and I say I don't ride a bike like that, only a dirt bike, and he says, "Same basic deal," and his words come out soft and sleepy, and he's older than he looked at first, they both are, and the burn of whiskey always makes me happy, and I know I said I'd be home, Darling, but things like this come up.

What I feel in that kitchen is the way humans are so flawed and so perfect, and I want to share bodies. You know your old dog? That's how I feel—I want to climb on people, breathe their breath, lick the inside of stranger's mouths.

I don't know these two, but who do we ever know, really, past the skin? How do we get there?

By the time I take the bike outside, we've been in the apartment so long, I forgot the sun would still be shining, but there it is. Lo and behold. Totally, setting sun in my eyes.

I think even the motorcycle is giving off pheromones! I like it so much, right away. My head is thick, my hopes are up. I put my legs around the bike, the engine gives off heat, and it moves fast enough to make decisions for me. When I try to brake, it makes the wrong decision—I twist my wrist back, notch up the throttle, hit a cement parking strip, then go over a walkway into the back side of a Laundromat, and fall, slow-motion, all of it.

So when I saw you, and you asked where I'd been those days, and I said, "Out," what I meant was, *out cold.*

I wasn't trying to be uncommunicative, sweet thing. Sometimes our greatest strength is our greatest weakness, right? I couldn't leave once I came around. They made sure I stayed up all night. We kept each other up, we took care of each other's bodies. I'm home now. You didn't need to leave. I hate it when you storm out. That's why—the shirt?

Yes.

Your shirt was dreamy. It's probably still there. Nobody would notice what a good shirt it is, and how it smells rich with the human scent of you.

Your shoes? I'm not so sure if they'd still be around.

But I'm here, with stolen pills for you, in my pocket, ready to make you homemade tortillas. This is love! This is how love works. Call me back.

THE ARBORETUM

Things started to change once Colin and I signed the papers. We bought a piece of land that locals had unofficially named the "The Arboretum." It was a narrow lot off the highway, in the shadow of Mt. Hood. An hour's drive outside of Portland in ordinary traffic, it was two acres of trees and an old farmhouse left standing in a strip of otherwise commercial development. It was a forgotten place, nearly abandoned, where the world was unpaved and luxurious, half-wild, rich with field grass and damp earth. I fell hard for the orchard out back. The orchard was like a cluster of people; each tree found its own posture. The pear trees and cherry trees were shorter, with stunted branches. The apple trees were particularly graceful. They cut against the sky in dark lines like ink drawings, sexy and decadent, with gnarled, long branches bent under heavy fruit.

I'd teach our children to draw out in the orchard, as we raised our babies in this earthly paradise.

They would know each tree like close relatives. The house would haunt their dreams when they grew up. I still walked the halls of my old childhood house, at night. Who doesn't? It would be a gift, to raise them close to the earth. Plus, there were no rules in that rural stretch—no covenants, restrictions or home owner association out to extract a fee and force us to mow what passed for a lawn.

I was ready to leave the city behind.

A tire swing made from a skinny Model-T tire hung on a frayed rope. I pushed the tire, let it rock back and forth. "Look, girls!" I called out. But they'd fallen behind, making their way through tall grass and over rough ground. They were still so young. I couldn't imagine what more a kid would need than land, fresh apples in the fall, and a good swing.

A crabapple sprawled like an open hand just beyond the side door of the house, fanning out in a collection of deep magenta and nearly black leaves. Another tree, tall and slim, was dressed in orange bark that peeled like sunburnt skin. There was a dense stand of pine in the way-back, and every tree called out as a friend, sentient and welcoming.

The front yard was shadowed by a weeping willow whose branches spanned a stretch wide enough to hide a whole stripped Cadillac behind a cascade of leaves. I know, because I walked through the lush curtain of its dangling yellow branches. When I first passed under the tree, the leaves were impossibly thick. Just beyond that drape though everything opened up and there was space to stand. It was a natural fort. And there was a Caddy, probably parked in the shade on some distant summer day, against the tree's thick trunk now. The air smelled rich with dirt. I leaned over the foggy glass of the Cadillac's half-open window to peer in. A cat sat in the front seat, only it'd quit being a cat a long time before. It was a skeleton tangled in the springs, where the seat had rotted away while the bones waited for a driver.

I wasn't afraid of a dead cat. My kids would learn about nature. They'd learn biology and the natural sciences, as outdoor children running free. I wanted that house and land so badly that I could feel myself almost drool, a tension set in my jaw, overly eager.

Colin was still deliberating.

I said, "Am I the only one excited about this?"

"Baysie, sweetheart," he said. "No need to be impulsive. Let's think it through." He pulled the top off a long strand of wild grass, surveying the lot. That grass looked like his tiny kin: tall and thin, hair standing up in tufts, blowing in the wind.

Impulsive is a relative term. I think faster than he does and know what I want.

We walked the yard. Next door, there was a pet store and supply called Celebrate Pets! Maybe in the spirit of domesticating live animals, enough cement and asphalt had been poured to flatten the wilderness. On the other side of the land was a Chevy dealership with a dismal, permanent party made out of balloons and flags. Behind the property line in back, more fields were marked with surveyors' stakes. Orange ribbons fluttered like neon moths, defining the boundaries of future roads and dirt pile-covered lots. Developers had leveled hills, filled in swamps. You could see what was coming: hell.

The Arboretum was the commercial equivalent of landlocked, cut off by parking lots. It was undividable land for county zoning reasons. It wasn't on the public water system either, and depended on its own old well. So it was an oversized, irregular lot with an aging orchard, saddled with a possibly problematic well and a decrepit house. It'd been on the market forever. It was our dream! I said, "You can barely see the pet store through the trees."

Colin said, "Deep, baby."

But I meant it. I laughed and threw a twig at him, giddy with the idea of escaping the sweep of Manicured Estates, those bland homes, most of what we'd found on the market.

Here, Mount Hood loomed tall and gleaming, covered in snow, off to the northeast. We were a thousand miles above sea level, above Portland, but below Mount Hood's gleaming rise.

Our toddler, Lucia, picked blueberries from a few bushes planted in a line. They'd probably been well tended once. Now they'd been let go. Feral blueberries! Such a dreamy thing.

"What is this?" Lucia said, in her tiny, stuttering voice. "What is this?" It was one in a handful of new phrases. The whole world was a mystery to her. I loved to enter into her questions, letting the world be new. Overgrown grass rustled. Bugs jumped and clicked, and the Chevy dealer's flags snapped in the wind. Everything hummed. I turned around, and said, "Nessie?"

Our nine-year-old. "Nessie!" I called again. But there was only Lucia's voice, still asking over and over, "What is this?" She poked her stick toward the grass.

Colin said. "A broken old barrel." He kicked something hidden.

I felt my heart quicken, my hand clench. I said, "Where is she?" The sun flashed against the leaves of an apple tree, there was nobody else around, she was gone. I yelled her name. Screamed it, really. Then Nessie dropped down from a tree into a patch of sunlight. She swung down from a low branch, using one arm and her other elbow against the crook of the tree, like a little monkey, then beamed our way and held her shirt like a basket that she'd filled with misshapen, black-spotted apples.

The first time we looked at the house, the owners were home. The woman was ironing a skirt in the kitchen. Her long, frizzy black hair was damp and gave off the sweet scent of apricot shampoo. She'd drawn on a hard line of red lipstick that caught in the wrinkles of her lips. The man took framed photos off the wall as fast as he could move, and pretended not to notice us making our way around the place. They weren't supposed to be home. I did my best to keep the kids from touching the family's shell collections and penny jars. The woman ran her iron up and down like she was murdering that skirt. The kitchen was outdated but comfortable, with adorable wood counters worn through years of family dinners. I touched the marks from a knife, where I imagined generations of mothers had cut loaves of bread and roasted meat, scarring the old wood.

We heard there'd been an earlier offer on the place already, but that offer was contingent on getting through zoning restrictions. The other interested party wanted permits to knock down the house, cut down the trees, build a big box store.

Our grey-haired hippie real estate agent, Mikal, tested the canned-pea colored stove by turning on a burner. The woman glanced at him, touching her kitchen, and she worked her jaw like she was chomping imaginary gum. The real estate agent knocked on a piece of paneling. He whistled gently to himself. The woman said, "We just want to get out of here," half-answering a question nobody had asked.

The realtor rocked up on his toes, in his Birkenstocks. He said, "We can lock up, if you've got somewhere you need to be?"

She gave a snort and pulled the plug from the wall so hard the cord snapped back and hit me in the arm, like a little viper. I rubbed the spot on my arm where the cord had snapped against my skin. Without apologizing, she took the skirt into the bedroom and closed the door. I think she meant they wanted to get out for good?

They had their lives—miserable, maybe—and we had ours out ahead of us.

Late that evening they accepted what Realtor Mikal called our "aggressive offer,"—meaning aggressively low because we were aggressively broke.

Colin and I went back to the house with an inspector. It was a strange house, modified over the years. I'd guess it had started with a Sears kit house in the late 1890's—the kind of architecture that was shipped out in a few major pieces on the train, then built up using local wood. It didn't have a full basement, but it had a half-cellar. The cellar doors were out in back, slanted against the ground. The inspector bent and worked a board out from between the handles on either door, removing a kind of make-shift lock meant hold the doors down, and keep them together. That board also looked as though it was meant to keep anything from getting out.

He opened one, slowly at first, until he flopped it all the way back on loose hinges, rattling the old metal parts and tossing off a rush of dried leaves. Then we walked, one after another, down broken cement steps, through spider webs and dust. The air grew colder with each step.

All basements are underground, but the raw edges of that cellar let the earth be more apparent. It was a little more like caving, or being buried alive. The inspector shined a flashlight over rough beams. Stalactites of sludge dangled from rusted pipes where drain water seeped through. I put my hand on a supporting post.

"Perfect wine cellar," Colin said. I took his arm and gave it a squeeze. He'd chosen optimism! I recognized his generous gesture, because that cellar was dismal. He knew how much I wanted the house.

The inspector said, "The pipes'll have to be replaced. You only got one bathroom, and it's on the ground floor, so that's not too much. And you might have some mold underground, little rot."

The low basement ceiling was a network of pipe, wires and beams. But upstairs, there was a bay window! Upstairs, there was light and air, and outside, those trees.

"There's a tree growing too close to the foundation, this side. Needs to be cut down," The inspector added. His flashlight hit a supporting post where my hand rested, and caught the gleam of high-gloss red paint. I moved away, brushed dirt off my palm.

What we saw, in the circle of light, was writing, like graffiti. It said, K-I-L, down the post. The "L" trailed off as though whoever wrote it had fallen.

Colin poked a finger through a rusted pipe overhead, and a glint of stained water dripped on his wrist in a dark smear.

I asked, "Kill?"

All Colin said was, "Put it in the addendum that they have to redo the pipes." He wiped his arm against his jeans.

Walking back to our car over the potholed driveway, I stepped on something like a root, or a piece of ginger. I picked it up, ran it between my fingers. It was a little metal man, a soldier, with a rifle raised to his shoulder.

I said, "Hey there, little guy. Attacking, or defending?" I spit on his face, to wipe the dirt away. His skin was painted the color of cantaloupe, with no eyes but the smallest dot of a round, red mouth. It was old, a kid's toy, and I wondered which war that soldier fought in the particular child's lifetime. Because the toy was metal, maybe made out of lead, I guessed it was older, before plastics took over. Korean war, or Vietnam, maybe. But there were always wars and soldiers. I put him in the crook of a dwarf cherry tree. I said, "He'll be our sentry."

Colin was already in the car. Trees swayed around me. Their leaves shook with a thousand hands rustling hello.

In the day, the Arboretum was fantastic. It was a refuge. Everything grew so well there! In the house, a line of avocado plants, each in its own coffee can, grew like mad. Even the girls were growing fast. Lucia banged the screen door open and closed, open and closed, and I watched as she toddled into the yard like a big kid now. Nessie, waiting for the school year to start, would take a book and climb into the apple trees as though into her own private, friendless, Eden.

Her hair dropped down like silken moss. She harvested pitted apples, brought them in and lined our windowsills.

After dark though, the floodlights of Celebrate Pets! and the Chevy dealer found their way through the forest. They bled through the curtains and stained our walls with the bleakness of a commercial wasteland.

The first night in the house, when I finally got Lucia to sleep, as soon as I slipped out of her room and back to our bed, she woke up. She didn't cry, but called, "Mama? Mama!"

Barely moving, barely breathing, as though trying to hide from our baby girl, I looked to Colin for help. "Your turn?"

"I teach in the morning." He turned the light off on his side of the bed. It'd been a long week for all of us, moving in. But true, he was the only one who had to face his college classes in the morning, teaching basic chemistry and forensic science.

I went down the hall. "Lulu!" I sang. "Time to slee-eep… Are you lying down?"

Her room was bright with the cool, electric white of floodlights. It took another hour of whispered lullabies to get her back to dreamland. Then, once I was back in our room, immediately I heard footsteps and shuffling. Lu was tall enough that she could climb out of her crib, but never had before. Colin was snoring, his mouth open against the pillow, looking so tired. I listened longer, without moving. The sound of a radio, pop songs and muffled D.J. voices, drifted through the walls. It was Nessie's radio, maybe.

Finally, I padded down the hall to where she slept in a nest of blankets. A helium balloon bobbed in the shadows. In her own room, Lucia was red-cheeked and warm, asleep too.

It wasn't the first time I'd heard one of my children's voices long after they'd gone to sleep. It was the echo of words I'd been listening to all day, mixed in with the apprehension that one of them might need me. It was a mother's curse, to hear those little voices, so dear, so dependent. I tried to sneak out of her bedroom, but right then Lu woke up. She turned over, sat up when she saw me moving away, stood, grabbed the bars of her crib and reached her hands.

She said, "Nonie!" Her old baby word: *Nursing.*

I said, "What?" and smiled back at her. "We gave that up, remember?" Back at the old house, she'd stopped being a nursing baby. "You're a big girl now."

But I went against every how-to book and picked her up. I couldn't help it. Moving was hard on a toddler too; our attention was always divided. She had to adjust to a new room. "My darling," I said, into the silk of her hair. I carried her into the hall, then down the long, narrow flight of stairs. She and I walked the house, looking for the radio, that whisper of static and voices. Sometimes I could barely hear it. Other times, it was almost loud. It was quieter downstairs than up.

"We're in paradise, Sweetie," I said. But there was a voice talking to us, in our house, that buzzing bee of late night chatter and pop songs. I held Lucia's hand, then whispered, "It's in the cellar." The plumbers had left a radio on. The sound must've been traveling through the heat ducts.

I held her close when I opened the back door to step into the dark yard, and hesitated over those cellar doors. They were heavy, but I could lift them. I'd take a careful step onto the dark cement stairwell, go down and turn off the forgotten radio.

I bent to work the board out from between the two door handles.

What if somebody were to come along, close the door and put that board back? We'd be trapped.

We didn't have immediate neighbors, only businesses and fields. There was nobody around, except Colin. I imagined him looking for us in the morning, assuming we'd gone for a walk, heading out to work while I pounded on those old splintered wooden doors in back, Lu in my arms.

The Arboretum's overgrown grass rustled. The branches of an apple tree shook as though an animal had jumped from one to the next. A wind slid up my thighs, in the night, under my short nightgown. Crickets and cicadas made a sound like distant laughing children, the laugh track to a sitcom that didn't end. It was like the grass was full of tiny giggling babies. So beautiful, and creepy. The tire swing dangled like a noose. I bent for the doors, reached the cool metal handle, and worked the board off, while I held Lucia tighter and tried not to jostle her. She put her trust in me. An apple fell and knocked against the ground hard. The sound was enough to send me inside again, heart pounding. Lucia was so warm, I held her tight, to calm my nerves now. Was it an apple? Something had dropped. The yard was a soft, unrelenting velvet black. I peered back out though the screen door. Finally, I saw two golden, glowing eyes emerge in the dark. A possum blinked and was gone.

The next morning, there was dirt in the freezer on our ice cubes. There was an ant frozen in one ice cube. The metal soldier from the driveway rested on a bed of ice. He was wrapped like a mummy in the wide, blue rubber band from last night's broccoli. I took him out of the freezer, held him by two fingers. "Nessie?"

"What?" She seemed genuinely surprised, mouth full of cereal.

I said, "Don't put toys in the freezer, especially when we don't even know where they came from."

She rolled her eyes, pointed to Lucia, who was busy chasing a slice of banana across her tray.

I said, "Lu can't reach the freezer."

Nessie and I looked at Colin. He was on his way out, already tired, already uptight and late for work, teaching at the college miles away.

The mail we got at that house came with all kinds of names on it. There were old-fashioned names. Hilda and Daisy. Emil, Evan, and Cleeve. Not Clive, but Cleeve. Then there were a few strangely religious names, like somebody called Gloria Deo. I stacked the mail and wrote on each one, "No longer at this address."

Stray cats came around, and I fed them. I put out scrambled eggs and canned tuna and once our leftover spaghetti. Some of the cats were feral, and ran, but others came right up to me. There was one with rich fur and sagging teats who looked like she'd just had babies, and I felt particularly attached to her. I'd put tuna in a bowl when she came around, run my hand over her fur, and she'd purr, and I'd say, "Oh, mama's hungry today," never quite sure if I meant her or me. Never sure if I meant hungry, or some larger longing that was growing in my belly like a third child.

After a few nights of Lucia waking up every hour—nights spent singing songs, telling stories, watching the weeping willow sway out the front window, its crown against the moon—I couldn't take it anymore. I needed to sleep. I'd go back to work too, eventually. I had to find work first, and so had to find the momentum to go out looking. I asked Colin, "Can you take a turn?"

He said, "I haven't been sleeping either." The darkness under his eyes showed how true that was. He said, "I have class in the morning, then meetings all afternoon." He put a pillow over his head. When Lulu cried, Colin pressed the pillow harder against his face like he was trying to smother himself.

The next day, I tacked worn-out towels over Lucia's windows to cut the light, but still light seeped through the thin spots. We couldn't afford new curtains, because we'd spent all our money on the house. That night, when she called for me, I called back, "Go to sleep, darling."

Beside me, Colin sat up in bed. He practically yelled, "Okay, that's it."

Then Lucia called out, "Mama!"

I sat up too. In the old place, she was a good sleeper. I said, "I can't tell if this is normal, some kind of age-related separation anxiety, or if she has an ear infection—"

He cut me off, saying, "She doesn't have a fever. She's fine. Let her cry it out."

"Maybe she's getting her molars." I could still hear the radio over the sound of our own tense voices. I asked, "Do you hear that radio?" It was playing Jeff Buckley. I could hear him crooning "Hallelujah" on repeat, off in the distance.

I hummed along, then sang a few lines.

He turned his back, tossed against the bed. "No. I don't hear anything."

How my dear Colin packed so much contempt into the name of the song was beyond me. He said, "You should get out, once in a while. Leave the property."

"I hate to leave our land," I said. It was true. Everything I needed was there, on those two acres.

During the day the whispering radio was masked by the freeway and the car dealer's speakers, but each night it came back. Between the static, I heard words. I heard the d.j., but also faraway voices saying, "Mama" and "Lu."

I always had to check, because what if one of the children needed me? I'd open Lulu's door, then Nessie's. I drifted down the halls and stairs on creaking floorboards. I tried not to wake Colin. He'd wake up anyway, and he'd glare. We were a system, one gear turning into the next, awake all night—mother, children, father, radio. That radio bothered me. I was the only one who could hear it. One night, I said, "Can you please check the cellar?"

He promised, "Tomorrow."

Colin moved down to sleep on the couch. Lucia was still calling, really calling this time, awake again. I followed the sound of her cries down to her room, where she was blotchy-faced and panicked. I took her in my arms, sat in the rocking chair.

Light from the Chevy dealership snuck past the tacked-up towels and splattered the walls. In the shadows, I saw the metal soldier on his back on the floor, his gun always lifted and ready, sleeping under Lucia's crib.

I did finally venture into town, to buy magnesium supplements and chamomile tea. I was in line at the register when an old woman gave me a big-eyed stare. She sat on the bench at the blood pressure machine, one arm in the cuff. Her sleeve was rolled up, showing her pale, spotted skin, strong old arms and blue veins.

Nessie had gone to read Archie comics at the rack. Lulu used both hands, and her chubby fingers, to pull out a stack of pamphlets on skin cancer and flutter them all to the floor. I said, "That's enough, honey, put those back." I said it loud, broadcasting: *I'm a conscientious parent!* I stretched to pick up pamphlets, while still using one foot to hold my place in line.

The old woman held her watery eyes on me. She hit a button and the blood pressure cuff swelled against her skin. Veins rose up and roped her arm. I turned my back. Too soon there was a tap on my shoulder. The woman was next to me, with her face close to mine. She said, "Slaves used to work that land." Her teeth were black and grey. Her breath smelled like apple cider vinegar.

I stepped sideways, and grabbed for Lulu who threw the stack of cancer pamphlets and ran behind a rack of reading glasses. I tried to go after her. The woman stepped in my way. She said, "Maybe not slaves, so much as prisoners. If you differentiate."

I couldn't see my daughter past the woman's skirt and bags. She blocked my way. She said, "I grew up where that pet shop is now. I saw some things."

I reached again for Lulu, and tried to smile when I asked, "How'd you know we're the new owners?" Lu had thrown herself on the ground. I wrestled her to her feet.

The woman said, "We called'em slaves. Northwestern slaves. Plenty of 'em."

I said, "It was a farm. There weren't any slaves," Like I was an expert. I wanted to believe. There were apples, and fields and bounty! It was paradise, Eden, the Arboretum, a sanctuary, and now it was ours, the lush land, damp black earth, where I'd raise my baby girls.

The woman laughed and showed how many teeth she had missing. She was crazy. She said, "A farm? All they grew there was desperate. It was a work camp. Had 'em chained. Dig up the ground good, you'll find the bodies."

That night, before dinner, I called Nessie in from the trees, but she didn't answer. I looked out into the branches and called again, then went in the house and asked Colin, "Have you seen Vanessa?"

I used her whole first name but not out of anger, the way some mothers do. I used that whole name out of love, remembering the day we named her. Darling baby girl-child. Vanessa, weighted under a name too long and heavy for such a small baby, but perfect for her as she grew into it, with dark hair, and her thoughtful way in the world.

Colin was reading the paper. Lulu pulled a dish out of the cupboard. I bent to stop her. "No, no, Honey. Breakable." She wrapped her fingers around the dish more tightly.

I'd put two grilled cheese sandwiches into a pan on the stove, and had a salad in process, torn lettuce on the cutting board, a parade of misshapen tomatoes in a line, waiting to be sliced. I loved making dinner, knowing each person under my roof would be nourished. But where was Nessie?

I went out the front door and called her name, all three syllables. I sent my heart out through my throat, yelling at the sky, and always afraid of the highway just off our property. Would she try to cross it? The back yard was out the other way, with its own possibilities. She could be anywhere, in any tree, in any ditch or field, and she didn't answer even though my voice was spreading across all available space, full volume. I ran down our driveway, calling. I longed for a smaller place then, a tiny spot, a one-room apartment where I could see both my kids at once.

I was sweating by the time I pushed through the overhang of the willow. But there she was, in the Cadillac, talking to the cat skeleton. A balloon bobbed in the car with her, like a shiny pink head. I rapped on the old glass of the half-open window. She jumped at the sound. "Dinner," I said.

Dinner. That age-old excuse to call children home.

Nessie put down the dull grey bone she'd been holding and said, "Why're you so mad?" She climbed out of the car, her legs dirty.

The love in my voice had transformed into a fast bite of fury. I didn't mean it. I meant love! I took her by the arm. "Didn't you hear me?"

"I was playing." She was only doing what I actually had hoped she do: play on her own, outside. Across the fence and through the scrim of willow leaves, I saw a salesman loitering over on the edge of the car lot. Nessie reached into the musty Caddy, for her balloon.

When we got back to the kitchen, Lulu twisted her mouth into a pre-tantrum scowl until she saw the balloon Nessie tugged along. The grilled cheese had started to scorch. The room was full of the scent of burned butter and bread. "Nobody else can smell this?" I asked, meaning Colin. He could flip a sandwich.

Nessie handed the balloon over, on its red cord. She said, "I took'em some apples."

Her hair was tangled in back, laced with sticks and leaves like she'd been rolling on the ground. Her lips were red and damp. She looked alert, almost fevered.

I said, "Who?"

Nessie smiled. The balloon turned silently, until it flashed the name of the Chevy dealership, showing one letter at a time.

Colin rubbed his eyes, and slouched at the table like an old man. He had ink stains on his arms from the paper.

I said, "Wash your hands. And do not hang out at the car dealership. That's not okay." What kind of flush was that coloring her skin, anyway?

The grilled cheese sent off a black smoke, ignored and wasted. I threw them in the sink. They hissed, hot and oily against cool drops of water.

Nessie was nine. She didn't need to hang around grown men. Salesmen, too. "Are you listening?" I said. Her balloon bobbed against the ceiling, nodding, as though only the balloon answered my question.

Days later, I reached for a pair of shoes in the back of the closet and found instead two blackened grilled cheese sandwiches. The air was bitter with the smell of scorched toast, my own harried cooking, a bad night at the stove. I recognized those sandwiches, with their mottled burn spots, as surely as I'd recognize the face of my own child—I made them, I burned them, I threw them away. They were laid out on a stack of shoeboxes, as though the boxes were a table, and as though the past wasn't over, my mistakes sticking around. There was one wrinkled napkin. A scattering of rubber bands. The metal soldier stood on the shoebox like a salt shaker.

Nessie didn't care about tea parties anymore. She wouldn't play in a closet. And Lulu? She wasn't coordinated enough to set a table.

That night, Colin slept again on the couch. I was up with Lu, looking for the radio, like it was a rare nocturnal animal. A DJ rambled in a fast, low, man's voice. He said, "I remember what the radio meant to me, but that was another time," and then his voice dipped lower. "Mama!" cut through or between his words. Real or imagined? I was there, if anyone needed me. I carried Lu downstairs.

Colin rolled over, away.

I asked, "Do you hear that?" When he didn't answer, I said it again. "You hear the radio?" I knew full well he was awake.

He mumbled, "It's the drive-thrus."

"The what?"

"Drive-thrus. Across the field." Slowly, he sat up. I sat beside him, with Lu on my lap. Lu ran a hand under my robe, under my T-shirt, looking for her *nonie,* my boobs, the first and best friends she'd known. I listened to the sounds outside, braided voices of faraway people ordering shakes and fries and chicken everything. Chicken *tenders.* Chicken burritos, chicken burgers. Wings, legs, thighs and even fingers. Chicken *fingers.* What the hell was that, anyway?

But I still heard the cry—"Mama!"—mixed in with other sounds, even with Lu on my lap.

Colin listened, his back hunched. His eyes were ringed with circles. He looked like his dad, his grandpa, some weary ancestor. He shook his head. "That's 'May I', not 'Mama.' *May I help you?"*

I heard another voice out there.

"A different drive-thru." Colin said. "They overlap."

"Please, just go downstairs. Take a look." I shouldn't have to be in this alone. It was time to turn the radio off.

It was unforgivingly dark under the house in the cellar. Colin carried a flashlight. I carried Lu. Nessa slept two floors up, in the deep sleep of a preteen, in a room crowded with leering balloons. The flashlight's beam danced on the cellar walls, and the roots of that tree growing too close to the house had started to creep in, showing in bits, like buried fingers. Then the light brushed across something. "What's that?" I grabbed Colin's hand, brought the circle of light back to what had caught my eye.

There was a child-sized wooden chair turned halfway to the wall in one dark corner. It was a red chair, with flowers painted on it. On the chair there were two burned grilled cheese sandwiches, and a collection of wide blue rubber bands.

Lu wriggled in my arms, tried to get down.

I said, "My god." I clutched Lu tighter, to hold her back, but from what? Leftovers?

Colin said, "Junk, from the last owner." He let the flashlight's beam fall to the dirt floor.

"Keep the light on the grilled cheese! Look at it," I urged.

But he tossed the light around the wall. "What are we looking for, the Virgin Mary's face?"

"That's our burned dinner, right out of the garbage. I've thrown it away twice." I had to steady Colin's hand, to make him shine that light on the burnt food like suspects in a line-up.

"We might have a black mold problem," he said. "And you need sleep."

I whispered, "I make our meals. All of them."

He said, "Now we're getting self righteous?" He was tired.

I said, "No. But I know those sandwiches." This was my language. The house was talking to me. It was telling me about my own mistakes: they don't go away. The trash goes out, but it seeps back in tiny increments, like the backflow of blood, the rush that causes a heart murmur. Why this particular trash? Because this was my mistake, an evening I was negligent. It was the night Nessie had been off by herself. I said, "From the night I burned dinner." Who was doing this? I said, "You're a scientist. That's material evidence, right there."

"It's not evidence," Colin said. He added, "We should make you an appointment, first thing, tomorrow—"

"With what?" I snapped. "What kind of doctor? Who talks about grilled cheese? This is between us, this is marriage. Family."

"A therapist," he said, with a kind of forced calm. I knew what he was thinking: He'd be the reasonable one, this round.

"This isn't about me," I said. "Or winning. It's about the kids." I wanted to do the right thing, best thing. This was their dreamscape, their future nightmare. "I want them to be happy—"

"They are happy," he said.

"—and safe," I added.

He said, "We couldn't be any safer."

"That's not comforting," I said.

He headed for the stairs, taking the flashlight with him, leaving me in the damp and dark, unless I followed close behind.

I took Lu upstairs, to bed. I was nervous and tired but afraid to sleep, had to think. I didn't want to live there anymore, in our paradise, alone. The house unnerved me, but with old, burned food? It seemed both minor and major. A grilled cheese sandwich was a small, ordinary, trivial thing, but it was also entirely material, very real, and so how did those sandwiches get in the cellar?

In her room, Lu started again, saying, "Nonie!"

I said, "No. You're too big. Nonie is for babies."

She said, "I need it!" Where was this coming from? She should've forgotten, already. She said, "I can't wait!" A new phrase.

When she said it again, I asked, "For what?"

She said, "I can't wait to be little again." Except "little" came out like "yittle." *I can't wait to be yittle again!*

A complete sentence. That was my daughter, precocious and verbal—everything a mother could want. Was it my job to tell her she'd never be *yittle again?*

"Yittle in the old house," she said, and cried and threw herself against me.

I said, "It was a good house, but we're not going back there." We weren't going back to the rental, and we weren't getting younger, and she wouldn't be little ever again. Life moves one direction. I put her in our bed, where Colin wouldn't sleep, and lay beside her until she sobbed herself into toddler dreams.

One night I walked out the front door into the yard, in the dark. The moon was a cool white. The trees rustled and laughed. A wind slipped over my legs, under the short nightgown I wore. Such a sensual world. I thought I was old, back then. I thought I was grown up. I didn't know all my big mistakes were up ahead of me, still to come.

Always the last one awake every night, I'd get up again and walk the house. Most nights I'd find myself downstairs, perched on the arm of the couch, watching Colin breathe. From there I saw how his cheek caught against the worn leather of our secondhand furniture until his skin bunched up like its own leather hide.

There were days when I'd try to talk to him about selling the place. We weren't comfortable there. Nobody slept well. He said, "So we'd move to some sealed-up suburban box, everything off-gassing radon?"

I didn't want that, either. I said, "There's something wrong with this house. We never used to argue. I think it's haunted." I dared to say that, out loud.

He said, "It's haunted by you, always up, always worrying. Go to bed."

But I was trying to sleep! Always.

Later, when he slept, he pulled his customary pillow half over his face to block out our little world. I pressed a palm against the soft expanse of the pillow...I could see the red letters of the basement's word in my mind's eye. I took my hand away again, trying not to K-I-L that bitter old man who had taken over Colin's slim frame.

I sipped the remains of his nightly glass of whiskey.

Nessie was upstairs, surrounded by her inflated bouquet of suitors, the bobbing balloons. She brought a new one home every day. For all I could tell she was ready to elope with a car dealer.

Whiskey helped. After that, I started pouring myself a nightly shot. I'd drink wine like medicine at midnight, or one in the morning, or four in the morning, to try to sleep, or at least take the edge off of being awake. I walked the halls with Lu in one arm and a glass of wine in the other hand, and would singw with the radio I could never find. Those nights were terrible, but they grew so familiar and looking back, I'd say they were even beautiful. I'd claw out my own eyes now if it'd help me get any one of those nights back, with small needy, dirty children and my angry husband and our molding house surrounded by fallen, rotten pears and new apples on those warm nights when summer edged into fall.

One afternoon neighbor kids pushed their way through the bushes. They'd learned Vanessa's name and invited her out to play, shouting "Ness-ssie!" They were dirty kids, and not always the same pack. Where did they come from? They played games in the yard, that kind of roughhouse pushing and shoving, all innocence for now. They trusted each other enough to play Blind Man's Bluff, tube socks stretched over their eyes.

"Take your sister," I said, but her sister, Lu, was too young. When Nessie ran out without her, I let it go. It was my fault they were so far apart in age. I wished I had them closer together—but if I had them in different years, would they be different children?

There was a night when Lu was finally asleep, and I moved to the kitchen table to flip through our stack of misaddressed mail. Marking each envelope and sending it back would be a small, calming chore. "No longer living at this address," I wrote on the top of the stack, then again on the next. "No longer living at this address" I wrote for Hilda, Emil, Cleave and Gloria Deo.

I heard a noise upstairs, and froze—Lucia, awake?

Still holding my breath, I wrote it on the next envelope, "No longer living…" when I saw, mid-sentence, the return address in bold block letters at the top of the envelope in my hand. It was from a group called "Parents of Murdered Children."

I put the envelope on the table.

Murdered children. I'd written "No longer living," across it.

That was our conversation, the envelope and me. I knew the house a little better now. We were on clearer terms. I heard the tiny voices: *Mama.* Out in the field, ghosts sang an opera, a tribute to slaughtered chicken, birds chopped and cooked a hundred ways. I heard the tick-tick and scratch of picnics in the closet, old children swift as mice scattering to dark corners.

That letter wasn't just mailed to somebody who used to live here, but to the parents of a child who used to live. I wanted to squeeze Nessie and Lu until they woke up, let them both be small and needy. Why not?

But they were growing too fast already.

Whiskey helped my nerves. I poured a glass of red wine. This house was giving me pieces: a toy soldier with his rifle, the radio always on, children picnicking in the cellar.

Terrifying things happen in even ordinary houses, with ordinary families. Terrifying things come in very small pieces, slowly seeping in.

I took a walk down the driveway on our land, just to feel the trees reach for me in the dark. I touched their leaves. Those trees whispered, *You are a conduit.* That's what they said! To me. And I understood—I was between mother and child, between the natural world and the concrete overtaking us, between the living and the dead, and I could hear history talking to me, showing me its stories in code.

It sounded crazy, but not as crazy as pretending our lives were new, and separate from all the people who had come and died before.

As a conduit I baked cupcakes—thirty-six of them—and covered them with chocolate buttermilk frosting, sweetest thing I could make. I fed the feral cats. I said, "Oh, mama," to the pretty, fat thing with sagging teats, and she bit my hand in happiness.

After dinner, after the dishes were washed, when Lu was finally tucked in bed and Nessie was wandering the house chewing on her toothbrush, I started making terrible food. Kids loved it. Nessie asked, "What're you cooking?"

"Mac and cheese." I added, "From a box. Brush your teeth, don't just gnaw on it."

She went for toothpaste, and called back, "Why're you making it?" I never let them eat that cheap mac and cheese with its glowing orange powdered sauce, unless Colin and I were both going out and a babysitter had to step in. "And what about the cupcakes?"

"Go to bed," I answered, not ready to talk with her about feeding murdered children. I was a mother, and good at it, and my reach could extend as far as need be.

That night, when Lu cried? I called up, "Go to sleep, darling." I poured whiskey, and let her cry it out. I did what the books suggest! I ignored her. When Colin fell asleep on the couch? I walked around him. And when the time was right, I went out the backdoor, arms laden with food, mother enough for everyone. I put the dishes and towels and candles on the damp ground. Dead children couldn't care about dirt, could they? And I wrestled the wooden plank out from between the two handles of the cellar doors.

Yes, it was dark down there, and thick with spiders and webs, but I found places for all the cupcakes, starting by stacking them on that tiny child's chair, then moving on to use a few of the old wooden beams and stray bricks. I put a candle in every one. Each cupcake was a tribute on my alter of food. I was no good at a séance, but I could host an amazing playdate with the afterlife. "Children?"

Those murdered babies needed mothering, if a blackened grilled cheese was all the food they had, and they recycled even that. They were crying out for love. I touched the roots of that tree that grew too close to the house. I ran my fingers over those pale lines of roots as though to press against the tree's hand.

I lit a match, then lit one of the candles. Those babies had probably missed so many birthday parties. I lit a second.

A mother's job is to hold the family together. A household is a stronghold. I'd build a bridge, make the children happy, and we'd all be able to sleep. I crafted a circle of tiny flickering flames. "Happy birthday to you..." I sang, softly. The same song came in over the distant radio. We were going to be fine. I poured my party wine. I didn't mind the dark. I actually grew comfortable down there, finally alone, waiting for the spirits of murdered children to come and need me. I rested my head on one damp board. "I know you're here," I murmured. "I got the mail."

I hadn't slept in forever.

Sometimes, a mother is first to strangle in her own tight fist of holding the household together. Most days I did alright, if you overlook those mornings when I was still pouring wine as Nessie got ready for school.

I did alright, if you don't count the séance.

The smoke alarms woke everyone up, upstairs. They didn't make a sound, in the cellar. I was asleep when Colin found me, in my ring of cupcakes and tiny burning candles. He shook me awake, saying, "You could've killed us all."

"Wha—?" I wiped dirt off my face. It was a luxury to sleep deeply, dreaming about other houses, other times. I said, "I was calling the murdered children."

He said, "You're drunk."

"Incidental!" I said, because it was. "We'd all live better here, if these little ones were fed." Couldn't he feel them, needing us?

I don't think he could, because he put out the candles.

He said, "You're lucky this house is leaking. If it weren't soaked, we'd be up in flames." Fire had darkened one damp board, fire and water competing to take that post down.

I said, "Only one post—"

He walked me upstairs. I knew what he was thinking: he'd be the reasonable one this round. Again.

"It's the children making us fight," I said, desperate for him to see it. The ghost children, I meant. Then I saw my own girls, big-eyed and scared, and knew how my words sounded. Our daughters leaned into each other, in matching pale blue nighties made to span the gulf of seven years between them. They'd always have each other—but I'd had them so far apart, they were essentially like two only-children. They were the best of Colin and of me. "Not you, darlings!" I called to them. "The murdered children make us fight. They can't sleep."

"Murdered?" Nessie called over.

"There are no murdered children," Colin said. Obviously a lie. He added, "Go to bed, girls." Only then, when he said it, did they turn away. They moved quietly as ghosts, with the wind lifting their nightgowns, and went off to bed, like he was the voice of reason and responsibility.

"They need you," Colin said sternly. "Lu, especially needs you. She's so little—"

Vanessa turned back, her eyes bigger than ever. She grew older right at that moment. I saw her heart. It climbed out her eyes to swoop in front of her like a bat. It darted into the dark sky.

This is how we entered into my era of medication. Out of love, I did what he asked! I saw the doctors. I talked about the burned grilled cheese. I took the medicine, and then the next medication, sometimes two at once, then three, then one. But no matter what I took, at night, I saw the children, and the soldier, and the stories of families gone far wrong.

What I'd like my girls to know is one thing: I was always doing my best to hold their place in paradise.

I loved them, unconditionally! I loved them, because they were alive. They were themselves. They had my life blood in their veins.

Maybe we could've bought a new house somewhere, a house without its history detailed in gouges in the countertops and misdirected mail. Subdivisions kept pushing forward all around us powered with the optimism of the new. That optimism had us surrounded by surveyor's stakes with fluttering ribbons bright and ugly as crime scene tape. The whole country, maybe the whole planet, had been divided and subdivided, paved and covered in bark dust. But I heard the laughing field and knew the optimism was thin. Beneath the pavement, the siding, the new plaster and streetlights, ghosts searched for last meals. They carried toys room to room. Miniature soldiers conjured up forgotten wars. I poured scotch over ice. I fought off the voices and did my job, was the mom. I wanted my babies to be lucky. Lucky kids grew up.

REFEREE

In this porn video already playing on the tiny TV when Mack and I saunter in, there's a guy in a gorilla suit with a cartoon-big white cock chasing what's meant to pass for a platinum blonde in a satin dress. Fay Wray and King Dong. The room in the video looks like a motel. There's bad, bland landscape art and a cheap bedspread. The apartment we're in looks about the same, only on the wall over the couch, where bad art should be, there's a hole the size of a head smashed in the sheetrock.

Mack's dad's place.

I put one cold hand to the hole in the wall, let sheetrock crumble under my fingers, and said, "So expressive!" I rubbed my chapped knuckles.

Mack said, "Have a seat, Nessa."

He stomped snow off his boots. Where we lived, we could see snow on the mountain all the time, but actual snowfall, like flakes in the air, on the ground, only reached us about once a year, for maybe a week. It was that week now. None of us, except the richer kids who skied, had enough warm clothes.

He said, "We're mourning and celebrating at the same time, so drink." He turned his backpack upside down, tumbling cans of beer onto the counter. It was a fake-wood island that stood between the linoleum part of the floor—*kitchen*— and the part with a rug, what was supposed to be the living room.

"What are you mourning?" I wasn't sure if I should care, if he was for real.

Mack cracked a beer and tossed one to Sanjiv, who was sprawled on the couch. He said, "Wasted youth."

I said, "You are infinite possibility." A star hockey player, he'd play for the Winterhawks. Everyone saw it was coming. He was in his element on the ice.

He belched.

Even when he burped, he was gorgeous, all dark curls and olive skin. He had black eyebrows and a curved slope to his nose and full, full lips like you never see on a guy. Mack's half-brother Kevin lay on a beanbag chair, his long body spread over the matted shag. They didn't look alike at all—like maybe they secretly didn't even have the same father?— but Kevin was hot too, butterscotch and hazel-eyed. They were boys rich in pot smoke, bed head, hockey scars. They were too big and lanky for the sagging plaid couch, the flattened beanbag. The sexy thing about hockey players is that they take what they want: *need met*. Space, time, whatever. They moved slow, drove fast, laughed when there was no joke. I laughed because they made me dizzy.

I weighed nothing. That was where we lived: an anorexic town. Girls worked hard to be less, expect less. When I wanted something, I'd say *no*. I'd say, *No thanks, no way*. But what I was always saying really, behind those words? One thing: *Love me, motherfuckers*.

The air was grey with smoke. The sliding glass door across the room was half open. There was a little balcony out there. Cold winter air blew in, enough that I could see my breath. On TV, the porn star skittered in her high heels and hid behind a potted plant.

Gorilla suit crouched and jumped, rubber cock swinging white and hard against a rag of fake black fur. In the apartment, I was the only girl. I tucked Mack's hair behind his ear, touched his chin. "Cartoons after school," I said, twirled away and stomped a chip bag on the floor. Empty.

I tugged on the pocket on the back of his Levi's but then dropped onto the couch next to Sanjiv, let my leg fall against his leg to leach heat off his body. My down coat was patched with silver tape. My jeans were wet to the shins, cowboy boots slick. I pulled a boot off, let packed snow fall, and pressed my bent knee into Sanjiv's thigh. I'd known them all for a while, but I'd known Sanjiv a little longer. They were my guys. I said, "Your mom knows you watch this?"

Kevin, on the floor, said, "Mom bought it." That was probably true. He didn't take his eyes off the tube. Kevin's body was a hard bargain of muscles and bones, where he rested against the beanbag. I wanted to fold myself along his side, curl into his hips.

Instead, I said, "You watch like it's educational. Shouldn't you all be jacking off or something?" Maybe I had limited ideas about how guys watched porn. What did I know? I picked up a chunk of snow that'd fallen out from where my frozen jeans tucked into my boots, and squeezed it over Kevin's head until the snow dripped with the heat of my hands, one drop against the soft pink skin on the back of his neck, the sweet forgotten place between his shirt and tousled hair, raw terrain, three freckles, a whole world, that warm pink baby skin. Kevin. So much beauty, in the hardness of his body. He flinched, ducked, and pushed my hand away.

"Ha!" I laughed.

Sanjiv made a noise in his throat and shifted. Squirmy, I was half in his lap. How'd I end up there, snuggled against the heat of his jeans?

Me and Sanjiv had been in school together since fifth grade. That was when my family moved to our house, the Arboretum, and his came from India or Indiana or California or wherever. I should know where he lived before, right? But when he moved to town we were kids. Nobody asked. In a town of mostly white people, we didn't know how to ask. Now we were too far past that moment for me to backtrack. All I knew was that he had relatives in all of those places.

Shy maybe, he was a mumbler. He talked more when he was younger, but he'd moved away from the habit. Now? I could've slid my hand down his pants, stolen the heat off his balls with my chilled fingers, he wouldn't have said more than a few quiet, slurred words. I put my hands in my coat pockets, fingered a folded paper and leaned back, ready to watch porn the way the guys were watching it, like it was a regular show, like I saw porn all the time.

I'd never seen porn but felt like I'd seen this one. It was like Benny Hill porn. Like Three Stooges doing Nasty King Kong.

That paper in my pocket? A note from Mom, worn soft as an old stuffed animal. She was back in the hospital.

Mack said, "Beer?"

I nodded and jiggled my foot against the carpet—it shook the whole building—then caught myself and stopped jiggling, because jiggling was like skittering, and I wasn't that kind of girl.

Mack and Kevin, they used to live on a leased farm. Their dad grew corn. They had apples too. In the early fall their dad would pay me and some other kids to pick apples. No matter how many apples I picked, it always only ever added up to about two dollars coming my way. He'd take the apples in his truck to a cider press on the edge of town. Sometimes I'd ride along with Mack and Kevin. The press was wooden, and damp. It had glass sides on the juicer section. You could climb up the side, hang on it and watch apples tumble into the machinery. They'd come out as juice and pulp, separated into two different tracks. It smelled like heaven in the little wooden shack around the press. It was partly the smell of mold on the old wooden floorboards, but also apples. Then their land was sold to build something called an Industrial Park, and we didn't go back to the cider press. The apple trees and corn were taken out. The farm house was razed.

I'd never been inside this particular one of Mack's dad's apartments, but it was the exact same as a hundred other apartments in the complex. Divorce Caves, all of them. It was the apartment the losing half of every divorce moved into. I'd babysat around there, different apartments. I'd waited by the white light of a microwave while a TV dinner turned in circles, meat and gravy and a dessert that'd taste like bad perfume. I'd gotten down on my knees, played with dolls and trucks and board games, long nights of Candy Land, chasing the lucky Queen Frostine card while a single a mom or dad tried to date in our dinky town. Every one of the apartments had the same half-kitchen, the same shallow balcony over a parking lot, the balcony just deep enough for mom or pop to sneak a late night smoke.

When they lost the farm, their whole divorce thing started. The land and the divorce seemed like one big scar.

Mack and Kevin, they had hockey dreams warbling on the horizon. They'd be the next Babych brothers! That was word around town. The Babych brothers were the Winterhawks' star players, before. When we were kids Wayne Babych had famously stayed not far from where we lived. He'd come from Canada and lived in a *billet*. "Billet" was a foreign word to me, but in the sports news back then. It was what they called local housing, offered by families for up-and-coming recruits.

Mack handed me a Pabst. For no reason I could see, Sanjiv jumped up like the couch was electric and he'd been hit with a shock. He pulled a tennis ball out of his coat pocket and bounced it off the wall. Gorilla suit grabbed the woman's dress and it tore, flimsy as toilet paper. White boobs tumbled out like a magic trick, doves from a scarf. Mack's brother, Kevin, flicked a lighter, took a hit off a crushed-can bong and filled the room with the perfume of pot. Sanjiv went out on the balcony, looked one way, then the other. When he touched an ashtray balanced on the rail the ashtray fell and broke against somebody else's patio down below. He knocked a dead potted plant off the edge, too.

"Settle, dude," Kevin said, his voice tight, holding in smoke. "Somebody'll call the cops."

Sanjiv chucked the tennis ball across the parking lot.

On the other side of the lot was patches of field, smaller than it used to be when I'd run through it as a kid, but still there, and across that field was our house.

Most times when Mack said *Come on over,* I said no, because these days, being around him made my brain slow. He scared me, because he'd grown into a God. When I saw his hockey-player shoulders, the scar on his jaw, his muscles, his curls, the way his dark hair shadowed his face, you'd think I was the one too stoned to pass P.E. His eyes were motor oil. His chew faded a white ring in the back pocket of his jeans. He smelled like clean skin, but in a cloud of smoke and old beer, like he'd just come from some party I'd never be invited to. He was a hockey player and a stoner and a good time and everything I wanted in the whole world.

I'd say *No, thanks.*

On the days Mack took the school bus, he made it his private ride. He made all the bus drivers basically into his mothers. They were all women, all older, with their hair pinned up into curls and their windbreakers on. He'd sweet talk and always knew their names and they'd laugh at his horsing around, shake their heads, shake that waddle under their old chins, roll their eyes. They let him on or off wherever he asked, totally against school rules. They put their jobs on the line for him. If we were both on the bus in the afternoon he'd usually get off in front of my house, walk through our fields and go over the fence where the squares of wire had been pressed down low to the ground, bent to accommodate years of people stepping over it. He'd say, "You coming?" and tip his thumb to his mouth, hand in a fist, little finger up. Drinks.

I always said no for the same reason that this time I said yes: I knew I'd be the only girl at Mack's dad's place. My goal now? *To go the distance, for love or money.*

On a balcony across the way, a little kid came out and threw half a white-bread sandwich over the edge. The bread separated in the air, letting a piece of ketchup-covered bologna fall free.

"I babysat over there, once." I said, and waved to the kid just as an arm pulled him back in through the clattering vertical blinds.

Mack's half-brother Kevin said, "That your lil' cousin?" He offered the crushed can bong, but I waved it off. Sipped my Pabst. The beer was cold as the air and sweet as Kool-Aid. King Dong had the porn star against a wall. Her dress was a pile of torn satin pooled at her feet but her high heels were still on. She made fake-scared faces, all *ooo's* and *oh no,* and her hands slid from her boobs to her thighs, then between her legs, rubbing up and down. Her fingernails were awful, but perfect. "What is this garbage?" I said, trying to be above it all.

Kevin twisted around again on the bean bag and said, "Which unit you in?"

Mack took a swipe toward Kevin's head. "Shut up, man."

Kevin said, "Wha—?"

"She's not in a *unit,* dude."

"Not that'd I'd mind," I said. I wasn't like girls from the new part of town, in the big houses, all fake white pillars, three car garages. We had a dirt drive. But our house had a name—the Arboretum. I could see the line of our roof when I looked out their dad's apartment's sliding door and across the fields. I pulled at the tape patch on my coat.

Mack took my hand. I followed him around the corner. He closed the bedroom door. I touched the scar over his jaw. There'd been blood on the ice, the night his chin split like a gutted fish, all fatty layers. "I was at that game," I whispered. I brought one hand to the back of my head, making a ref's call: *Head contact.*

I saw when the other guy hit him.

Mack said, "I was the instigator," and looked sheepish, gave a shrug.

I swung a hand to the side, a ref's call for *roughing.* Hockey was not a big sport in Oregon. It was marginalized, left to the outsiders, except for the Winterhawks.

I said, "Let me call the shots. You, can do anything. It's all up ahead."

He was strong, and tall, with an easy smile. I'd say he had a pretty smile, with those lips. He was every mother's favorite bad-boy son. With his helmet off, knocked out, Mack's hair had spread on the ice like a dark halo. There was a bright dash of blood. He was carried to some faraway place. I wanted to go with him. I said, "What's it like, to be knocked out?"

I sort of hoped to try it, sometime.

He said, "No art to it. It's coming to thas' a bitch."

I said, "I mean, when you're unconscious—"

He pulled his coat off and threw it on a pile of clothes on a chair. Kicked dirty Jockey's under the bed. We put our beers on the nightstand side by side, two cans beaded with sweat. Cozy. I said, "I could be a ref or a linesman." I went through a dance of calls in a series of fast arm gestures: *Penalty shot, high sticking, icing, goal!*

He pushed up his sleeves. There was a mess of scab and lumped skin on his arm. I touched it, fingers light. He tried to coax me backward, onto the bed. I didn't give in. "What happened?"

He shook hair out of his eyes. He said, "I shot up carpet fibers. That easy, and I almost lost my arm." He laughed, like it was a big joke.

"Washout," I said, and tried to give the ref's call, flinging my arms wide. "No goal, no violation. Easy mistake."

He tapped his forehead with his index finger, like he'd learned something. His eyelashes were black spiders. "I learned. Don't spill your stash," he said. "That mistake cost me hockey."

Those were serious words. I asked, "You're not still playing?" How'd I miss that? Mack had a way of ducking out, staying at his mom's across town, going who knows where. I said, "You could get back in. They love you."

In a forced, low voice he said, "Hockey is a character building sport, son." He pushed me backward onto the bed, letting the mattress knock against the back of my knees. I practiced saying yes, let myself be laid out like a comforter. He said, "An athlete cares about his body, on the ice and off. Apparently, I don't." He pressed against me, bones and hips, under his weight. I tried to follow, not lead. To go the distance.

I said, "You still—"

His mouth hit mine and it was too open, too wet, but the smell was there, the party. I was under his tent of smoke and beer, his whiskey-colored skin, under his weight.

Mack tugged at the button-fly of my jeans. Long johns, wool socks, t-shirt, sweater. It was layers over layers, same as guys wore—winter uniforms, farthest thing ever from the porn star costume. Feathers floated from my coat.

Something crashed in the front room. I dropped a hand to the bed. Mack didn't flinch, didn't stop pressing his open mouth to mine, his tongue against my tongue, fingers digging for skin. Kevin said, *Jesus, man,* on the other side of the wall. Sanjiv's voice came through as his usual murmur, only a little more muffled.

Another smash, and there was the sound of rubble falling between sheetrock down into the wall. I pushed away from Mack, against his shoulders, but his weight on mine held me on the bed.

Our teeth hit. His mouth was a gag. My words came out wrecked, foreign and chipped, like words barely translated, meant for a language with no words at all. Smothered.

Another crash, and this time a hand broke through the wall over Mack's head, with bloody knuckles tangled in wires. Sheetrock hit my face, with grit like sand in my eyes.

Then Mack got up slowly, patiently. He let dust and rubble fall off the broad planes of his back. He was huge, a monster of a man, shaking off fallen pieces of the building itself. He was the babysitter this round, and he stood tall when he opened the hollow door.

Sanjiv's knuckles were marked with blood as red as roses. Holes bloomed in the plaster. That art, his self-expression, was paintless—but not painless—graffiti, drawn in his own hand. I wiped Mack's spit off my chin. Kevin said, "Dad'll shit."

Mack slurred, "Dad's a faggot."

Kevin said, "You're the faggot."

Kevin threw himself at Mack, reached for Mack's throat, but Mack was bigger and he knocked Kevin over, then the two of them went down together, hit an end table and spilled a beer. I stayed back. The muscles in their arms and necks strained against their skin. Every one of their muscles called out to me, like every one of them was mine. They were so beautiful. These were farm boys without a farm, athletes without a sport. I said, "And here we are, game tied, gone into a sudden-death playoff—"

The fight kept going.

I said, "Hey, Mack. No." I threw an arm to the side, made the ref call. I said, "Roughing! One more fight, game's over."

Mack had Kevin by the shoulders, but Kevin threw him. Somebody's foot put another hole in the thin wall. I said, "Minor penalty, off the ice!" When Mack knocked Kevin into the couch, I said, "Butt-ending!"

Their arms were locked, each holding the other's elbows, holding each other at a distance but close too, like they couldn't get away and they couldn't come together, and they were the most beautiful guys I've ever seen. I really did a few things about art, and Mack and Kevin were Classical statues, wrestling. If those boys were only naked, they'd be the models for every great marble statue of sparring gods.

Sanjiv rubbed the palm of one hand over his bleeding knuckles and went out on the balcony. Gorilla Suit ass-fucked the phony Fay Wray until the tape screwed up. The picture jumped up and down. Mack got the upper hand. A vein on the side of his neck was thick and blue. Kevin's eyes were round, little walnuts, as he struggled. A piece of my silver tape stuck to the side of Mack's coat now.

I put a hand to my lip, and it came back red with blood. My chapped lip had split, from kissing. I took a Pabst from the counter and held the can to my mouth like an ice pack, then slid another can in my coat pocket. The can was so nicely solid. It fit my pocket like it was meant to be there and weighed me down like a sinker. My head was light—that can of Pabst weighed more than I did. I was helium.

I slid a second can in the other pocket, to keep from floating away.

Mack slammed Kevin into the TV, knocked the TV and its little table over. It wasn't late, but it was dark out. "Alright," I said, like I was trying to stop the fight—like I even could. But the thing is, I wasn't. I couldn't. I didn't try that hard. I put my finger to my lip, drew a line of my own blood on the wall in the kitchen corner.

There was a magnet on the fridge made to look like a page from a notebook, with a felt pen dangling on a string. *To Do.* There was no list, like somebody had nothing to do. I wrote: *Call Vanessa.*

I wrote my phone number. Blue ink off the board stained the side of my hand. I put a stamp of the side of my ink-stained fist beside the words I'd written, and it looked like a baby's footprint.

Then I left, down the hall, down the rattling metal apartment stairs.

Snow was drifting down like dust. Those fat white flakes seemed the strangest dream a person could have. It had covered the world! In a few days, it'd be gone. My foot sunk through the drifts between the field grass. In the blue light, all that iced-over snow had the crack of punched plaster. Our house was tall against a black and blue sky. A gutter jutted out like a splinter. The roof split around the chimney. Snow leaned against windows. My sister Lu would be home with dad. They were probably watching T.V. and working on dinner. Lu and Dad, they got along.

Lu had decided she wanted her name to be Carrion. I thought she meant Karen, but she corrected me. "Carrion," she said, and did a leaping sort of dance in the living room. With her arms outstretched, she said "It's the most beautiful name in the world."

I was a kid, just older than she was now, when we moved into that place. I remembered living back in the city, Portland, before she was born. Then at the Arboretum I'd spend long days out in the fields weaving chairs out of sticks and field grass that was still rooted in the ground. I'd weave chairs so tight that I could sit on them. I imagined a chair could grow into a couch if the rooted grass were green. Now snow glittered white against the dark blue sky. The fields had been diced by cement, some of them built over completely, then the economy tanked and the construction stopped. What was left was still marked with orange flags, ready for contractors, for more divorce caves.

Why wait for divorce? Why wait for builders? I moved in right then—sat in the ice-capped drifts. I swung a foot side to side, knocking the snow away. There was my kitchen, my living room.

I did want to be a hockey referee. At home, I'd always been ref between my parents. I could put myself between the fights.

What if my snowdrift chair could grow into a couch. What if my mother were around. I said, "Mom, I think Mack likes me." I took a handful of white snow from a clump of tall grass, and put it against my tongue. An anorexic's ice cream. The snow came away red, the crack in my lip. Tiny snow drifted against my jeans and wove a silk blanket, satin-white and soft as the porn star's dress. "Maybe Sanjiv, too. He's alright, isn't he? I mean, in his weird-guy way." He was good-looking. I could cope with his obvious anger problem and total lack of communication skills.

Snow came down in a dizzy swirl, and for the moment the dizziness in my head made sense. I sipped the beer, ate snow, closed my eyes, and snuggled close against the ice pack. My head was so light. Wind sang through the field grass. The same wind brushed hair off my face, soft as my mother's hand, and when the falling snow started to clump into flakes, each thick flake came down with the love of a frozen kiss, like somebody was saving up, freezing their warm love for later.

I pushed new snow into a pillow. Lay on the ground. Then I worked the note in my pocket around a damp can of beer. Unfolded worn paper. My fingers were stiff. I could hear my mother's voice in her handwriting. In cursive soft as a lullaby she sang: *Oranges. Pine-Sol. Gallon of milk. Bread, spaghetti, canned soup.* At the end, she wrote, *Go the distance for love or money.*

The last thing she did before she went in the hospital this most recent round was write that note. Well, she lit their bed on fire after that, so that was that one exact last thing. When she found what she needed in medicine and talk therapy, when they got her balanced out, after she'd gone the distance of her own internal marathon, she'd come home back to us carrying bags of Pine-Sol and love, milk and money.

NEIGHBORHOOD NOTES: ART SHOW

Maybe there's a time up ahead, or there was a time, or there is this time right now when you're in a place with too many people, it's sweating-hot and you don't know any of them. Say you're in a crowded, make-shift gallery in an Old Town alleyway. You've walked down there alone to meet a friend who hasn't shown up. You wouldn't have gone except you thought you wouldn't be alone and now you're wedged between strangers and outside it's dark and the art on the walls inside is made out of duct tape and it's sexy and sophisticated in its crazy-small details, naked bodies drawn in layers of tape, duct tape labia and testicles, and it's childish and hot and plastic and grown up at the same time and mostly you feel lost because everyone else at the opening seems to know each other and the woman running the place has a massive head of curly hair and a giant cooler full of ice and beer, so you reach into the ice and pry loose a can of PBR. That beer is a way to make yourself at home. It's a swig of high school. You will fit in. At the same moment that you pull the tab, the woman in charge looks past you at a pack of skinny punks near the door. They're maybe your age?

Teenagers veering toward twenty. She yells, "Cut the underage drinking. This is my place."

You are *underage*. Drinking. She's not looking at you though, because when you're alone you're invisible. The city is a new thing. You're figuring out how life works. Where you grew up you had the kind of yard that people here call "land." They say the word with a strange drawn-out distancing, a reverence, like you owned a whole country or as though their feet aren't actually on real ground too, but also like maybe you were primitive? You had indoor plumbing, mostly.

You're an outsider, here. Lifting that beer is about stepping through a doorway from outsider to inside. You raise it with high hopes: belong.

The gallery owner has lost her cool. She's red-faced when she hurls a can of beer at a guy, and you watch the can sail like a baseball. Anger? Well, that's familiar territory. Maybe you are an insider to certain corners of this scene.

The can rushes past too close to your own head showing a serious velocity. It finds its way across the slim open space. When it makes contact with the target's forehead he drops the open beer that was in his hands straight to the floor. He turns to look, all wounded animal eyes. A red welt rises at his hairline.

Move through the crowd until you're by his side. Next thing, you're talking to strangers. "It's better if it swells, instead of putting pressure on your brain," you say. "Hold a cold beer to it," you offer, and lift your can toward his head. You're a well-trained, highly experienced party paramedic.

He has the beer that was thrown at him in his hands. Obliging you, he lifts it to the bump on his head where his skin is red and rising. But then the welt is still swelling when he almost immediately quits ministering to it. He cracks that fresh beer open instead, acts like it was only being passed across a table. He ignores the gallery owner like family. He ignores his own head and the pain he must feel. He opens that can with a hiss and the gush of foam, shaken, a beer shower. The whole moment passes fast as a mile-age marker clipping by on the side of a highway. It's in the future, then happening, then over and gone. It will happen again in other buildings, other crowds of people when you move forward then hang back.

MUSTARD

Our dad, when he taught forensic science, said it was the art of looking at a problem and tracking backward, analyzing the smallest pieces to find out where things went wrong. When he actually did lab work, it usually involved investigating tampered with or otherwise faulty pre-packed food. He'd analyze unknown objects found in a box of cereal, a can of soup, a carton of orange juice. He'd determine if an item was molding mouse feet, somebody's fingers lost in an industrial accident, or only an ordinary clump of burned cereal ingredients that had fallen off industrial machinery into the Wheatie-O's mix.

I was fourteen and still at home when one of his graduate students moved into Nessie's old abandoned bedroom. Maybe my parents just wanted to populate the place? This guy showed up with a suitcase and he stayed. He slept in her twin bed, under her blue and purple flowered comforter. It was so wrong to see his big body lumped under the blanket where my big sister used to lay flat and read Tin Tin books, even reading to me on the lucky days. I tried not to look, hoped he'd close his door. Whatever was going on in that guy's life, nobody told me. Nobody asked my opinion.

My best bet was to be invisible and keep out of his way. Sometimes I'd ask mom, "How long is he going to be here?"

She'd say, "Be nice, Lu." Once she said, "We don't know, do we?" like life was all some big question and she wasn't really in charge. She was freshly home again, medicated, humming and making dinners. For mom, it was a good stretch. She'd murmur, "Our land is a refuge." I think she really believed it, like housing this guy was doing good work. Other times she'd say the same thing only to herself, quietly and more like an incantation, trying to make it true.

We had one bathroom. When the student was using it, I'd stay away. When I needed it, I'd lock the door. The worst spot in the house was the kitchen because you can't lock anybody out of the kitchen. In the morning before school, I'd pack a lunch while it was still dark out. Then I'd put a frozen waffle in the toaster and wait, tapping a knife into the butter. Usually I'd take a dry waffle back upstairs and take a shower, but now this guy was in the kitchen, always making coffee. My parents never got up early, but he did just to make small talk while I was still in my worn-out, polyester nightgown.

That nightgown was so old it was wearing through, nearly transparent. That guy in our house? Suddenly being dressed mattered.

After the first couple of days of him hanging around, I started getting dressed without taking a shower. It was a cold winter. Then I didn't see any reason not to sleep in my clothes.

There was a phrase my dad liked to quote: "Physical evidence can not be intimidated." It was a saying, from a leading authority in his field.

Apparently I wasn't physical evidence. My body wasn't? Because I was intimidated all the time.

In the morning, he'd toast an English muffin, and put his hands over the top of the toaster like it was a little fire. If I didn't get there first, I'd be stuck waiting for a turn. It was like I had a new uncle, or a way-older brother. A pain in the ass. He'd make noises, like

"Mmmm, mmmmm..." and groan, and push butter around over the muffin. He'd spread this expensive imported marmalade over the butter, and lick the knife. It was all very ritual.

When I was chewing a dry Eggo, trying to get my boots on, he'd say things like, "You're a shy one, aren't you?"

I wasn't shy. I didn't like him. It was creepy the way he looked at me like I was a grown woman, when I still rode my old banana seat Schwinn. I still liked Bubblicious, the best bubblegum ever.

I played volleyball. I tried to study Spanish.

I wasn't some Lolita girl but he looked at me like I was, and his look was trying to turn me into the show he hoped to see. He thought I was my sister, perhaps. She was wild, while I was tame. If she were home, she could stand in for me. She could stand in front of me, like a shield.

He did one good thing—filled our fridge with like sixteen kinds of mustard and said, "Have whatever you want!"

If I'd been really into mustard, that would've been generous!

After school, he'd be the only one in the house, there to meet me. One time I came in and he was at the stove. He said, "Try this vindaloo. Learned how to make it on my travels." He said that, "my travels," like it was mysterious and important, and he waved a wooden spoon toward me.

I'd done a report on Mumbai in fifth grade. I said, "What was India like?"

He said, "England. I learned to make vindaloo in England."

So he'd done a semester in England. Whatever, right?

He took a big bite of his own vindaloo, off the spoon, and made his groaning sounds, and said, "Mmm... mmm... this is how to live." Then he swung the spoon my way again.

I got out of there.

After that, he always had some kind of food going—usually something that meant he'd been cooking a long time, and that meant he'd been in our house all day. He'd come at me with that wooden spoon. When he pushed beef bourguignon on me, I squeaked, "I'm a vegetarian!" and ran up to my room and closed the door.

When he made curried lentils, I said, "I'm totally allergic to legumes," and got away fast. The man smelled like sweat and salt and the longer he stayed in our house the more our house smelled like him. Now that I'm older, I think maybe he smelled like dried cum, but I didn't think that way back then.

I was kind of a dork.

One night, he made dinner for the family. Rabbit. It was a little rabbit body, on a plate. It looked like a stripped down prisoner. He said it again—"Now this is how to live!"—as he passed the plate to my dad. I was going to throw up. My dad handed me the plate, an animal with one leg cut off, and I couldn't take it. I dropped it on the floor. I started to cry. Mom said, "What is wrong with you?"

Like there was something wrong *with me?*

But I saw the smirk on that guy's face, our grad student. He'd made me nervous, and he liked it.

So I came home one day, and the house smelled like him, and it smelled like meat and I tried to pass the kitchen without talking to him, and I was pretty much chanting, in my head, *don't talk to me don't talk to me,* and I saw him at the kitchen table. I'd never seen him look quite so collapsed before. It was like he'd had a really bad day. He had his glasses off, on the table, by his hand. His shoulders were slumped.

I sort of felt sorry for him.

I thought I could tiptoe past, get a Coke out of the fridge. I'd grab a Coke and go. I moved so quietly.

He didn't hear me, didn't move. I pulled the fridge door open, and the suction of the seal on the fridge made a sound, like making out, pretty much, like kissing, and it seemed loud because everything else was so quiet.

I looked, but he hadn't moved. From that side, I could see his mouth was open. His eyes were closed, but the lids were purple. His lips were purple. And it took me a while, but I realized that he was having a problem—he was dead, or dying. I said his name, loud, now chanting in my head, *talk to me talk to me talk to me.*

I didn't want to touch him, but did. I touched his shoulder. He dropped his head all the way to the table, and it made a terrible thunk. I screamed, and got away, and first thing I did was call my mom at work, but she didn't answer. I left a message.

Dad was in class, teaching. There was no way to reach him. Vanessa? Traveling Mexico then Central America, last I heard. She barely been in touch with me anyway since back when I was playing with dolls, a little kid, by which I mean maybe a year before, a lifetime ago.

So it was me and the dead student guy, home after school, surrounded by trees and land and the sound of the drive-thrus off in the distance. I was too young, didn't know what to do. Call 911? It wasn't exactly an emergency. He was already dead. I sat at the table and hoped one of my parents would call back. That's when I saw the plate. He'd made a plate of food. It was beside his elbow, almost hidden behind his arm. A sausage sandwich.

That was the meat smell, filling the house. The stove was still hot. He'd made a sandwich, then died. It looked like a fat sausage on a potato bread bun, and I could see the deep brown lines of one of his favorite mustards, spread along both the bun and the meat. I imagined how he'd spread that mustard—he'd say, Mmm... Mmm... and lick the knife, the way he did. It was his last meal.

When I got my courage up, I called the police, told them I was home, with a dead man. I said he was sitting at our kitchen table, that I'd come home, that I didn't actually know his last name, but he was staying with us. Then I was off the phone again, alone and waiting.

That sausage looked so alone. I reached out and lifted it. He always wanted me to try his cooking. I'd turned him down so many times. The sausage was still warm. I wanted to do something right. I put it to my mouth, breathed the steam off the meat. I let my teeth come together around it. When my bite broke through the casing, warm grease ran out, into my mouth. It was a good sausage, full of fennel and pork. I chewed, and swallowed.

I felt stiff, the way I moved when I took that first bite, like I was eating something in church. He'd made that sausage so carefully. Food was his thing. I took another bite. I did. I ate it. I ate the dead man's hot and meaty sandwich. It was good.

If I were my father, I would've analyzed that food. I would've broken it down into the smallest pieces in a laboratory and looked for poison or ordinary fats. I'd look back, sifting through the smallest details to find out exactly where this guy's life went wrong, until his careening troubles converged with my life. But I wasn't my father, I was a teenage girl.

It felt very ritual to eat that meat. This was my own ritual offering, now. He was a guy with rituals and I joined in, in his honor.

I wish I hadn't done it, though.

It's been thirty years. I feel like that mistake is still with me. I ate a dead man's greasy sausage, and what if some part of it is still in my body? Lodged in my intestines, or resting as a yellow fat deposit under my skin, along my ribs, on my belly. I'd have liposuction if a doctor could promise to find exactly the fat cells plumped by that single hot, dripping sausage. I want everything about it to go away.

When you see women who don't eat? Or women who cleanse, detox and purge? I think they've done something like this. They've eaten in a way that's left a memory, a creepy ghost, a body inside their own body.

The weird thing is, that's not how it felt that afternoon. The mustard, which he'd carefully chosen, was tangy and ripe. It was perfect. He was a lonely guy.

If I were dad, I'd yell at the girl that was me. I'd say, "You're eating the evidence!"

I wiped grease off my mouth with the back of my hand.

The grad student had poured himself a dark brown beer. It was there in a glass, on the table. I dragged the glass over, took a sip. It was the first beer I ever had. It was awful, sweet and thick and room temperature. Now I'd guess he'd learned to drink stout that way in England, but back then, I expected it to taste more like a Coke. And when I drank that beer I hated it, but took another drink, and I thought about what the man said—"This is how to live!"—and I didn't stop drinking for about twenty more years.

That's what I was doing when the cops showed up, when the ambulance arrived. Fourteen and hoisting a warm beer. I toasted to the dead man, *Cheers!* Then they hauled his body away.

MISS AMERICA HAS A PLAN

Down in the booze-soaked corners of Los Amigos, I found the regulars scattered at side tables and playing pool. But there was a new man too, at the bar. I tried to look away. My eyes came back to him. Warmed by an amber beer light, the rumples of the man's white flounced shirt screamed secret history. He could've have bought that shirt at Forever 21, had it handmade in Venice, or stolen it from a Shakespeare festival.

Who dressed in soot-marked flounce?

I'd been traveling for months, spending my savings, and now was hanging out where it was cheap. Los Amigos was a dirty and dim bar. I liked it, especially on a Sunday. The bartender was always this woman who I'd guessed worked there because she wanted the excuse of a paycheck, to be out in a dive on her own and in charge. She wouldn't go in alone if she weren't working. Her husband might not let her. She wouldn't stand behind that counter and pour drinks without a pistol. I'm American though, and American women drink by themselves just fine.

The new man rested his feet, in boots, on the wooden planks of the floor with a confidence beyond that of anyone I'd ever met.

I said a timid, "Hola." My Spanish was a revived high school class I'd been making use of up and down Mexico.

He nodded, and said, "Sit."

It was a command. He said it in English, as though he knew me. I climbed onto the tall chair he indicated.

The bartender had black hair bleached blonde, with long dark roots. Her shirt read Sonic Youth. Her apron said, "No hay resacas si sigue bebiendo." She held a pint glass in one thick hand, gave it a toss, caught it again, and scoffed at my willingness. I saw the roll of her eyes.

I wouldn't admit even to myself that maybe, secretly, I hoped I was the first to stand in the light of this man's blousy charisma. Maybe I was the first tourist traveling his path. I'd met guys like that since high school: overlooked. Hot, though in a way nobody else noticed. He had a fleck of napkin caught in the growth of his rough shave. Who else would see the charm of a man with lint on his face? It was like I'd found a steal in a Goodwill bargain bin, my raw diamond.

I'd polish him. I'd polish him hard.

This was in Guanajuato, which is to say officially Estado Libre y Soberano de Guanajuato, but nobody used that name.

Nobody used names much at all. Not my name, anyway. It surprised me then, when he asked what my name was.

"Maria de Socorro," I told him. *Maria of help.* Of aid. Of relief. Succor.

Or sucker. Maybe.

Why tell him my real name? I was shaking it off. I wasn't Nessie, Nessa or Vanessa now. I didn't have to be that girl from the land of sticks, surveyors' lines, and concrete. Where we sat wasn't his country and it wasn't my country. It was a good bar with cold beer and no police.

That's all I ask of a place, anymore: cold beer, no cops, one hot guy.

Travelers, together. The map of wrinkles around his eyes was as familiar as family. I said, "I've seen you before."

He said, "Sure. Picture the evening news." He made a gesture, as though slicing himself in half at the waist. "Historic uprising." He made the quotation marks sign with one hand.

I said, "What's that?" He didn't look like a newscaster.

"I'm very 'televisual.'" He made the quotation marks again. "Telegenic, according to *Newsweek*." His accent was decorative, and didn't interfere with his English.

That's when he told me—not a newscaster, he was the news. He gave me the rundown. He said there was a *little revolution!* And he blew through narrow lips, making a dismissive sound. He lifted his beer in its sweating bottle and tipped it, then drank. He added, "Kicked out. After all I did for them."

He'd lost control of a whole country, sure as a car skidding down an embankment. "I am now," he said, "a deposed dictator."

My knees went wobbly, my spine hot: the baddest of bad boys, hotter than a stoned hockey player. Yes, I have a weakness.

He smiled, and turned to me, and his lips were very red for a man's; he was Freddie Mercury. Freddie Mercury was alive, and in Mexico. Freddie Mercury had been, once upon a time, his own historic uprising, now deposed.

I swallowed, then said, "You were in Queen?"

He said, "Queens? No. I stay out of the U.S. I have a cousin there, though."

So he wasn't Freddie Mercury. His name wasn't Charles Taylor. It wasn't Manuel Noriega, the pineapple. It wasn't Maximiliano, Mustafa, Rafael, Idi, or Raoul. He was not Muammar, and not Hosni. That's all I can say—his name is confidential.

He said, "These days, I'm a shit magnet."

What did that make me? I refused to take it personally. He was hurt. He was a man who needed a country. I was a woman who needed a man. I'd be his country. He'd be my dictator. I saw our future unfold like a history book.

He looked at my feet. "Are those Israeli?"

My sandals.

I felt the need to stay neutral yet engaged. What was his relationship to Israel, pro or anti? The Gaza strip was in need of medicating, that's all I knew. Medicating for despair, anger and impulse control. Medicating for loss and love and the rest of it. Who was I to judge the world? I was a scrawny chick from the middle of nowhere, who grew up in an old farmhouse off the side of a road.

I pulled my foot up until I could see the bottom of the sole, and looked for a brand. There was the worn tread of walking in a foreign country. A bottle cap surprised me, rammed into the high wedge heels. They were a comfort-stride cork heel. I could run in them when I had to, and still go out dancing. They were party shoes, of no particular political party.

He reached over and pried the beer cap from my cork sole. When it fell, it was a soft tap and rattle against the wood floor. His was a sweet gesture. He rubbed his fingers together to dust off grime. He said, "See those men near the door?"

Two men, at a table. Of course I saw them.

He said, "They're listening." He tipped his beer bottle to one side and let it roll one way, then back, his hand on the bottle's thin neck.

The men were red-eyed, probably high, and had the thick waists of young drunks.

He whispered, "They're everywhere."

"Who?" Those two men couldn't be everywhere, but yes, young drunks basically dotted the landscape.

My dictator shook out his dark curls. He said, "What do you know about revolution, except from movies?"

I said, "And books." I felt smart, until I said it, until the word came out small and thin, and so I offered what my high school

English teacher called *supporting details.* "Castro learned about revolution from Hemingway. *For Whom the Bell Tolls.* He learned how a small contingent can overthrow the ruling party." I nodded as though back in class, as though I hadn't given up on school a long time ago.

His nod was slow, qualified by doubt, as he turned to where his jacket hung on the back of his chair. He took a reporter's notebook from a pocket, found a pen and wrote it down: *For Whom Bell Tolls.*

There it was! I'd helped a dictator.

He read his own words over again. He scribbled something else, below the words. I let him write. A good woman knows when to stay out of the way.

It was two fast beers before I got up my courage and asked: "War crimes?" When you fall in love, you have to know dark things. And I was falling.

He laughed. His teeth were lovely. He was warming to me. He put down his pen. He said, "War crimes is a metaphor. People who haven't been there never understand."

He spit over his shoulder, onto the wooden floor.

I spit over my shoulder too, only more discretely, away from him. Practicing. I wanted to know how it felt to spit on a floor.

My spit landed on the back of my denim jacket. I wiped it with my palm, and felt my face go hot. I'd practice at home.

This man was my teacher, my father, my rock-and-roll crush. He ruffled my hair and said, "Some day, little one, maybe you'll manage your own country. You'll move beyond the books. Then you'll understand war crimes."

How did he know? Yes, I wanted power. I loved the very thought of it. But my power would come by association. My power would come by giving in to his.

The bartender put a finger in my beer bottle as she reached to take it away. She waggled her finger, the bottle dancing, and asked, "Más?"

She did that on purpose. There was still a good swig in the bottom of the bottle, but her fingers on the lip? Her finger inside it? It was practically gynecological. No thanks. She waited to see if we'd order more.

I waited to see if he'd buy.

He put his pen and notebook away. He said, "I'm broke. The military budget is over."

Didn't they get a severance package?

I pulled out a Visa card from my tiny purse, laid it on the worn wood of the bartop. The bartender looked with a steady gaze that conveyed so clearly her words: *Are you joking?* She didn't bother to say it out loud. The flair of her nostrils told me all: *No credit here.* I lived on credit. She uncrooked her finger to drop the bottle in the vat of empties.

I said, "My credit is great." I'd maxed out so many times, they raised my limits, back in the states; I could buy a whole mall.

The dictator said, "Give Miss America her credit." His words were a slur.

So he knew I was American? Even as Maria de Socorro, my attempt at acculturation.

The bartender put a hand under the counter, reaching for either her soda or the pistol. Either way, we were done. Negotiations over.

I lifted the speck of napkin from the rough cut of my drinking man's beard-growth and tossed it on the floor. "Let me walk you home."

He laughed. I thought he laughed at me—walk a dictator home? —but no, he pushed against the bar's counter and climbed off his tall chair. "Adios, Los Amigos," he said to the bar.

He'd leave with me!

The bartender leaned against the wall and dried a glass with a rag.

My heart picked up. He was wobbly. He needed me. I was his support. I pushed against the heavy wooden door until it opened.

He stumbled; the floor was uneven. Outside, a small dog ran up to our ankles. My dictator said, "There you are, Little Lick."

He crouched, and both his knees crackled at once. His jeans were punk rock snug. The dog gave my dictator long-tongued kisses all over his face and the dictator closed his eyes and let it happen. He smiled, and said, "We call him Lichtenstein because he's so very small."

Then he stood and kicked the dog. Or he didn't kick it exactly, but gave it a good solid push with one booted foot. He pushed the dog this way, then that way, as we walked. The dog ran ahead and came back for more.

The dog loved it! It ran at my man's side, tongue out. That dog was in love. That dog was proof: this man was loveable. He was kind, even in his gentle kicks of military combat.

He murmured, "Are they following us?"

The night was dark, the Sunday streets empty. There was nobody, except a couple of old men, smoking. My dictator saw them and turned down a narrow alley. "Quick," he said.

Was it wise to go down a narrow alley with a drunk and paranoid deposed dictator? This was new terrain. And me, without a pistol. I wasn't the bartender, with her weapon. I was an adventurer, a student of no school, giving myself credit for any experience at all.

He was older than I was. He knew the alleys. I followed like the dog at our feet. My currency was my body. I'd spend it how I liked. Why not? My heart beat harder.

The dog came back for a kick but moved under the deposed dictator's feet too fast and the man stumbled over Lichtenstein. He might've fallen, but I stepped in close, put my shoulder under his arm, his arm around me, and he didn't hit the ground. I wobbled in my possibly-Israeli cork high heels.

I said, "Sir, I will be your human shield."

He said, "Let a falling dictator fall." He was drunk and in a blue mood.

I said, "I have a better plan."

"Miss America has a plan!" He liked it, if he liked anything, in his bitter buzz.

I unbuttoned his pants. I slid the zipper down. In the back alley I released the scent that is what it means to get to know a man. There's nothing like that moment: cock unwrapped, the first time.

He was sweaty. He'd had long days.

I slid my hand down along the line of fur that grew over his belly. He leaned back against the cracked wall of a building. My fingers reached lower. What I found: he was soft, not hard.

He said, "Human shield, I'm no threat to anyone these days."

"Hush, hush. It's the booze. I can erect you," I whispered, like he was a statue, a sculpture, a building on the verge of collapse. I thought it was what he'd like to hear.

He said, "It's the decline of civilization."

That's what he really wanted to hear: civilization there, in his cock.

I tried again, with politico sweet-talk. "The dollar is still strong."

"Your dollar, propped up by foreign interests."

I had his foreign interests covered. "I'm interested, Mr. Fahrenheit," a pet name plucked from a Queen song, the code of Queen lyrics. He didn't let on if he recognized it. I said, "Let's go to your place." I tugged his pants closed.

We walked stumbling steps together in the alley, his arm over my shoulders. He said, "We can't wake my mom."

"Your mom lives with you?"

He said, "Only temporary. Until a country lets me in." He seemed to grow smaller, there at my side.

Where was my danger zone, my adventure? I'd loved men like this before. We kissed then, long and damp in the dark alley. I kissed my dictator.

When he pulled away from me, I murmured, "You're making me live." Another Queen line.

He whispered, "I used to make people do all kinds of things."

His words gave me chills. I moved in closer. "I'm here to polish my diamond," I said. That diamond in the rough. I loved him for his faults as much as I did his jawbone, his hair, his political power.

He stumbled backward and tripped on boards piled there. Lichtenstein was underfoot, and the dog yapped as the man went down. I went down too, one hand to his head, holding him close. We sprawled on the bricks and packed earth.

"Miss America, it's too late," he said.

I lay on top of him, ran my fingers through his black and grey curls, and said, "No hay resacas si sigue bebiendo." It was from the bartendress's apron: No hangovers if we keep drinking. The only way out was forward! "You'll find a new country." I licked his face. His stubble was rough under my tongue. I licked his face again. He rolled away. Lichtenstein joined in the mix, ran his tongue over my dictator's cheek.

"I'll be a dictator's wife. You'll be my commander." Our future was delicious, and it was so clear! "I'll look good at your side."

"That you would," he agreed.

I had a vision: We'd climb the political ladder. I'd channel my repressed drives into conspicuous consumption, a beacon for the hopes of the people. Maybe I'd buy shoes, like Imelda Marcos. I'd move so far beyond my possibly-Israeli sandals. We'd make love and babies. We wouldn't know who to trust, but we'd be in it together—and that's a tight marriage.

I'd write magazine articles on politically-induced monogamy. Why not? A fine housewife's hobby. His Shakespearean shirt fluttered against the dark and cluttered alley. "We'll be televisual together," I said.

Shadows fell across us, a flicker in dim light. Somebody passed at the mouth of the alley. He said, "We could both be killed."

I whispered, "Sure. In grade school, a boy choked on Jell-O, it's that common." I laughed, drunk on our future. Death seemed a small risk. "We can have the world."

He said, "We have the world. This is it." His fingernails were dirty, as he traced a line over packed dirt, between bricks. He rapped hirsute knuckles on the bricks we lay on.

"We can have the moon." I looked for the moon in the slice of sky over our alley, though it wasn't there.

My dictator's head rested on a stack of boards. A rusted nail poked through one plank. "Young Lady Liberty, my Miss America, you're too young to remember Rome. But here we are, the fall of Empire. This one's yours."

We were tangled, arms and legs, the family dog, a short, shared history. I said, "We're a triumvirate!"

He said, "You don't know politics yet."

I offered my best party trick, stood, and hoisted my skirt. I slid my underwear down my thighs, to pee against the wall, pee like a man. I have good muscles. My urine, that hot human truth, drew a slim dark river over the old bricks of that alley. I raised the hand that wasn't lifting my skirt, raised it like the Statue of Liberty, as though holding a burning torch. "Give me your poor, your muddled asses."

He said, "Really? And what would you do with them?"

I laughed loud. I was still a free agent. I lay alongside him on the dirt and brick, kissed him deeply, beer-sweetened mouths open. I was Lady Liberty and I was Maria de Socorro, there to help. "I don't know," I said. "But you're mine. What we have, my dictator, my war machine—what we have, you and me, is a grand love. Where can we go?"

He said, "My mom's cool with it."

I had bigger plans.

The earth between bricks was so dry, it was like fired pottery. The rivulet of my urine took the shape of Florida. I said, "Florida!" and pointed. Our future? My deposed dictator half sat up, to see what I saw. Would Florida welcome us? But by the time he looked the spot had morphed, its ragged edge expanding.

"Zimbabwe," he said, with less enthusiasm.

Our future wasn't finished finding its shape yet. There was South Sudan, then Costa Rica, then Venezuela clear as day. Stop! I hoped for Venezuela, and held my breath. It was like a roulette table in that way, but the mark kept moving.

A silhouette blocked the mouth of the alley. Enemy or wanderer? The streetlight came back to the alley, the interloper had moved on. My dictator extended a single finger, stretched his arm, reached. He touched my urine. It was an intimate move. It was dirty.

I loved this man. He drew a complicated, jagged line, a country I couldn't recognize. "Las Vegas?"

"Congo." His sly smile offered a challenge.

The Congo? Perhaps the worst place on earth to be female. At least in the top five.

Clearly, our relationship was suffering from a cultural difference, or his lousy childhood, or my failure to communicate. I ran my hand over his drawing, put my fingers in my own urine, tried to change his mind. "This is what you've done to me, what I've become." Yes, I tried guilt, even as I surrendered to his influence.

He said, "Stay here." He jogged to the end of the alley.

I rested my head on the board, closed my eyes, and waited under that moonless sky. In our future together, I'd sign my name Lady Liberty, as he christened me. He'd come back with an apology; we'd forget the Congo. He couldn't possibly mean it.

I heard his feet over loose stones. My head was throbbing. I listened to the lullaby of street sounds. I could hear actual music, a bar in the distance. And other than that, the alley grew so quiet.

When I sat up, nobody was there. I walked to the end of the alley, called my man's name. He'd disappeared; "Dictator? Honey? Sweet Pea?" My voice cracked, from smoke and booze.

"We can try Congo," I offered, ready to make concessions. I spoke to the dark. But I knew, already, I was on my own. The world was one big political party. I, American in body and spirit, healthy, debauched and dedicated to travel, had no date. I felt a simmering discontent. What good was freedom when I wasn't free to hand it over, what use was the currency of my body if I couldn't spend it?

I left the alley, headed back toward the smoke-filled rooms where I'd find another entrenched leader, a dictator, an accomplice, my shill, deep in the next dark bar.

NEIGHBORHOOD NOTES: BOTTOMS UP

The alcoholic diabetic across the street left home in an ambulance in the night. They carried him down the long set of stairs from his door to the street and put him in the back, in the dark, with the ambulance lights crafting as many deep shadows as illuminated spaces. We thought he might be gone for good—and that wouldn't be good. Why does anyone say *gone for good,* unless they mean it as a good thing? He came back three days later, two feet shorter. Poor man, he'd lost both feet.

How do we even talk about a thing like that, those two feet, gone for good?

SEE YOU LATER, FRY-O-LATOR

I woke up when it was still dark outside, except for a weird white glow that seeped in past the curtains. It was my sixteenth birthday. We ignored birthdays, in our house. Mom said they were bad luck. The temperature had dropped in the night. We lived in a cold, windy corridor. We'd had an early fall blizzard. That was the light—a November Mourning Moon, still out, reflected on snow.

Mom loved the Mourning moon, and said it was her friend. That moon, she said, whispered to her when she couldn't sleep, which was always.

I used one sharp fingernail to etch a cartoon birthday cake in a layer of ice that blanketed my window. The glass looked like an old TV without reception, opaque and mottled. I scratched a dash of candles on the cartoon cake, phallic and listing, and gave each candle-cock a paisley flame. The flames were a school of sperm. *Fuck me,* I wrote backwards, a message to anybody out in the snow—like there'd be anyone in the pitch-dark winter fields. It was all apple trees and pine trees. Grass. I scratched a happy face. A happy face was the same from either side of the glass, speaking the same language from in the house or out.

The grad student who lived with us had died two years before. Vanessa had been moved out forever. Mom and dad were a closed system, busy with each other.

I pressed my hand to the ice and held it, and the ice welcomed my skin. My hand left a print. I was the Ice Queen.

The truth is, I was shy. I was a melted heart. I wanted to be brave like Nessa, who was fearless enough to leave this place behind. But me? Every time I went even just to school, I had to talk myself into being around other people.

Maybe I'd never leave.

I'd gone to bed fifteen and woken up sixteen. Mom and dad had gotten up and gone somewhere during the night. Mom was probably having her annual birthday allergic reaction. She either regretted that I was growing up, or regretted that her kids were born? Either way, there was always crying. Once she piled bricks on our storm cellar doors. I thought, what dead thing is down there? Dad had brought her back inside, acted like that was normal, all part of a longer conversation between them. We, their kids, were that living conversation.

Dad treated mom like a forensics assignment: he was out to solve the problem. He listened to her. He did. He'd be an expert witness someday, if anyone ever asked.

The refrigerator was wheezing and asthmatic. The house was cold. The windows were dark with snow. Each window on one side of the house only showed the cross-section of a snowdrift, the way the glass of an ant farm shows a slice of an ant colony. It was like we were a science fair experiment. The experiment was a question: How to be a house when you're not equipped?

I wasn't an ill-equipped house. I could be adaptive. I would be pure ice. Then cold would be immaterial. Who needs insulation? Who needs shoes, boots, a winter coat?

I opened the side door and our dog, Charlie, brought in a rage of snow. She dragged a bad front leg. The snow around the door was specked with blood, where Charlie had been waiting. That was her habit—she chewed her leg like a coyote caught in some invisible trap.

With the door open, I could see where my parents' footprints broke the first snowdrift just beyond the door. A layer of new snow had already settled over where they walked and left the compressed spots of their footprints softened with powder. They'd turned back at least once. Turned in circles. Debating? Fighting? Maybe.

Farther off, a couch-shaped drift really was our old couch underneath. We'd put out to air last spring. All summer at night I'd sat on the couch and read magazines while crickets sang, while my parents sang in the house, fighting, swearing, boozing it up.

If I were a savage I could read the tracks of my parents' path. I'd adapt again. *Savage Ice Queen: The Movie.* I could stand in packed snow barefoot. And I was in the snow barefoot, nightgown ruffle blowing against my ankles. Cold only feels cold at first, before it fades to numb. I bent down, tucked my knees inside the nightgown to keep a thin line of flannel between damp snow and the heat of private corners, and looked for evidence. My parents had left, and not in a straight line. One but not the other of our two cars gone meant they left together.

That's so obvious! The Ice Queen was a laugh in my ear, in my mind. I was the Ice Queen. I looked for subtle clues. The second car, the Old Car, was a sedan-shaped drift, a match for the snow-upholstered couch. Why did I worry where my parents went? I had what I needed: a house, a car, a job. A dog. The American Dream. I'd overslept, missed the school bus, but a learner's permit is as good as a driver's license when you come from an ice cave miles outside town.

I bundled my nightgown and lifted it. *Savage Ice Queen, pees in the wild.* Steam cut through the snow between my feet; the bright yellow stain made a hole in the ice crystals. The air filled with the muffled scent of vitamin B I took to turn around a split-end problem. My own heat was warmer as it rushed out; warm air brushed my ankles, and tiny drops splattered. It was the chemistry of urine over ice, body heat transferring. My own experiment.

***

Ryan, the stoner, sat closest to the door and tried to trip me as I slid into Chemistry late. Blank faces turned toward the late-opening door, not like they cared, but just asking: *Who? Who comes so late?*

Me. Cheeks flushed, still hot from digging the car out. I'd had to work it out of a snowdrift. My hair was wet with melted snow. My favorite teacher, Mrs Hapenstanz, worked away behind her teaching counter like the host of a cooking show, with a Bunsen burner and metal tongs. Her elbows jutted out. She swung a test tube back and forth over the burner's blue flame. Lisa, a paper-thin slip of anorexic weightlessness, was passed out in the back row. I saw Ryan's outstretched foot but kicked it on purpose anyway, letting my waffle boot slap the side of his waffle boot, orange laces kissing. Snow fell on the black and white linoleum, off the frozen leg of my jeans. Mrs. Hapenstanz gave me a quick eyeball. Ryan smiled with only one side of his mouth. I sat next to Rachel Swoops.

If I were a gas, I'd be helium-light, settling into my seat. My muscles burned from shoveling snow.

"Einstein's new trick," Rachel whispered.

"What's it supposed to do?" I hissed back, a lousy whisperer. I peeled off my coat, then pulled down the sleeves of a sweater to cover my wrist where the skin was marked with pink lines, burns from the grid of a fry rack from my job at Huff Burger. They called me *Fry Rack* at school. *Fry Girl. Fry Rat, Fried Rat, Grease Monkey, ha!*

Rachel shrugged.

"Girls," Mrs. Hapenstanz said. Her voice broke the crazy way her voice always did, singing up and down even in a single word. "Pay attention." She added something to a beaker, one liquid into another, the first as yellow as my vitamin B. She held the beaker at eye level, right in front of her nose, until she went cross-eyed trying to make sense of what she saw, frowning and squinted.

She'll need Botox, Rachel wrote on her notebook, and pushed the notebook my way.

Scientists invented Botox, I wrote back.

"What this *should* have done…" Mrs. Hapenstanz said. I couldn't help it. I laughed. I loved it when she said that. Every time, every experiment. They never worked, and I liked it that way.

"Lu, please." She started again. "It should've turned to a greenish gas. I'm not sure what's gone wrong..." And I couldn't control it. Why did I like this? It was like being tickled, seeing science fail, the parts not adding up. Mrs. Hapenstanz, pure optimism, shook her head like even a small failure was unbelievable. I giggled, hoped she wouldn't notice, tried not to laugh and snorted instead.

Rachel, already close to flunking, acted like she didn't know me, with a hand to the side of her face. Mrs Hapenstanz said, "Lu, enough," like it was a command for a dog.

But she wouldn't send me out. What I knew, and what she knew, is that I did my homework. I memorized Avogadro's number, the calculation of a mole. I had the periodic table taped inside my locker. In a room full of dyslexic anorexics, stoners and party girls, I was our Nobel Prize candidate, or close enough. I pulled the sleeves of my sweater down, stretching the knit to cover the burns. *Fryolator* it said in the pink graphics of a burn scar, in backward cursive along the inside of my arm.

After Chemistry was lunch. Ryan saw my keys. "Driving now, Fry Girl?" He soft-punched my arm, my sleeve, where fry rack tattoos lay hidden below.

I nodded. Rachel looked surprised, more used to me late-night sneaking the car.

"Cool," Ryan said. And it was.

***

After school, before work, I let Charlie out. She stopped to nose the frozen yellow piss in the snow—mine. There was no sign of my folks, nothing about my birthday, still only the one set of tracks leaving the house now mingled with mine both coming and going. A splintered chair in the bushes looked run over. My parents were like lupus, MS, or rosacea, the body attacking itself, a leg trying to divorce the hip, the brain. I was a free radical, bumping up between them. It was already dark out, a winter day as short as school, a school day as long as winter.

I brought my Huff Burger uniform into the kitchen, closed the kitchen doors and turned on the oven full blast. But heat didn't matter. I could strip down in a blizzard.

The uniform was a brown polyester shirt that zipped up the back and wide, flared pants. The shirt had a built-in bra, a swerve in the striped fabric where my body was supposed to fill in the gaps like there was a formula between hips, waist, and boobs: if one, then the other. My shirt stayed loose in empty points. There were tiny red dots in a constellation under both my eyes, like miniature burns from splattered grease. I ran a fast line of concealer over them.

The old car, musty and vinyl, had a dash that was cracked like dried mud in spring. I headed down our long dirt drive and the car's tires slid into the grooves made by my parents. I pulled onto the highway. I could see the road through holes, where the floor had rusted all the way through. Cold slush flew off the spin of the tires and bit my ankles. When I hit a patch of black ice, the car danced in a slow sideways glide. The front wheels grabbed for asphalt, but the back wheels didn't care. I stayed calm, rode out the skid until the tires found asphalt and gravel.

***

"You're on fry rack," Jeff said, before I even had my coat off. He ran a finger over his mustache.

I said, "No, I'm cashier."

He crunched up a paper bag and threw a long shot to an overflowing trashcan. Missed, hit the rim. "Nope. Rack."

The Rack. It sounded like a medieval torture device.

The schedule was posted on the wall between the walk-in freezer and stacks of buns. I didn't want anywhere near that fry rack. It was a beginner's station, plus it was all grease and quick moves, and I worked it way too often. Up front, Dana leaned against the register guarding her spot. Her hair was a curling, butter-yellow pom-pom out the back of her hat, with no split ends. The boob gaps in her uniform weren't gaps, like she was proof of the if-hips-then-boobs equation. Jeff said, "Had a complaint about you last time. A secret customer. Said you weren't smiling."

A "secret customer" meant a company spy. They wrote up these little reports. Like I'd smile more now, written up? *There's ways to make a girl smile.* That's what I wanted to say, with Ice Queen sophistication: words could ring with the hard crack of an ice coating breaking over powdered snow, carrying the sweet taste of deadly sap trapped in a Poison Sumac icicle.

The Ice Queen would speak like my sister. Brave.

He threw a fifteen-pound bag of onion rings at me. I caught the bag, felt its white plastic all slippery with frozen grease. *The Ice Queen never fumbles.*

I fumbled, dropped the bag and left a cold grease stain in a darker patch of color like it was wet, down the leg of my uniform pants.

Dana smiled, gave an eyelash flutter and tugged at a gold floating heart on a thin chain around her neck.

Jeff said, "Ten minutes, dinner rush," and went to code Dana into the register.

A low whisper gargled out, "You know they're screwing each other." The voice came from around the corner, behind the grilling machine, behind Burger Assembly. That corner was a house of mirrors with warped stainless steel boxes in every direction, and in that corner, from everywhere, I saw the reflection of skin and uniforms and hair. A grunt like me, a woman named Karen, was putting burgers on the conveyer belt.

There was a time my sister thought I wanted to be named Karen. Because she called me that I still felt the name as a little bit of who I was, even though my sister was wrong. Hello Karen!

This Karen was newly huge, her face encircled by rings of flesh. She'd transformed herself. I hadn't worked with her in a month, but heard rumors: she had to trade up uniform sizes three times. I'd traded down twice, shrinking, contracting with the winter's cold. Those were the ways to go in a world of cheap fast food and employee freebies: eat it or don't. We all had these bodies to tend and fuel.

Karen wheezed like our fridge. I knock a bony elbow into the edge of a counter, and it was like stick against stone, two hard surfaces. She slammed a handful of frozen meat patties against the steel edge of a machine to break the stack apart. Her sausage fingers, taut and red, were reflected more times than I could count in the stainless steel of everything, like a kaleidoscope. My own fingers were red, too, and like sticks. We were these struggling body-machines, doing our jobs.

What Karen didn't get is this: if you don't eat, your stomach turns into a hard knot instead of an empty space. It turns into an answer instead of a question. I started questioning all food after the student died, after the sausage, and the answer was? Minimize.

I don't know if I had the answer right, I only knew my own trip.

The truth is, even before the college guy's sausage, my sister Vanessa had shown me the beauty of needing less. She was so hard! She could do without anything. I wanted to be her. She'd left us behind.

I put my hat on, got in place.

Heat came off the deep fry oil. A few steps over, cold rose from the drink station's ice. The two made a sickening corridor of hot and cold struggling to mix, and not in the sweet way of tornado weather but more like a house fire blasting in winter. There was an orange heat lamp, glaring and bright, and a white light over the ice. In metal cursive script, on the side of each fry basket, it said *Fry-O-lator, Fry-O-lator, Fry-O-lator.*

"We're closing tonight," Karen said, breathing hard, lips squished in her new face. "You and me."

Closing meant locking up at 2:30 in the morning, cleaning, and getting off the clock by three. The company didn't pay for work after three no matter what so closing with Karen was good—she was a fast robot. I tried to be the same.

I put a basket of rings down and two baskets of fries. Grease snapped at my arms like a biting rat. My job was to tear open the big white bags, take two steps sideways, grab a new metal basket, fill the basket to the marker and sink the whole thing in grease. Fries have to be hot and ready. When a timer beeps, that means the fries are done, and then a rack rises automatically up from the grease. My job was to jump for it. One second is all management allows between when the timer rings and when fries are dumped under the heat lamp. All night long the floor mats grow slick, then slicker, with splattered fat.

The beep started, I reached for the basket handle, dumped fries in the bin under the orange heat lamp, and let salt snow down over their hot skins.

On a fast break, I stood in back near the manager's office and called home. I traced a finger over my scarred arm. It was so scarred, it had started to look plaid. On the schedule on the wall my name had been crossed out and replaced with Dana's name, for all the register shifts. I could see, through the narrow space between the burger counter and the shelves, to where Dana and Jeff trap flies in the microwave. Dana laughed, a broken cackle that maybe sounded charming to somebody else's ears? The trick with flies is, they don't have enough water in their bodies. Microwave a fly and nothing happens. A fly is its own kind of superhero.

It's a superhero by deprivation, being able to do without. I admired those flies.

On the other end of the phone line, in our snow covered ice cave, the phone rang. My mother's voice came on, apologizing: "Sorry, we're not in right now, but if you'll leave a message..."

"Mom?" I asked the answering machine. "Dad? You there?"

On the way back to my station I slid a chicken sandwich into my uniform pocket. The sandwich was dead, left under the lamp too long. My dad, if he came home, would take the sandwich apart like a mechanical thing and warm it in pieces, each piece balanced on a knife over a burner one at a time.

The dinner rush trickled in, then hit in full force; the lobby jammed with kids and old people and then all the families from some football game that'd just gotten out, and the orange heat lamp at the fry station made my eyes so dry they went blurry.

I poured fries into paper bags, moving fast, orders in and orders out. A ribbon of white receipt paper pumped out at my station, giving me directions. Fry Rack was a dance, both arms swinging: scoop fries, grab the salt, drop the small paper bags of fries into the bigger paper bags, tear the order off the roll and drop that in the bag too.

Dana's register jammed, or maybe she needed change. I don't know, but Jeff was up there, keys in hand. He reached around her hips. He put one hand to either side, around her waist. He put his mouth to her neck. I saw his lips move. She turned, giggled. The crowd pressed against the counter. Dana smiled, his hand on her ass. Where was our company spy? I didn't lose pace.

Deep in the rhythm, another fry timer sounded its steady bleat. I turned, dropped the aluminum fry scoop into its rack, hit the timer-off switch, grabbed for the handle on the fries as they rose from the grease, turned halfway back around, and boom! Jeff cut past me, all managerial now, in my way, his body in front of my body.

"We need at least three baskets down. Two rings. The orders are backing..." He grabbed fries from the bins, shoved fries in his mouth. As he skirted past, his knee hit my knee, foot to my ankle—on purpose? He ducked sideways, and kept going. Both hands full, I skidded on the spot between the big black floor mats, where grease layered over the fake tile floor. I slipped, swung an arm to grab for anything solid, slid into the mechanized basket as it rose, and with a hiss there it was, a pink brand rising over my skin. There was no time to look. Orders came in fast. Jeff was gone, back to counting receipts or browsing porn or whatever he did in his office. I put my burned hand to the ice trough in the drinks station. Held a round cube. The metal basket had left the kiss of a hot, pink grid, *y-O-Lato* seared backward across my palm.

Late that night, I took six bags of trash out to the locked dumpster. The dumpster was surrounded by a brick fort, with a locked metal gate in front, like Huff Burger trash was pure gold. Streetlights reflected against snow. Those lights kept the night from ever being as dark as it was outside of town, out where I lived, in the fields. Between the streetlights and the snow, the night was glowing blue. In the blue-white light, I looked behind the brick walls around the dumpster, checked for crazies, then moved with Ice Queen stealth over frozen asphalt, under the parking lot lights and a big, dark, glittering sky.

It was past midnight. My birthday was over. *You can come home now, mom!*

Karen locked up. Our cars were last in the lot. She drove a rust-eaten clunker, small and squashed. My car, twice as big and twice as old, had seats inviting as a sofa, but the lock was frozen and wouldn't take the key. Karen scraped her windows while her roller skate-mobile warmed up. I warmed my key in one hand, blowing hot breath on it. I had to force the key, first in, then side to side. Karen got in her car, and the car dropped lower.

When I turned the key in my ignition, nothing happened. No heater, no engine, no radio. The Plymouth clicked. I gave it a minute. Karen took off, wet tracks in the snow. I tried again. The lot was empty now, except for me and my car, and then snow, new drifts over old, and the black spots of exhaust and salt that marked patches of ice and gravel.

I reached under the dash, popped the hood, opened the door. Soon as I did, one car came spinning down the highway. The hum of chains against gravel and ice carried from far away. Headlights moved toward me. I closed the door again, ducked low. The car edged past, tossing slush like damp confetti in a sad parade. The tail lights moved into the distance, red and warm, then finally gone. When I opened the door, a night wind cut through the wide, flapping legs of my uniform.

I knocked snow off the Plymouth's hood, lifted the hood and looked inside, until I heard another car coming. Then I got back in and locked the door.

The car moved past. It skidded to a stop. There was the high-pitched whine of a car in a fast reverse. The driver pulled into the lot backwards, tried to brake, and the car slid until he'd passed me again. I looked in the rearview.

Slowly, the car pulled forward, inch by inch, until we were driver's side window to driver's side window. There was one man inside. His was an old car, a Nova to my Satellite. He rolled his window down. I wiped condensation away from my window, and peered through the cleared space.

The man pointed down, then turned his hand in circles: *Roll down the window.* I shook my head, behind fogged glass. A Plymouth Satellite is a comforting wall of metal. Except for the holes in the floor. Tiny planets of new snow glittered in the wind.

"Car trouble?" He shouted. He wore a dark stocking cap pulled low.

"No," I yelled back.

He said, "Pop the hood," and gestured with his gloved hand, thumb pointing at the night sky. A strand of yarn splayed from his frayed glove. It was just him and me, dark gloves, stocking caps, a long stretch of empty highway. And I was the Ice Queen. I'd sit there all night, stay in my car, wait for him to leave and hike along the road on my own. Ice Queen patience. *Superhuman endurance.*

Then what?

He said, "I'm good with cars."

I could walk all night and into the day. I could go home, to an empty cave.

A Huff Burger bag blew along the side of the freeway. The bag was light, as though underdressed for the cold, and moved fast as a lost kid running to someplace like home. I could do anything. I could stand up to burns, to cold, to this freaky stranger, if that's what he was.

If I were Dana, I'd have a house and parents in it. I'd have boobs.

If I were my sister, I'd have friends throwing a kegger somewhere just down a side street, a blazing bonfire, a pack of misfits big enough to be their own country.

The man got out of his car. He put his gloves on my fender. "You'll freeze out here," he said. What did he know? I was already a sheet of ice, a frozen branch, a twig. I could freeze in my own house, if I wanted to. The man's eyes darted down the road.

I was an icy slip of nothing. I was invincible.

I reached low, pulled the t-bar to unlatch the hood. I stayed in my car, watched him rustle through his trunk. He connected jumper cables, started his engine.

He called out, "Give it a try."

I turned my key. *Click.* He walked around to stand outside my window. *Click.* He disappeared behind the hood again. Like he knew what he was doing. A fine ruse.

I could see his hands working, through the gap between the hood and the car body, his skin grey-white as it reflected the lone parking lot light. It wouldn't be hard to steal my carburetor. "This cold weather," he yelled out. "Need all your Cold Cranking Amps."

He scraped corrosion from the battery, cleaned the connections with a screwdriver. His hands were chapped, a cut across one knuckle. A cotton glove blew off the fender. He didn't see it go.

"Try again," he called, and stepped to the side. He rubbed his hands together, blew on his fingers.

That glove would be one of the world's small mysteries, resting alongside the highway frozen into the slush, snowed over until spring. People would wonder: *why take one glove off here?* The man would puzzle over where the glove had gone, left with only one of the pair.

The glove would be like my parents, gone without reason.

I turned the key. He shook his head, pulled off his stocking cap and wiped his hands on it. His face was flushed, dark hair blowing forward.

I had a pen in the car, and I put the pen in my coat pocket. I'd stab the man in the eyes if I had to. That was my plan. Armed with the pen, I got out of the Plymouth, walked across the snow, and picked up the man's glove where it lay in slush. I put the glove back on the fender with its mate. Mystery solved.

"Thanks," he said.

I fingered the pen. Kept my eyes on him.

He reached for the gloves, pushed them down into his pocket, and started scraping terminals again. "I don't know. Might be electrical." His breath was a white cloud. He wiped his nose on his hat.

I said, "The battery's almost new," and watched my own breath cloud, then fade.

Beyond the smell of exhaust, there was something else in the air. Cinnamon, or vanilla. His pant legs flapped in the wind. Polyester. They were navy blue, with a paler blue stripe. I asked, "You in a marching band?"

He looked over my way, then went back to chipping at corrosion on the battery terminals. He said, "You look cold."

Cold? I said, "I can stand in snow barefoot." Savage, and proud of it. "I can reach into hot grease with my bare hands."

He laughed, and shook his head. "Nobody should have to stand in snow barefoot—" He hit something inside the car with the side of a wrench. Tapping. "—or reach into hot grease. Try it again. Might be your starter."

I didn't move to start the car. But in my pocket, I let go of the pen. I took my hand out, and opened my palm to show the brand, the geometry of a fry rack grid against the constellation of grease-splatter burns. The backwards cursive, *y-O-Lato,* was blistered and raised, the burn still new. I had that word written on my arm, too. The machines were marking me as theirs.

He leaned in close, squinted to see under the flickering streetlight, and said, "Jesus!"

The strange thing was, as he said it I saw my hand as though it wasn't mine at all but was someone else's, a red and raw thing, like our dog Charlie's leg. He said, "What's that about?"

I nodded at Huff Burger. Closed my hand. The skin was stiff and hot. I put my hand back in my coat pocket, and then it was mine again, but not like it mattered—just skin and bones, immaterial.

"Listen, you need a ride somewhere?" His car sat waiting. There were no other cars on the road. Everything was icy and muffled.

"I'll walk."

"To where?" He looked up and down the road. "You smell like French fries."

Fry Girl.

He said, "It smells good."

I smelled something sweeter. "Smells like doughnuts." The air was sweet as a bakery. But I didn't eat anymore. An Ice Queen doesn't eat. Even an anorexic can't compete with ice.

I needed food the way a fly needed water: barely.

"Panda Pastries," he said, and nodded down the highway. Far down, there was a giant, revolving, doughnut-bellied panda sign. Sweet, frying dough. Perfume. Sugar. I said, "Never smelled it from here before."

He pointed at his car, took the few steps, opened his car door and showed boxes, pink and marbled with grease stains. He pulled one box out and had to use two hands because the box was that heavy. He sat it on the hood of his car. When he opened the lid, I saw a field of crullers and maple bars, powdered sugar-coated cake doughnuts, chocolate-filled, éclairs. There were oversized fritters and coiled springs of glazed dough, bars and doughnut holes. He said, "Have what you want," like he was offering me the world.

I kicked the snow, and said. "Is this like, 'Hey little girl, want some candy?'"

He shrugged. "My embarrassment of riches. I take 'em back to the dorm." His blue striped pants, I saw now, weren't real clothes. He was wearing Panda Pastries gear. "They call me *'Nuts Man,"* he laughed. "Cause I provide. Go ahead, dig in."

I didn't need food. The doughnuts smelled so sweet! But what did I need with sweet? Then I saw, in one low corner of Mr. Nuts Man's greasy box, a cupcake. It was a white cupcake with blue and red letters across the top, and a scatter of sugared dots like confetti. *Happy Birthday,* the cupcake said. That little cupcake reminded me of mom. She'd almost killed us all once, in a strange cupcake bonfire in the basement. That was the start of her problems, as I remembered it. Birthdays had always been hard. I asked, "Whose birthday is it?"

"Nobody's," he said, and shrugged. "We just make 'em up."

It wasn't my birthday anymore, after midnight. I flicked a finger at the box, like that crap was only for suckers. Fatsos and softies. That cupcake was a trap, laid in my path. This guy was a softie. The Ice Queen lived on cold air. I breathed in. But even the air now was sweeter than before. I said, "And you don't mind?"

"Mind? No way, have all you want." He leaned against his car.

"I mean, you don't mind being called 'Nuts Man?" And for some reason, as I said it, my eyes welled up. My throat was tight. I choked, reached a hand to my neck.

"You okay?" he said.

I said, "That smell!" I coughed. "Maybe I'm allergic." My voice broke, my eyes clouded. Even my hands started shaking. Could I be allergic to a smell? It was the smell of a kitchen. An oven used for more than heat.

He ducked down and looked up, as though to see my eyes. "You're too cold. Let me walk you to a pay phone."

A pay phone. I shook my head. Who would I call at three-thirty in the morning? Rachel Swoops? Her parents would think I was on drugs. My parents, who knows? I had a sister out there, someplace. She was braver than me, though, and long gone traveling. I could call our chemistry teacher, my favorite class. Mrs. Hapenstanz at least would understand the failed science of a dead car and a late night, and all that human error. My lips felt fat, but I wouldn't cry now. "No need," I said, and I held my own hand.

He said, "Troy," and he held out his hand. I unclasped my hands, and reached out.

"Lu," I said. His hands were at least as cold as mine. Somehow, that was nice.

Troy drove me home. I held a pink baker's box on my lap. The car filled with the smell of burgers, fries, and doughnuts. In matching polyester, our coats and winter boots, we passed through crowded suburbs on either side of the highway.

"Keep going," I said.

When we got to my house outside town, there were no cars in our long drive.

Troy pointed, "That drift looks like a couch."

Still nervous, always nervous, more used to being entirely alone, I braved up and asked anyway, "Would you come in?"

He shut off the engine, climbed out and followed me around to our side-door. "You have a dog." He meant the frozen spot of yellow snow. My morning experiment. That was like a lifetime before.

"We do," I said. And as I turned to look for Charlie, one hand out with a key for the door, I slipped on ice and slid, the fry-rack dance, and the world swam underfoot. I grabbed Troy's shoulder, he put a hand to my side, steady again. When I caught my balance, I pushed open the door to the house and we moved from dark to darker, from the night sky to our cave.

"Your parents don't believe in furniture." He kept his coat on.

I shrugged. "We used to have more."

The dog was inside. "She's hurt," Troy said. Her shoulder was damp where she chewed, where she looked for metal pins buried deep in her bone.

"Ages ago," I said.

He said, "But she's bleeding."

I shrugged. "Self-inflicted."

Charlie followed us into the kitchen. I closed the doors and turned on the stove. We had a table and chairs. A ceiling light. I poured brandy from a bottle above the sink, one short glass for me and one for Troy. My parent's brandy was a bribe; I didn't want him to leave.

He looked in the fridge. "There's nothing here," he said, like he'd never been in an ice cave before.

"There's milk," I said. "And beer. And this." I pulled the cold, dead chicken sandwich out of my coat pocket.

"Pass, thanks," he said, sweetly.

It had started to snow again outside, big damp flakes that covered our tracks. Troy moved for the front door. I said, "Where are you going? It's a storm."

He went out, just like that, and then I was alone in the house again. I felt like a five-year-old, afraid to go to sleep, and at the same time like a grown-up with a house all my own. Neither way felt nice or right or settled. I picked a rag rug off the floor and gave it a shake. Dirt fell. I put the rug over my lap like a blanket, waited for the sound of an engine, or the lights of Troy's beams against the snow on our driveway.

The screen door rattled open. Troy stomped snow off his boots. He slid one big, pink box onto our wobbly kitchen table, opened the lid and flashed a world of crullers, éclairs, cake doughnuts, and fritters. That cupcake, my own little birthday, sat in one corner all dressed up with nobody to sing.

Early morning, I showed Troy to my parents' room. Their floor was carpeted with dirty clothes and towels. Cold candles dripped hardened wax onto saucers. A chest of drawers had the drawers out, the bottom of one drawer splintered like somebody had stepped right through it. Their bed was a mattress on the floor, and had been since the year mom burned their bed. That fire was long gone, but the room still smelled like a campfire, and would forever.

"Sure they won't come back?" He lifted a book off the blankets and touched the worn sheets.

"Maybe eventually. Not yet." The air smelled greasy and sweet. It was *Fry Girl and 'Nuts Man, Episode One.* He started to unlace his boots. He slid one boot off, showing a black sock. The mattress had two gullies—the shape of two people, sleeping side by side. Troy, when he slept, would roll into one like an old habit. I ran my hand along the other. This was a new story: me, sixteen, older than I'd ever been, with a warm man soon to be sleeping in my parents' bed.

He asked, "What if they do?"

I said, "Wake me."

NEIGHBORHOOD NOTES: USED GOODS

A five-drawer dresser, composing itself out in the alley—decomposing really, nearly composting its tiny pressboard feet where they stand in a cool puddle—wears a paper bib shouting "Free."

Watch out for splinters when you run to meet it, little lover! So many plans rush in, each thought golden as marriage: You could put your underwear in the top drawer, once you wrestle it home, dry it off. Every drawer in this dresser is entirely different from the one below, the one above. The first drawer has grooves notched to match a cousin piece of furniture long, long gone. It's a foster drawer, tucked cozy in a new home. One drawer is painted yellow. Another is made of thin, unpainted, cherry-stained wood.

The dresser is a place for gathering the lost and found, like a church or a block party.

Dear dresser, chest of drawers, you highboy, lowboy, chiffonier, you're beautiful! But how do you hold yourself together?

These are very good and used used goods, a place where all mismatched socks can feel at ease. Now this traveling dresser, moving like a hitchhiker, needy and broken, has found a new home. When you open a drawer you'll see a pen and a book of matches. You'll find an uncapped needle. You can use it. Go ahead. It's fine. How do we know it's fine to use? Because other people have.

THROW A FRISBEE IN THE PARK

Sean was talking to this dark-haired girl outside their Renaissance Art History class, in the wide hallways of Portland State University's Neuberger Hall, when they figured out that they'd both turn twenty on the same day in exactly one week. Their professor was late. A few students took off but the rest stood or sat, scattered and waiting. Sean and the girl were part of that group. They leaned against corkboards that were fixed to the walls covered with event flyers and crisis line notices with dark ink drawings of crying ladies on them, and a curled fringe of phone numbers to tear off. The girl said, "My birthday has always been horrible. Every year." She chewed her nails. On her arm? There was a tattoo that'd been badly removed, or the pale lines of old scars. Either way, it was cursive, written backward, an old script or font that seemed to say *y-O-Lato?* Sean wondered if it was something in Latin. He tore off a number from one hot pink page and rolled the strip between his fingers.

He said, "So, what's your name?"

Lu. She said it in a way that was drawn out slowly, her voice soft and gentle. Totally hot. She said it like a girl a little disconnected, maybe one whose brain had grown used to being high—his dream girl, all the way. He was pretty sure she'd be better at packing a bowl than she was at looking him in the eye. When she did manage to look right at him, Sean felt special, like she'd gone out of her way. Then her bangs fell back over her eyes, and she cocked her head.

Lu and Sean each held a copy of their Renaissance art history textbook, a big brick, thick enough to stop a bullet. His had the cover ripped off. Hers was the wrong edition, older and cheaper, with about six names written in ballpoint pen on the front, and a yellow sticker that said USED. She had a naked Rockabilly girl tattooed on her thin upper arm, three green dots drawn near her wrist, and a short piece of blackberry vine laced over her clavicle. The tattoos looked random as the scrawl on her textbook's cover, like somebody had been doodling on her skin. He'd let himself think it, but would never say it: she looked like she'd been passed around.

She blushed when she talked, if that's what you could call it. It wasn't a soft flush on her cheeks. It was more of a red patch that climbed up her chest, and behind her ears, heating her skin as they talked.

So their moms were in labor on the same day, bringing them into the world. It was like they should know each other. He didn't want to think about specifics: his mom, twenty-two years old, on her back, legs up or whatever. Her mom, however old she'd been, half-naked in a hospital robe. Maybe her mom had her guts cut open, with that other kind of delivery. All he knew was that they were two women who'd been knocked up and were fat and bloody. He didn't want to think about his mom that way mostly because then he'd have to think about himself as a baby, totally pathetic, and Lu's bloody, bald head, new to the world.

He just wanted Lu to keep saying anything, saying *Really?* moving her lips up and down, flashing her narrow teeth, flushing. Nodding, *Yes, mine too!*

Her hair was shaved up one side and long on the other and her short fingernails were painted black. She was skinny, flat-chested, almost like a guy but not in a bad way. Mostly she looked like she'd been raised inside, in a house without sun in some middle-class nowhere, all dry cereal and TV. Now she was out in the world. She picked at the worn corner of her book, a book that had been dropped a few times. She looked at the cover and said, "What's 'Renaissance' anyhow? There's no rebirth. You're born, you live, you get one round." Her voice was soft and spacey. That's what the class had told them Renaissance meant—rebirth. She said, "Renaissance is a thing invented a long time ago to make people feel like they're on the right track. Like they get a second chance."

He nodded, unsure. His mind was on her neck, the way it was long and pale, and the way she held it, exposed, straight-up vampire bait, and that climbing hot flush. He asked, "Wanna do something next week? Skip class, hang out. For our birthdays." That was strategic: *during* class. The time she'd be least likely to have other plans. *For our birthdays.* Bonding. He pushed it, and added, "For our rebirth."

Laughing, she didn't turn him down or accept, but only said, "Hang out?" She tipped her head to the side again, tipped it toward where her hair was still long, like that long hair actually pulled her head sideways. Where her hair was cut short, it stood up in dark brown bristles and showed her clean, white scalp. Her eyes were greenish brown. She smelled flammable, like turpentine and oranges. When she lifted one arm to move her hair behind her shoulder, she flashed a sudden patch of bright red blood blooming on the soft skin of her underarm at the edge of the naked Rockabilly chick tattoo.

"You're bleeding." He winced when he said it—too much to think about, her body and blood—and he had a fast urge to smoke a bowl right then, to self-medicate.

She ran a hand over her jaw then down her neck, checking.

He pointed to his own arm. She held her arm up, tried to see by looking underneath. When he pointed this time, he touched her skin, and electricity completed a small circuit. He pulled his hand back. She ran her fingers over the spot, where the blood stayed put. She tried to scratch it off with her fingernails. It was brighter than blood, he saw now. "Cadmium red," she said. "Paint."

So she was a painter? She brought her arms back to her sides, and collected herself, like a bird settling back on a branch. She added, "If we hung out, what would we do?"

She made his invitation sound sketchy. He was a farm kid. He grew up just outside Portland in a town called Boring, and now he'd lived in the city for a few years, but still was trying to fit in. He'd gone back to school, wanted to meet girls—girls like this one.

She grew up outside of Sandy, she said. Not far from him! Still.

She made him feel like a creep. He didn't know how to date. Where he grew up, you played Minecraft at a girl's house if you were lucky, and if her parents were gone you got drunk enough to make out. Now he tapped his book against the wall. Boom, boom, boom. Thinking. Boom. A flake of plaster fell to the floor, the wall giving up that easily. He unrolled the strip of pink paper in his hand, with the campus rape hotline number on it, and when he wrestled a pen out of his back pocket, he turned the paper over, pressed it against the wall and wrote his own number on the back. "Throw a Frisbee in Washington Park," he said. "Something like that?"

***

Boyfriend seemed exactly the wrong word for what Lu had hanging around already, because 1) the guy she was seeing was at least ten years older than she was, not a boy; and 2) she wasn't any good at communicating, and she knew it and 3) she grew up in a family where she wasn't supposed to start dating ever, her mom couldn't handle reality, her dad always thought Lu was perpetually ten years old, so she was awkward with the whole picture and even the concept.

Fortunately, this new guy Sean, hadn't asked if she had a boyfriend, because when guys did ask—and they did, always ready to plant their skinny flagpole if she wasn't already taken—she never knew the right answer. It was the worst kind of test.

Her man Travis, he wasn't afraid to ask questions. He'd ask ten questions in a row, like an interrogator. He'd been in the Air Force. Maybe that was where he got the confidence.

Later that same day Lu and Travis were in her one-room apartment, naked and sweaty, stretched out on her mattress on the floor. She peeled one of the oranges she'd bought at the Vietnamese grocery, cheaper by the crate. The orange's peel was loose and came off in one piece. Travis's eyes were on her thin fingers as she peeled that skin, then put the peels in a tidy pile, on the bed, beside her bony hip. He was always watching. She kind of liked it. Travis peeled a white sticker off the orange's skin. *Little Cutie* it said on the sticker. He pressed it to her thigh, but it didn't stick because of the sweat. He said, "You have paint on your arm."

She said, "I know. Cad red." She ate her orange, biting through the segments, letting juice run down her throat. The room was small and narrow and nearly empty, except for an old refrigerator, an end table, and a jammed-full closet without a door, where she kept everything else she owned. A pretty patch of late-afternoon sun lay over the bare wood of splintered floorboards, echoed by white squares of new, stretched canvas leaning against one wall.

"Cadmium," he said. "That's poison."

She ate her orange, and said, "It is not." She laughed again. He was crazy, always telling her new ways to die, *weaponizing* everything. She didn't believe half of it. "Maybe this is my birth control patch. Pure poison, seeping into my bloodstream." She ran her hands over the paint spot.

Stretched out on his back, Travis tugged at his curled chest hairs, and said, "In the '50s, the Army drifted zinc cadmium sulfide over the Midwest. Thing is, they couldn't control its drift. Spread a thousand miles, clear into Canada. The U.S. is still apologizing to them. Kind of a bust."

Maybe he was right, or crazy, but either way he knew things, had traveled, and she respected that. She'd barely been off the property where she grew up. He was out of high school when she was in grade school.

He said, "Now the military has two tests going on. One is to show there were no health problems from those secret tests. They say cadmium, at the levels they used, is fine. But the other work? They're looking for a replacement for cadmium in weapons casing. Because cadmium is poison, and they know it." He picked at the paint on the soft back of her arm, taking care of her, and didn't give up until it came off, even as he scratched her arm.

She said, "Did you work with cadmium?"

He reached for an open bottle of beer, where it rested, sweating in its own condensation, on the floor beside the mattress. He said, "I don't know what I did. A lot of things. But what are you doing, next week? Got a birthday coming up." He'd changed the subject.

She said, "You're doing it again." Like a nervous tick, when she asked about the past, he always asked about the future. Every time. She was always honest. She said, "I'm going to the park. With this guy, Sean."

Travis sat up, moving his back up the wall. His muscles flexed. He said, "Come again?"

When he moved like that, she could smell his body in the air, his sweat and semen, their afternoon sex, the heat of him. Mostly, she liked that he cared.

"He asked me. I said yes. It's in the middle of the day," she said, like that made a difference, like it wasn't a real date because it wasn't at night. When Travis was silent, she added, "It's the only plan I have. Nobody else asked me to do anything, not even my mom." Not even him, she meant. It was her birthday.

Travis said, "It's a date. Who the hell's Sean, again?"

And she thought, *Who the hell are you, Mister?* But his eyes were blue and his hair was thick, and his arms were strong and sinewy. He had a Nevada tan, desert tan, wherever he'd been living, wherever he sometimes went. He was gorgeous, that hothead. She put an orange segment in her mouth, held it out toward his mouth, leaned in, rolled on top of him, her body over his, and he bit into the orange, gulped it even, made his mouth ready for more, for her, like he'd been starving.

***

Travis was a drone operator stationed in Nevada for longer than he could take, and none of what he did made him feel good about himself. Actually, it made him feel like he had rocks in his mouth, under his tongue, most of the time. It made him feel like he'd eaten cement. He tried not to show it.

He'd been the eyes of the job, a sensor they called it, keeping a steady watch on a screen. He saw things, *sensed* things. He worked alongside a partner, in close communication. When the pilot released the drone, Travis would work the cameras, the eyes and lasers—terminal guidance. Their squad killed over a thousand human targets, making the world a safer place.

When he left the Air Force and came back to Portland, he signed up for community college classes down the hill from his mom's place. The school was in a forest. It was that green, Oregon green, right in the city, and he could breathe again, away from the Nevada brown and office air, the rank air of a cramped room. He could get to school on the city bus. Sometimes he rode his bike, like a kid, and it felt good. He liked not operating anything—not a car, not a Predator, not a Hellfire. Coasting. Everybody on campus? Mostly they were closer to the age he'd been back before he joined the military. Now, he drank too much. He knew he did. So what?

In the military, his work held a spot on the kill chain. He was part of the strategy, one more body and mind in service, deciding how to invest time, money and lives. It was about precision, even when that precision didn't always pay off. They did their best. Now he was ready to float. He didn't want to invest in anything too fast, not even himself. Out of Service, he'd think, like a sign on a busted soda machine at the far edge of campus.

There was an intentional lack of precision to his days, his plan, his open-ended questions.

Still he had the creepy feeling sometimes that he was on somebody's screen, far away. He could be a target. We were all on someone's radar imaging. The government could dust pure poison over its entire population and nobody would know where the problem started. His skin crawled if he let himself think.

Other than blotto in a dark bar, the community college campus was the best place to be, where he felt the cement in his gut grow lighter, more like the pumice he'd hiked over once out by Crater lake with his dad when he was a kid, when his dad was alive. He liked sitting in classes. Listening. Sometimes he had a hard time staying still in a classroom, though. There was a mixed feeling that came up inside of him, possibility and despair duking it out. The classes were about turning himself into somebody else—an anthropologist, or a computer programmer—except he knew he would never be anybody else. He was a drone operator. He saw the screens in his sleep, where he'd worked for twelve-hour shifts at a time. Now he took Ambien, a hypnogogic that left a person near-hypnotized and didn't always make him sleep; sometimes it only made him leave his body, his plans. He took Adderall in the day. He'd made a deal with himself to only look forward, and not too far. He navigated an emotional fog like driving a car down a dark, socked in road, or guiding a Hellfire against infrared. He stayed in his shallow okay zone.

The sprawling buildings and acreage of the community college made up a tiny world where nobody freaked out if you talked to strangers. Lately, all he had were strangers. After a while he transferred from Portland Community to Portland State, downtown, looking for more of the same. He started hanging around Smith Center, with its Food Court and the Park Blocks where religious freaks and students loitered. The Park Blocks were a green zone, to his mind. Not in the military sense, but a place he could hide and hope. It was all trees and wooden benches, where homeless people sometimes slept. Hanging around that school was the same as dropping at a bar—you didn't need an invitation, didn't need friends, could make new ones.

The day Travis met Lu he was in his best suit—dark blue, pinstripes, a necktie. Women his age would see right through his sweat and pretense. Any woman his age, she'd say, "What, you work at Men's Warehouse now?" Yeah, a woman would know a cheap suit was like an easy costume, but the girls didn't catch on.

The first time he saw Lu, he'd been in the Student Center buying a coffee to take outside. Lu reached for the communal cream. When she saw him pull his Adderall vial out of his pocket, she'd smiled and said, "Exams?"

The term had only just started.

She'd walked with him outside, sat in the Park Blocks, talked him into buying her friends a bottle of bourbon. He was old enough to buy booze, and they wanted booze, and that was a perfect equation. He remembered how she'd said, "You look lust—" and let the sentence hang in the air, before she said, "...lustrous, in the sun." It was beautiful, young woman flirting.

He was up for it.

They pooled their money, those girls scraping together worn bills. They pulled dollars out of backpacks and old lady-style purses that smelled like the Goodwill. They dropped coins into his hand. They were a small sea of tattooed skin and smoke, roiling in front of him. They counted their money two and then three times, like they could find ways to stretch it, and they still didn't have enough so finally he put in a few dollars of his own. It didn't matter. Buying kids booze was against the law but hell, it wasn't the worst thing he'd done. After that, it turned into a thing—they'd see him and wave, and they knew his name and let him be one of theirs, one of them. They cut a small place in the world for him to belong.

Then he'd started dating Lu, if that's what you called it. He had sex with her, and stayed the night in her one-room place.

Now he was naked on Lu's bed in the heat. April. He sort of wanted to throttle her, to shake her. A date? Christ on a cross. She was making life harder. But he also knew she wasn't his at all. He was far away. Even inside his own head, he was far away from himself.

The drone work made distances unreal. He'd stare at a screen, eyes peeled open. He could feel close to a target in another country. He watched families celebrate holidays, get together for birthdays and weddings. He missed his own cousin's wedding back home. He started to recognize the shape of each stray dog that cut through an alley. He could watch people going on with their lives, and his life was on hold. He saw teenagers grow up. He watched villages, saw couples—*copulating* even, once, out in a field, and that was the word he used, in his head: copulating. He couldn't say *fucking* because that brought it home, and he sure as shit couldn't say making love without gagging on the words. He wasn't allowed to look away.

With Lu, he felt close but also like he was watching her on a screen, or she was watching him, mediated by some time and space continuum that mystified him. Her life was an alternative universe. Once she'd broken a bottle on the sidewalk. They were walking in a light rain. Their paper bag got wet and gave out, that easily. The bottle smashed against the cement. He felt his stomach shatter along with it. She'd said, "It's so beautiful." Broken glass glittered against the wet sidewalk, and the wine was a dark river, but beautiful was the opposite of what Travis had thought, until Lu said. From then, he wanted to let the world be her world, not his. Sex with Lu? It was a fantasy. She was sexy as hell. Still, the whole thing was a placebo with a shot of whiskey on the side: half a cure. It was good, but he wasn't getting better.

Sometimes, he'd get a word lodged in his head: transmissions, say. Everything was a transmission. Like STDs, sexually transmitted, and drones, missiles, weaponized transmissions. Transmissions, transmission. The language messed him up. The word had worn its way into his skin. He'd grown up with his brain in different worlds. His mom was a librarian, he thought he liked computers and baseball, and now he cared and didn't care at the same time about everything, and his mom was old and anxious and he was not playing baseball. He sat up, reached for his jeans, but before he pulled them on he said, "So you're doing what, with this guy?"

She rolled away, onto her back, and stretched out long, eating her orange, her skin evenly pale, head to toe, except for the tats. She had a tattoo on her shoulder of a hummingbird that'd been outlined but never inked in, half-done, plan aborted. That shoulder was turned toward him now, showing him her back, the bones of her spine, her skin. Her voice was muted as she answered, facing away. She said, "Maybe toss a Frisbee in the park."

Why was he hearing about this just now? There'd been a delay. He wasn't sure if this was an attack, or what kind—a threat, or a blip—and worked to let it go. Lu lived in the world he'd fought to preserve. The sun outside the window was dropping toward the West, out over the ocean, far away, and as the light shifted the room looked grainy and the colors dulled, and it was too easy for it to all melt into an image on a screen. He saw Lu in infrared, a flash burned against the back of his retina, like somebody had flipped the camera. She was there, in light and shadow. He touched her hip. The warmth of her skin settled his heart. He dropped his jeans back to the floor, without putting them on.

There was a knock on the door. They looked at each other in the dimming natural light and Lu got up to pull on a loose dress. When she opened the door a slim crack, there was a woman with a plastic baggie in her hand. "Hey. It's you," Lu said, and opened the door the rest of the way. It was Candy, an upstairs neighbor.

Candy said, "Hey. I got this bag of 'shrooms. I'm gonna make tea. Trip with me?" She had thin brown hair and a weathered face and it was hard to tell if she was older than Lu or had just smoked and drank in the sun at more music festivals. She had about thirty earrings in her ears, or maybe not that many but who counted?

Lu turned to Travis, with her bare feet and pale legs in the room's grey light, and Travis felt himself pull away, disappear into the bed, the floor, the sheet over his body like he was already a corpse. He held a hand up, gestured no thanks. Because psychedelic mushrooms? There was a time he would've said yes. Before. But now, he had no interest in accessing the recesses of his wider mind. It flat-out scared him.

***

All that week, Sean thought about the way Lu smelled—volatile—and the way she looked—mellow—and that paint on the soft skin of her arm. They had a plan. He'd scored. She didn't call. That was good. If she called, she'd have a chance to cancel.

Travis tried to pretend it wasn't happening, that the naked girl who let him fuck her, who let him go down on her, wasn't really going out with some guy she met in a hall. *Find, target, launch, engage...* His training rattled against the inside of his brain. It didn't help. He contained himself, even when his military brain cut in, aching to neutralize the adversary, gain information, build the kill chain for this slo-mo attack.

How big a breach?

If he had an Xbox he could play games and zone out, except that didn't work anymore because after twelve-hour screen days in the military—all that white hot stillness, refusing to blink, that contained panic and pure responsibility—games made him sick. He couldn't be around Lu, either. He committed to avoiding her, to protect himself from panic and that urge to move toward action. Then he'd show up late at night at Lu's place anyway, buzzed, when the Adderall was winning and he'd flushed his Ambien on impulse.

The closer to the beginning of the Kill Chain that an attack can be halted, the better. Strategy was more effective the earlier it was employed.

Lu would get to know Sean. Travis couldn't stop it, and it wasn't his business, but it was, too. He wrestled with his urge to dominate, and to let go. He felt that struggle in the way he held his jaw, a civilian with military training, like a machine he was supposed to turn off but it fed him. He felt the weird space between people: from here to there. Bodies might seem close, might even be physically close, but brains, central control, were always worlds apart.

One afternoon in the Park Blocks outside Portland State, he ran into Lu and her friends and they started pulling out dollars, in a sign to buy booze that he could drink with them. Lu said, "Hey, Sexbot." Usually that made him laugh, he knew she meant it as a compliment, but this time around he walked the fuck away before they could hand him the dollars because who was he, anyway?

Lu felt herself turning into a total pleaser, not cool, but Travis was so beautiful when he was happy. Maybe she felt guilty? Except the whole creating happiness thing was exhausting, and it was impossible if he didn't even come around, and then sometimes there were nights when he'd show up totally wasted and in tears and she had no idea what to do with that strong man falling apart in her bed—he was so much older than her and her friends, why didn't he have it together?—and she'd call her friends and ask for ideas. She'd whisper, "Dudette. Help me out. This isn't what I signed up for." It was always late at night. Her friends never came over when she called for help. Travis's face would seem to fold in on itself, creating a raft of lines around his mouth, his lips drawn down, the most real frown she'd ever seen. His face would be so suddenly wet with tears, like they sprung from his skin like sweat, not just from his eyes. His skin would get hot too, she could feel it, with something like rage, that took over, like fever, and then everything she said was wrong.

She wanted to use her body to prop him up. It was a physical urge, to make him act like the man she thought he was. Maybe she loved him?

One night when he was drunk—he didn't hit her, but he put his hand on her face, reached out, and it was like he'd misjudged the distance. He wasn't slapping her. Not really. More like he was in a hurry, and thought she was farther away.

Another night they came in late and Candy was dragging a garbage bag of clothes over the building's worn yellow carpet down to the basement laundry, singing classic rock, maybe the Who, maybe the Police, or some mixtape mash-up in her mind. Travis said, "She never leaves, and never works. She's a paid informer. A spy for the Feds." He said it more like a joke than in a paranoid way, Lu thought, or hoped maybe.

In Lu's room, Travis started saying, "You're going out to throw a Frisbee? That's a date," and Lu got a little tired of picking up the pieces of his feelings.

"I can go to the park with Sean. It doesn't hurt you," she said. It was the park! It was fine. She didn't owe Travis her life. Half the time he wasn't even around. Travis was a guy who bought them booze, and now he was a friend, and they had sex and he smelled good. Even if Travis himself asked her if she *had a boyfriend,* she wouldn't know the answer. She would have said, *You tell me.* He wasn't stepping up.

On a night when things were okay, Lu and Travis went to play pool. Lu was carded and couldn't get in. They stayed out on the street talking, making out, drunk in the dark. They went into an alley and Portland was so small, they were like pool balls themselves, knocking into each other, because Sean was right there, already in the same alley, taking a leak. Sean was shaking it off, zipping up. Lu said, "Sean?"

And Sean answered, "Lu?"

"Jesus," Travis said. "Let's get out of here." Travis was unnerved by how Sean looked so far away, down that alley, a ready-made target, standing upright between the vectors of the buildings' brick walls.

Back on the street, they were silent at first, then, as they walked, Travis said, "So that's him."

Lu hit Travis on the arm. She said, "Why didn't you invite me to do something?" For her birthday, she meant. She said, "I've had a life of bad birthdays. Every year."

Her sister never remembered her birthday, or maybe even Lu at all. Her mother was allergic to birthdays, and what kind of mother is that? Her dad was checked out.

"You have plans," Travis said, because by now he was committed to being moody and difficult.

Lu went home alone, a mutual decision, and in the apartment lobby everything smelled like nail polish. Candy was there, painting her toenails. She said, "Boy trouble?" Her lips were thin, and flat, but her eyes were big and sincere and she looked at Lu like she cared.

Lu must've looked like she'd been crying. Maybe she sort of was.

Candy said, "I get it. He's hot. Smoke?" She offered a Pall Mall, tapping the pack. Lu reached for the cigarette Candy offered.

The women went up three flights of stairs then out a fire escape to smoke together in the dark, where the big, lit sky and the city's low skyline showed there was still space in the world, even as Portland grew crowded with people and the new buildings everyone called infill. They intertwined their fingers, Lu's right hand in Candy's left, and Lu practiced smoking with her left hand because she had a hollow spot in her gut and wanted to hold on. Travis would have to understand.

None of them changed course.

So early on the afternoon of Lu and Sean's matching birthdays, the two of them met at a place on Burnside and climbed the West Hills together with a neon green Frisbee and a bottle of Prosecco rattling against two plastic cups in a paper bag. They walked up a set of narrow cement stairs. Within a block, the city dropped away and they were in a sprawling green corridor of manicured wilderness.

Lu worried and tried not to worry because she was also incredibly happy, really, as they moved past the park's landmarks. There was a bench dedicated to a guy, a writer and revolutionary named John Reed, where she used to write in her diary back in high school. That bench looked as nondescript as any other bench around, even though John Reed was a big deal way back, Portland's own major player, pivotal in the Russian Revolution. There was a cement column for Sacajawea, who helped Lewis and Clark push all the way to Oregon, to wipe out Natives right there, in the West. They passed a playground and kept going into the woods, further back on the trails. She felt okay—like she probably wasn't going along with an axe murderer, that kind of okay. They weren't exactly alone. There were people in the park, mostly moms, kids and dog walkers.

She thought, what if this guy, Sean, what if he's a rapist? You had to think that about everyone at first. She imagined describing him to the cops, like if she were raped but lived, and didn't want to think about other possibilities. She took an inventory: Her height, maybe? Brown-blonde hair. A white guy, kind of cute, pretty ordinary. At least Travis knew where she was, and who she was with. That was her safeguard.

It was the way she'd heard about hookers always telling somebody who they got in the car with, right? That wasn't how she saw herself, but how else did you date?

Travis would get over it. He'd be mad. It wouldn't last. He'd never acted accountable to her, anyway, and they weren't married. Everybody would live.

She and Sean got off the path and pushed their way through a line of bushes, then past a Holocaust memorial where brass sculptures of toys and roses were embedded in the ground, made to look liked they'd been dropped, in honor of dead children. It was spring. The sun cut through the trees. They found an open space away from the path and Sean put the bottle, still in its bag, at the base of a tree. He could have put it anywhere on the ground. Instead, he rested the bag against the roots, as though the tree were holding it, like the bottle needed to be held. She knew that feeling.

"Over there," Sean said, and motioned for her to move back.

Playing Frisbee gave Sean permission to look at Lu, across a short distance. He didn't have to feel stupid for staring. She was wearing this dress that went all the way to the ground, with big flowers on it, and Converse. She was skinny and her arms were long and nothing about her seemed at home in the sun. She wasn't flushing now, though. He wasn't having the same affect. How to bring that back on?

He liked it. He liked her nerves, and sort of wished they were jammed together on a couch playing Minecraft in a dark basement, his natural terrain. The thing about Frisbee was that in order to play together, they had to get farther apart and he wasn't sure that was what he wanted after all, except this way at least he could look at her. They were here now and they moved backward in opposite directions so they could get in a good throw over distance.

Sun through the green Frisbee was so bright that it was practically hallucinogenic. The first throw felt awkward, stiff, but crucial. He wanted to look cool. Sean pulled his hand back, held the Frisbee, and let it fly. It moved through the air in a way that was both fast and slow, slightly floating, aloft and heading toward Lu. She put up her hands and caught the Frisbee. She slapped it between her palms, and then moved it to one hand, and threw it back. Each time, it seemed like luck when the Frisbee stayed airborne. It was luck to catch it.

For Travis, it was one of the days when the urge to get out of class was stronger than any hope of self-improvement and he picked up his Anthropology books and left. Outside, in town, an old church reached a wooden spire toward the blue sky and somebody had hung a sign painted on a bed sheet along the roofline. They'd written, in spray paint, STOP THE CHEMTRAILS! People, little people, with no idea what they were talking about, were trying to speak up using an old sheet and a can of spray-paint, but who were they talking to? Somebody, somewhere, in a dark, rank basement bunker of a room might read that on a screen. Who would care? The air was warm and the sun was bright and the day would get hotter before it cooled off. It felt like a day of secret weapons testing. Portland's clean air was laced with things that'd kill you. Mostly benzene but other poisons too.

He stopped at a store, picked out a card for Lu and wrote inside, "Happy Birthday. Almost old enough to buy your own."

Then that didn't seem right. He crossed his words out and the card looked worse, like he was re-using it. He threw the card and its blank envelope in the public trash. The envelope should be buried with its card. He felt somebody watching, seeing him waste that thing he'd just bought. Not God. Maybe the government, the U.S. or an enemy or both, or only the lonely Google Earth and all the satellites overhead.

This was a test. Not a military test, or God testing anybody. It was a test of endurance.

The Frisbee caught an updraft, warbled and swung upward then fell back toward Sean. Lu couldn't catch it, but ran forward, then stopped, digging her Chuck Taylors into the damp ground. The beauty of this game? No keeping score. They weren't playing Frisbee golf or Ultimate. Lu swooped low, lifted the Frisbee off the grass. He took a gamble, asked, "You get high?"

Travis lived with his mom for now because she'd been diagnosed with an anxiety disorder while he was in the Air Force and she didn't always get her meds right. Nobody said it, but Travis felt like his enlistment sent her off the rails. By going away, he'd done his mom damage. She'd absorbed his anxiety, the nightmares he shoved down. It was hard to be near her; she was emotionally porous. So when he didn't feel like going home to her hotbox of a house in the 'burbs, he walked downtown instead and out of habit, he veered toward Lu's apartment building.

The front door, into her apartment lobby, was locked. He rang the buzzer, confirming what he knew: nobody answered because Lu was in the park. She was out throwing a Frisbee. With some jackass.

Some jackass who'd scored time with her. Some jackass like himself, like Travis.

She lived on the ground floor and always left a window open, without a screen, where she sometimes sat to smoke. He walked through the line of Arbor Vitae, pushed himself past the scratch of branches, felt them claw at his face, and ducked. It was easy to raise the rattling old wood frame window and hoist himself in, climbing the rough brick wall with his sneakers, holding on to the window's ledge, no problem, same way he'd done as a kid, same way he'd done a lot of places. Then he fell to the floor on the other side, and was alone in her room, surrounded by that scent of oranges, turpentine, and oil paint. He was home, in her home. He was in a cloud that was maybe toxic, maybe not, but it was the scent of Lu.

He picked up a shirt she'd left on the bed, pulled it to his face for animal reasons, then put it back where he'd found it. The coffee pot on the small piece of counter next to the sink was turned off but still held warm coffee, telling him Lu had woken up late, hung around, just left. It was weird being alone in her apartment, like he was hiding, so he opened the door to the hall, acted like he had a key and had come in that way. This was not surveillance. He was only stopping by.

Candy dragged a vacuum cleaner down the hall. Her vacuum had the word FREE written in Sharpie over its plastic shell. That vacuum, with scrawled writing on its round dome, was like a gutter punk he'd seen with a forehead tattoo. Travis could guess she'd picked it up on a street corner. Candy drifted closer, leaning against the doorway, like a person sneaking up on a stray dog, not sure of its temperament. "I don't bite," he said.

She asked, "Is Lu around?"

He shrugged. "Somewhere."

"She knows you're here?" When he didn't answer, Candy added, "Lu's my best friend."

Lu would not have said the same. Was Candy protecting the place? Protecting it from him. That cement in Travis's stomach climbed toward his throat. His mom needed him, he should check on her. Candy's hair lay in long, limp tendrils around her shoulders. He wanted to cry into her dirty hair. The canister vacuum sat at her feet like a dog. He offered, "Does that thing work?" He'd make himself useful. Good works, the antidote to being him. Candy brought it into the room, tugging it forward as she walked.

He reached for a bottle of whiskey, where it was stored on a shelf alongside a few glasses over the room's small sink. The bottle was half-full, and he'd paid for it. When he opened it and held it out, Candy took the bottle like strange guys had been handing her booze her whole life. Maybe they had.

She took a swig. Travis said, "Sit down. We'll tune this thing up." He kicked a rickety chair, showing her where she could sit. "Stay," he said.

Sean rolled a fatty in the sun on the upturned Frisbee. He was in his element, same way he'd spent afternoons on the back acre out in Boring. *Transferrable skills,* he thought, quoting a high school guidance counselor. He licked the paper, sealed it.

Lu said, "Old school," meaning the joint. Nobody smoked pot that way anymore. She took it from his hands, and he flicked a lighter.

He said, "Rolling papers travel small, no bulk, and I like it. It's how I learned."

She held her hair back, leaned in, touched her lips lightly to the edges of the paper and drew smoke into her lungs. She passed it back, and he took a hit.

A man came stumbling out of the bushes, then disappeared into the same line of bushes again, his eyes on his cell phone the whole time. There were the sounds of children playing, one yelling something over and over that sounded like "Kohlrabi!" but could have been anything. There were people everywhere, but the bushes and trees and wide-open spaces let them each feel alone, and even those people who did stumble through never looked twice at the pot.

Their game of Frisbee found a new pace, sometimes so slow and then Sean wondered how long had they been playing, anyway? Lu had a grass stain on her dress and didn't care. He wanted to take his clothes off, run like a dog. He threw the Frisbee. It sailed far to the left of his aim. Lu watched it sail without moving toward it. It landed deep in the bushes. Because she hadn't even tried, Sean said, "Too bad. If you'd caught that one, I would've paid you twenty bucks."

"Really? Ha!" Lu barked, and walked slowly, ducked under a branch, and disappeared into the bushes. Sean called, "Watch out for dead bodies."

The bushes shook. "And live bodies," her voice floated toward him, out of the woods. Then she reemerged, in a flurry of leaves.

She threw the Frisbee toward him and he watched it float over. She said, "I forget about the park. It's paradise."

He said, "How can you forget about it? It's huge."

The vacuum roared but didn't pick up anything, even after they'd wrapped Lu's masking tape around an air hole, trying to increase the suction. Travis took it apart, using a butter knife, mostly, turning screws, working with what they had. Finally, he said, "It's dead on arrival." He fell back on Lu's bed, with grease on his arms.

"Maybe." Candy looked at the vacuum, her loss.

Lu could come back any minute, and Travis knew it. She'd find them there, in her space, drinking her booze that he'd bought. Maybe he wanted her to find them.

He could be Candy's friend, too. He was a free agent. Travis would keep the party going until Lu found them and then she'd know he made friends, easy, she wasn't so special, but she was lucky he hung around. She took him for granted. He saw the scars on Candy's wrist and arms, pink marks about the size of a dime. He took her by the hand, turned her arm in the light that came through the window. "What are you, a cook?"

She said, "I worked in a bakery for a while, at night." She said it like she was lying. He could tell by the way she half-closed her eyes and the way she raised her chin like she had something to prove. He'd seen chemical burns before. She'd tried cooking meth, was his guess. Of course she had. Who put her up to that? Whatever she'd been through was still with her, the way his life shadowed him.

The Frisbee was held aloft, cutting an arc from Lu to Sean. They'd hiked further into the park, away from Portland, and the sun was moving toward the west, behind the hill. Back in town Travis and Candy had finished the half-bottle of whiskey and emptied a six pack they found in the fridge. They'd opened the curtains and generally moved in. Travis heard one word in his head, his personal curse, *transmission, transmission.* He lifted Candy's hair and brought his mouth to her neck because he knew she'd go for it, chicks always did, but he was thinking about Lu.

Sean stepped back, ran to catch the hallucinogenic green Frisbee, and had it in his hands, but it bounced off his fingers. He let it hit the ground, and said, "Want to hike down, find a pizza?"

Travis pushed Candy backwards onto Lu's mattress, and Candy was more than willing. They let the whiskey do the talking. Her head hit the pillow, but a book too, and she used one arm to push Renaissance Art History out of the way, and Travis helped her. Make love, not war—fucking was the best distraction from being pissed off, so those hippies were right, except Travis couldn't pretend there wasn't an element of war in what he did now.

He would win. This was a war about getting fucked or being faithful, and why hold back? He undid his belt, his jeans. Candy helped him push them down.

Sean twirled the Frisbee on one finger. Lu said, "Yes. I'm starving."

It was always easy to find your way back because the park slopped mostly one direction, running like water into the city.

Candy's hips were so bony they hurt, like being hit with a hammer when they brought their bodies together, but they slammed into each other, mostly his body into hers, bringing his hips back then forward, knocking human bones and skin. Missile off the rail, he thought. Deadly payload, he thought. *Weapon release, weapon release, weapon release, weapon release.*

Then it was over and Travis rolled onto his back, and saw the line of silver earrings in Candy's ear, and he thought, Why is she even here?

Sean spun the Frisbee on one finger, and felt his knees, his bones jostled, as he and Lu almost-jogged back down the sloping grass toward the city.

Candy dug her fingers in the front pocket of Travis's Levi's, where they were still down around his legs, and he pulled them up even as she found a hard pack of Camel filters there and she offered him one of his own smokes and he took it, yeah, nodding.

By the time Lu and Sean showed up with a pizza in a cardboard box and that Frisbee in hand, Lu's room was full of smoke. Her sheets were covered in grease and there was a massacred vacuum cleaner in the middle of her small floor. Travis and Candy were smoking at her open window and Lu said, "What's going on?"

This was what he'd wanted: Lu, home. But that feeling of cement in Travis's gut came back, hard and heavy. He felt the dull tug of a post-booze headache moving in. Lu pulled a pink slip of paper out of her pocket, threw it on her spindly table. It was a phone number, Sean's name. Travis panicked. *Find, fix, track, target, engage, access…* He said, "Lu—"

Sean put the pizza down. He said, "Um, I think I need to get going—" because even the air in the room had a warbling energy to it, and he was not a fighter.

Lu looked right at him then, in that way Sean had wanted her to, making eye contact, making him feel special. She said, "Stay. It's my place."

Travis said, "You're ruining my life." He pointed a finger at Sean in that small space.

Sean said, "Hey, buddy. I don't even know you—"

Travis said, "Doesn't matter," because he had killed people he never met, and so he knew a few things.

Candy said, "Trav, let's go."

"Trav?" said Lu.

But Travis shook Candy's fingers off his arm when she tugged on him, because who was she kidding? It was like the worst kind of double date. He said, "I could fucking kill you," to Sean. He wanted to show there were consequences. He wanted the booze to lift and leave his brain. He wanted a drink.

Sean moved toward the door. Nobody stopped him, so he took off, backed out the door, left Lu to her life, that life that he didn't know about. Candy left too, without the vacuum.

Travis said, "Lu, I didn't mean it." He said, "Things were good between us. Why do you have to do this?" He started talking fast. He washed his arms in her sink, tried to wash the vacuum cleaner's grease off like it was the sweat and sperm of sex itself. It was *messing around…*

"I didn't do anything to you," she said. He didn't look good, so angry. "Go home, sleep it off." But he didn't go. When they talked,

Lu heard how the words kept going, knocking into each other. They changed tone, arguing, pleading. It was exhausting.

It was one room, two people, and a conversation that ran in a circle.

Hours later, he was still there, saying, "It can't be over between us." And then even later he said, "It was real, between us." He didn't mean to yell but needed her to hear and everybody felt so far the fuck away. The world was small, and receding.

She said, "Why is everything *between us?* What about me? Just me. I'm sick of worrying about you. Get out."

Travis saw her flash in infrared, drawing a heat-seeking missile. Predators circled cities, filling the air. Hellfire was out there waiting to be unleashed when a sensor gave the word. He saw Lu, her face on screens all over the world, shouting, *Me, me, me,* and her insistence rang out like idealism. What did she think, she was autonomous?

He said, "I know, I made a wrong call—"

She said, "Wrong call?"

He said, "I'm sorry. I was crazy—"

He'd filed worse after-action reports. That's what they called them, *after action,* after missiles, after drone strikes. He had that same panic now, the need to be precise and get it right.

She cut him off, asking, "What makes you think we were so serious, ever?"

It was all serious to him. It had always been serious. He wiped the sweat of panic off his forehead.

Moving across town fast, Sean's feet slapped the pavement. His heart beat in the same rhythm. He could've been killed. Who was that guy? He thought before that maybe he'd make out with Lu. He'd get to know her. It could've been nice, good, between them. But he wasn't on a suicide mission. It was like the way sometimes a girl's dad was home, waiting up, but that was not her dad. A boyfriend? Why would she not say that? They'd hung out all day. She'd brought him home to that guy.

And in the box of a studio apartment, as Lu and Travis argued, as they tried to control themselves, to control each other, tiny spirochete bacterium, those simple lives, were already working their way into Travis's system to build a syphilitic future that would drag him to the VA clinic, then the pharmacy. In another part of the building, another apartment, on Candy's mattress, up a flight, the unmanned soldiers of his drone sperm found their target egg and slammed into it with enough force to change their sperm and egg worlds into a zygote, merging before they'd cleave and split in their own drama, making a syphilitic embryo, microscopic lives enacting the original violence, destroying themselves to build a new life. A spider hung high up on one of the old walls of Lu's place, watching, and down in Nevada working sensors who were still in the Air Force watched over houses where couples had the same arguments in other languages, and there are always more lives involved in every minute we're together alone, and Travis felt his mistake like a weapon he'd used on himself.

Months away, out on that continuum of time, Candy, out in the hall, would touch her rounding belly, then go back to painting her toenails in her toxic cloud.

For now though, late, in the apartment, Lu said, "I need space between us, between me and this. All of it."

Space is never empty. Emotions have vectors and velocity. You can crush a person from a distance. Sometimes the first weapon is the act or art of pulling away. Travis wanted to grab her. Lu was infrared. The world was littered with raw arms, blown-apart bodies. He could see it on the inside of his eyelids. He said, "Everything that matters? It happens between people." He launched his words, wanted to believe they were a missile but knew his voice was only a piece of truth tied to his own heart, delivered like a message tied to a rock thrown through a window. What mattered most right then would be her words, her heart, her weapon.

She said, "You're on your own."

After that night, the Park Blocks outside Portland State University would be agitated with their energy as they avoided each other. It would be for him, anyway. It would be for Sean, too, who felt like somebody had pulled a gun on him, the same kind of anger. It might be for Lu. They'd pass and bump into each other and feel it. Lu would see Sean and say, "Hey," and he'd nod and get away fast. Once, they talked. Lu said, "He doesn't own me, you know." She said, "We can throw a Frisbee in the park again. Hang out."

Sean said, "Um. You've got a few things to work out, maybe?"

He found another girl to play Frisbee. To smoke dope. To go home to a studio apartment and a mattress on the floor. They'd all watch Candy's kid grow up, around town, because Portland was a small, crowded city, and sometimes a child has more parents than anyone can count, even when it might feel like the kid has none, when a baby might grow to be its own angry, weaponized, unmanned vehicle, with its own life and trajectory. Travis would love that boy, a person with his—Travis's—own eyes, and he'd hate him, too. It was the way he felt about himself. It was his life, spiraling forward, in the shape of another person.

None of them could change course. The future was in motion.

HONEYMOONING

On the train, I spent both nights awake, in the empty club car after they'd quit serving. I rode with my feet on the window ledge and a book in my lap to put off conversation, although mostly there was nobody else awake and the only conversation was the one in my head, making plans about what I'd do next as soon as I got back to Portland. I'd been down in Mexico then came up through Arizona. I went over to D.C. and Chicago, made a loop through the mitten of Michigan to visit a few friends I barely knew really, and now I'd head home. The train stopped in each town, allowing for three days and two nights suspended against the slow promise of a future approaching. The nights were even more full of this feeling than the days.

I'm not afraid of flying, but I am afraid of moving too fast. After kicking around for a while, I needed time to make a plan beyond finding Mack. That was the only Portland plan I had. A white sheet of paper I'd been using as a bookmark was meant to be a letter I'd mail to my sister, if I found her address. "Dear Lu," I wrote at the top. The timing of our mother's breakdown, when we were both so young—but I was older, always older of course—that had left us to fall in opposite directions. Dad was good to Lu. He'd said, to our mom, "Lu in particular needs you!"

I was nine. His words? They said I was free to go. Goodbye. I missed my sister, dear little Carrion. I had no idea what her life was like.

I watched the moon through the window. It was a beautiful, floating illusion of a still point in the universe. Dark shadows passed over the plains, mountains and water.

The second night, at three in the morning we stopped on the east side of Montana. A man and a woman boarded there. I heard them make their way, loud and crashing, down a car of people sleeping before they found the club car, the last car with lights still on. The bright lights had been dimmed. I sat in the orange glow.

When he saw me the man said, "Here's a girl who knows how to party." He said, "Not like the rest of them crabby-ass deadbeats back there," meaning travelers sleeping. It was late going on early, coming into morning soon.

I don't know where he got that insight—I only had a little ice in a plastic cup on the windowsill—but I didn't deny it. I pivoted back and forth in my chair, anxious for the train to roll, ready to be moving, smiled, then looked at my book like I meant to read.

The man dumped my ice in the trash. He offered, "Brandy?" then didn't wait for an answer. The woman laughed. The train started and they both nearly fell. The man reached for a chair that swiveled under his hand, and the woman grabbed at the man's fleshy upper arm. Peach brandy sloshed against the side of my cup.

The woman told me, "This is our first vacation ever," and they laughed again, taking off their winter coats. Underneath, the woman wore a wispy blue dress with cap sleeves like wings at her shoulders. She had on high heels, as if she'd meant to be going to a party. The man only wore jeans and a yellow T-shirt that pulled, showing a stretch of hairy stomach as he reached to steady himself.

The man said, "We didn't even tell our work. Just upped and left. Hell, it's Christmas, more or less."

The woman said, "Nobody even knows we got married," and she giggled and swigged from the bottle. "We worked in a pizza place, back there. But not any more we don't. We're honeymooning!"

Honeymoon. The word sounded sweet and ancient, full of promise. I gave up pretending to read. They hadn't noticed anyway. They were talking straight to me.

She said, "We told his folks we were visiting my parents this Christmas, and told my parents we'd be at his folk's place. Wait till they find out. Tom just said, 'Hell, we need a vacation,' and here we are, on our way."

The man said, "I'm Tom and she's Nancy. Nice to make your acquaintance."

"Vanessa," I said, claiming my own name, my real name, as I shook their hands. Nancy smiled like she couldn't believe life. I couldn't believe they'd skipped out on work, even though I too had quit a going-nowhere job after eight months of five-days-a-week. What I learned, during the eight months full-time, was that I hadn't yet found a way to make a living. The train started picking up speed, rocking its way across Montana. Tom pulled a Yahtzee game from his duffel bag. I told them that I didn't know how to play.

Tom said, "Shit! You don't know what you're missing."

And there, in his words, was the story of my life. I missed everything and everyone. I missed the places I'd traveled to and left behind. I missed my mom and our old ratty farmhouse, and my sister, who didn't keep in any kind of touch. I missed every tree and field around our old place that'd been cut and razed for a new parking lot. I had a growing list.

I let them teach me Yahtzee.

Over eight years I'd quit all kinds of jobs. I quit as a waitress and as a bar-back. I quit being an art model and quit in sales. I quit taking tickets at the door of a nightclub, and barely lasted one month serving lunches in a hospital cafeteria. I quit because I didn't like the limitations—because I didn't know, never knew, always wondered exactly what I was missing!

"You on vacation?" Nancy asked, as Tom set up the game.

"About like yours," I said, unemployment being one thing Tom, Nancy, and I had in common. The peach brandy was sharp and sweet. I had to drink it slow. As the train jogged a rough corner the drink spilled over the rim of my cup, stinging a chapped place between my thumb and fingers, running to my wrist like perfume.

We drank brandy and played Yahtzee until the sky started to lighten and the train slowed somewhere near Whitefish. The moon was now paper-thin and fading. That moon was sky-tinged, the way you could see right through it to the blue of the evening light, and it was hung like a damp tissue as though pressed against glass. The train stopped. There was a tavern within walking distance. That tavern, on the edge of town, had all its neon beer signs turned on, hanging in two small windows cut in the dark wood walls.

Tom said, "How long do we have? Let's go get a drink."

Nancy hesitated. There was one person outside, far in the distance: a boy running behind a remote-controlled car. The boy had his hands out in front of him, elbows straight, holding the remote control. The car bounced off curbs and tumbled through ditches. The boy's legs swung in wide flailing arcs as he followed the car, running past the town's bank, past one dime store and the post office. The streets were broad, flat, and empty. The boy with the car in the town's barely-visible dust of dry snow looked to me like Christmas, like vacation, meaning a day worth waking up early for and a way I never felt anymore except on the train, being already up and between jobs, on my own vacation anyhow.

Tom stood up and said, "Come on. Let me buy you a drink. You girls both just need another drink." He held out his hands, one to each of us, to pull us to our feet. On the way out a porter near the door said we had twenty minutes.

"If you're late," the porter said to Tom, as though Tom were now our leader, "this train won't wait."

Twenty minutes was plenty of time.

Inside the tavern was dark. There was a pool table, and other tables with chairs scattered around. A row of mostly men and two old women sat at the bar, people who possibly worked at night and came out for beers in the A.M. I put a quarter in a machine and got a handful of mixed nuts while Tom ordered a pitcher and three glasses. We sat at the end of the bar.

Tom looked at the walls and at the ceiling. He said, "So, this is still Montana."

Nancy laughed and put her hand on his knee. Her eyes were half-closed. She was watching Tom stack change against the counter. The beer was good, cold and thin, and cut through the taste of being up all night. The pool table was open; with time I would've started a game. A tavern is a place made easy to spend all day. I didn't even know if the town we were in had a name. The town didn't seem much bigger than the tavern itself.

My Portland plan was to stay with Mack until I got organized. If that didn't work out, I had an old friend named Tino who was never far away. I'd sign up with a temp agency. I'd done that enough times. Always a temp, permanently impermanent. I'd find an alarm clock and set it for the morning and try not to turn it off before I woke up. I had half a college degree and knew how to fix a jammed copy machine, and every office needs that all the time. Mostly, I liked that Portland was waiting for me, just over in the distance, full of work and apartments and people. Pure potential.

Then I heard the low rumble of the train's engine, the groan of metal pushing against inertia, against air, against its own weight.

I said, "What time is it?"

And a man at the counter said, "Train's leaving. Better go catch it."

Nancy, wide awake now, eyes open, said, "Shit," and grabbed her purse.

Tom tipped his head back and slammed his beer. I left half of mine on the counter and ran out into the lot in front. The sun, just over the horizon, reflected on the sparse patches of snow and the hard, dry ground. Our train moved to the west.

I said, "Shit," repeating Nancy. I didn't know what else to say. Tom and Nancy ran up behind me and the three of us stood in silence, next to a broken refrigerator with its door off the hinges. Everything I owned was on the train, in the compartment above my seat. The paperback I'd been reading now rode with Yahtzee, in the club car, my place marked with the unfinished letter. There was a pay phone next to the cinder block station, but I didn't know one person to call inside a thousand miles. My sister? She'd probably be asleep, like a normal person. The boy with the remote-controlled car circled back on his own path, kicking up a trail of dust.

Tom cracked his knuckles of one hand against the palm of his other. I was cold and Nancy looked freezing. One mile to the north was Canada, and even Canada meant just more of where we were already.

As we stood watching, the train seemed to stop, to park in the distance. I couldn't tell if it was actually coming back, or only catching more of the sun. Then I was sure, it was coming back. A man in an Amtrak uniform came out of the station and watched as the train moved backward, onto the platform. It was bringing back my bag and my book and my letter.

I said, "What are they doing?"

He said, "Brake check. You've still got ten minutes."

Tom groaned and made a gesture like he was throwing a hat at the ground. Nancy swung her purse and kicked one high-heeled foot. She said, "Jesus!" Then, "God damn! Thought we were going to honeymoon in this dump."

My knees were shaking, I was that relieved.

But because they wouldn't let us board the train again yet, and with ten minutes as plenty of time, when Tom and Nancy turned, I turned too, the three of us heading back to the tavern.

"We've still got half a pitcher left," Tom said.

The tavern air was warm. The dark was a relief, respite from the glare of the early sun. Our pitcher sat on the counter, the glasses untouched. People inside were waiting to laugh, knowing we hadn't gone anywhere yet.

"We've got ten minutes!" Tom bellowed, joining the joke.

The line of regulars slapped the counter softly with their wrinkled hands.

The bar smelled dank with mildew. It was the smell of the club, car smoke, spilled drinks, and grease. It was the pizza parlor Tom and Nancy meant to leave behind, the smell of jobs I'd had, the way I was living. It was the scent of life in a cheap limbo. I could travel and sip a drink forever. I reached for the same red vinyl stool I'd been sitting on earlier and it swiveled under my hands, spinning toward me. My knees buckled from riding the train too long. One craggy, glassy-eyed woman, an early morning drinker on her own long vacation, still laughing at the joke of our traveling train, the waning of our honeymoon, smiled my way and said "Watch out. You forget yourself, you'll end up living here." She rested her hand, gnarled and roped with veins, directly over mine.

THE FIRST NORMAL MAN

An art museum is a sacred space. I still feel it, even though I've been a guard for twenty years. I've walked long halls of Early American primitive paintings, and Baroque European furniture. I've seen Duane Hansen sculptures, lifelike and freaky, and all kinds of art come through. The Native American galleries in particular, in the museum where I work, are kept invitingly dark. They're part of the permanent collection. Those rooms smell ripe with wood and floor polish.

I tug my beard, run a hand through my hair, and pace through the rooms slowly, all too aware of the squeak and roll of my black work shoes.

There's a machine under a PlexiGlass cube ticking away on a pedestal in one corner of each room of the museum. It's made of brass and wood, with a needle and a roll of paper running through it. Visitors move along the path of exhibits and some stop to look at that machine from the top, then bend over and lean in close to see it from the sides. They study the equipment for finer details. Because in a museum everything is art or artifact, right? Put a sandwich on a pedestal, or set a can of Coke in the wrong spot, and visitors think it's significant.

That machine is called a hygrothermograph. The museum is all about climate control. The hygrothermograph keeps track of moisture in the air and temperature fluctuations. In the Native American wing, climate control protects wooden masks from cracking and baskets from mold or decay. Those baskets would've been trashed by now back when they had a shot in the real world. Here, the hope is that they'll be preserved forever.

After two decades as a guard, I've started to feel like those baskets: preserved. I still ride the bike that I picked up in college. I fit my old Levi's, and they don't wear out; most days I spend in uniform anyway. I haven't even put on mid-life gut rolls. I'm an early-edition hipster, a Portland artifact.

I walk the length of a glass case full of beaded leather shirts. Each shirt is brown as dirt beneath its beads. Somebody's fingers sewed those beads on. By now that person has been dead for decades. I don't know which part makes the shirts more valuable—age, details in the work, or death, of a whole generation by now, maybe even the near death, cultural death, of a way of life—but the ghost of my own white shirt floats over them as a reflection in the glass. My blue blazer shows up like a dark pool. It truncates the white in that reflection, as though somebody cut off my arms, and either side of my chest. *Half a man,* I think, and give my reflection a title. I could be a painting, or a looping video installation. My beard makes my jaw blurry in the reflection, and the light makes the rest of my face look like a skull. The room is quiet except for the tick and hiss of the hygrothermograph tracking the minutia of environmental change. The museum is working on funding to upgrade those machines to a digital version. If they ever get that money earmarked, I'll miss the old tick and hiss, the brass and wood of ancient technology. Maybe the old version can be preserved, on display. On weekdays, guard work is a quiet, isolated business. Every sound is as good as a conversation.

I bring a pen, and a narrow notebook that fits my blazer pocket. I have an idea about writing a graphic novel called, "Security." I've written the title on the front of my notebook where it looks like official work notes. The graphic novel is my exit strategy, my next career. Sometimes I secretly sketch cartoon versions of the museum's art, learning from the masters.

I carry a radio latched onto my belt. When a voice rattles over the radio, saying, rotate, my job is to walk to the next station. If another guard walks toward me, again my job pretty much is to walk away, to the next station. We're not supposed to do what supervisors call "bunch up."

There was this guard named Stacy around for a while. She was big, with the kind of body that made me want to be R. Crumb, to draw like R. Crumb. I could never decide if she was sexy. She was definitely built. She had crazy hair, always pulled up high into a ponytail, curling like ivy. I'd see her before work out on the museum's marble steps, peeling a rubber band off her wrist and wrestling that ponytail into place.

Stacy was a compulsive talker, exuding a fatal degree of loneliness. When she could see me, it was like I had a magnetic pull. Maybe she was that way with everyone? She'd call my name. "Hey, Sean!" she'd say. "Sean, do you think—" and "Sean!" using my name as leverage to forge a connection.

Trying to stay in the range of her assigned spot, she'd drift, edging closer to me then moving back. She'd make faces from a distance to catch my attention, hissing, "Psst! Sean!" Eventually she'd come all the way down long halls of Early American Impressionist paintings, with their ornate and gilded frames, or past the brown and orange striped canvases of the Clement Greenberg Modernist collection, wherever we were stationed. She'd get out of her assigned space, lean in and whisper. I'd smell coffee on her breath. I could tell she drank it with cream, no sugar, bitter and milky. The things she said? She'd talk about patrons, our supervisor, lunch, her feet or her ankles being tired, her new shoes, the old days when she'd lived in Paris, lived in Guatemala. It didn't matter what she said. She kept reaching out like that, with words, putting both of our jobs at risk.

It made me nervous, because we were warned more than once to not bunch up. I needed the job.

What really made me nervous about Stacy? She carried a kind of loneliness that felt almost contagious. She wanted too much.

I'd try to move away from her. She'd follow me. I'd feel her coffee breath against my skin, hear her hiss-whisper. I'd say, "You know, we're supposed to keep space—" Then one day she didn't come in. She left a white shirt with her name inside the collar hanging on a rack in our guard closet. Fired, I'd guess. Better her than me.

I would never want to be Stacy, to be that alone, clawing at strangers for conversation. I did okay. I'd been dating a girl named Lu, until that fell apart. But Lu was hot, and we were still friends. She called me the First Normal Guy She'd Ever Dated. That's how she introduced me. Still.

Me.

Cool.

I saw myself reflected in her words the way I was reflected in the glass of the cases: like art. Lu's vision made me into something worth saving.

Stacy's blazer's been reassigned. Her old shirt still hung in the guard closet. I see it when I check in or out. It's yellowed at the cuffs and emanates this amalgamated scent of her skin, even months after she's moved on. It's like she's there. Where she wrote her name in the back of the neck with a Sharpie, it looks like it was written by a kid. It's an artifact, her shirt.

But I miss her conversation, more than I thought I would. Without her distractions, I feel like a dog in a yard with an invisible fence when I walk the length of my assigned corridor. That's what I'm doing mid-week, quietest day of every week, when I stop to stand by a row of masks and totems. It's so quiet, the tick of the climate control equipment is the only sound, until finally the silence is broken by the gentle slap and roll of footsteps. I see the arm of another blue blazer far down the hall. It's a coworker off in the European gallery. He's hidden behind a life-sized Rodin sculpture of a standing naked woman, and maybe he's coming, to relieve me? I hear the word in my mind, anticipating it coming in over the radio: *Rotate!* But no. My colleague moves out of sight. He's pacing, too.

Further off, kids' voices come into earshot. They sing up and down, boys or girls or maybe both. It's a burble that moves in a narrow range, high and happy, like water over stones. It sounds like too small of a group to be a whole class. Listening carefully, I try to guess who's coming. My bet is that there's a silent, hopeful, loving, resentful mother skulking along with her own pack of pre-schoolers. She's edifying them with art, waiting for her children to be old enough for school, when she'll get her day-life back. There's a mom, sucking in her breath and hoping the kids don't break anything. My mom was always eager to get us on the bus, anyway. As the sounds moved closer, I put my feet apart, hands behind my back, assuming what I'd call an official posture.

The voices are disembodied sound. Where are the bodies? I'm ready.

I wait next to a tall display of a wooden face in the middle of what looks like a wooden, radiating sunshine. It's a "transformation mask." That mask hovers like a buddy at my shoulder. I almost want to talk to it, joke around the way I used to with Stacy, but I'd feel like Tom Hanks, in a Castaway moment.

I miss Stacy, with her desperation and her coffee breath, but I'm relieved to be out of the circle of her anxiety, really. She was always pulling me in, on the edge of trouble, with her compulsions and her loneliness. She used to be some kind of party girl in France. She used to be thin, she said. She always seemed trapped, now, in loneliness and age.

What's weird is how hard it can be to stand still. I'm a bicyclist, and have been forever, since before the city filled up with bike lanes and decked-out commuter bike snobs. My thighs are all muscle. When I stand around all day, into the afternoon, I start to feel like a good bike pulled to the curb. I'm every car that's ever idled, a motorcycle gulping its own exhaust, lurching toward open road. I'm paid to stand, and I get this feeling my body is waiting for my mind to figure out what I'm supposed to do with being alive.

When I took the job, it sounded so easy. Twenty years of standing still, it's a particular kind of quiet pain.

One red-letter day I kicked the same guy out of the museum twice. He was maybe Samoan. You could say I'm big for a white art school downtown nerd. He was big in a more significant way—a way that could kick my ass. He had a ragged scar down his cheek, and that scar said he'd seen worse problems than me and my radio. He walked right into the coat check, stole my wallet. That's right—my wallet. Out of every valuable thing in the museum, he stole a security guard's booze and bus money. I saw him with my backpack in his hands, and I stepped in front of him, told him to wait in the guard's closet, where we were wrapped in the smell of Stacy's yellowed shirt, and somebody else's sack lunch. I radioed the front desk, told them to call the police.

There was a round of static. My supervisor's voice came back, saying, "Call the *what?*"

We didn't have a lot of genuine emergencies.

The guy with my wallet and I, we both heard it. Those radios aren't built for discretion. "The cops," I said, hands shaking.

The city's jails are overcrowded. They don't hold petty criminals very long, far as I can tell. They didn't hold the wallet thief any longer than it took to run paperwork and rack up some fines. The same guy was back in the museum by late afternoon, like he hadn't finished his rounds. I was near the front desk then. He skipped the admissions line. I said, "Sir, you need to pay your entry fee." If he'd paid, I would've let him in. That's part of the job, right? No hard feelings, I had my wallet, and I had my eye on him. I work with the systems in place. But he didn't pay. Maybe I'm not a big guy, but it's not a big town. He'd had his time with me once. He turned and walked out.

Lonely Stacy's old blazer? It smells like cigarettes. It was up for grabs and I took it when nobody else did. If it's a woman's blazer, I can't tell. She was a big woman, and curvy, but the blazer fits. Sometimes, there's not as much difference as you might think between the bodies of men and women.

The kids' voices get louder, then they come around the doorway. The mom I'd expected turns out to be a dad instead. These two baby girls kind of step sideways and dance around by his knees. He pulls them close, saying, "Don't touch anything."

He's doing my job, there.

The secret thing about me and about any guard bored out of his mind, is that we actually sort of want somebody to touch the art, cop a feel. It'd be a reason to bust out. It's our big moment. I'd say, *Sir, please don't.* Otherwise, there's not a lot to do.

Now this guy, the one in the gallery?

I recognize his profile immediately—I know him.

He spreads a hand over one girl's blonde head, like a hat. I think, those are his kids? I don't have children, and still feel like a kid myself most of the time. All three stop to look at the transformation mask, made out of wood and shells. The mask has wires to make it transform, like a face puppet. I have this urge to say, *kids, that's the face of dzunuk'wa, a witch. She eats babies...* It's true. Hidden inside the mask there's another face, a man with a John Waters mustache.

It's a witch, a woman, but it's a guy too. Transformation can move in any direction.

But I don't say that. Security guards are invisible. We're not docents, there to lead tours. If you don't talk to us, we can't talk to you. That's the protocol.

I feel weird. I want to throw him out, but he's not breaking any rules. I want to pass him my phone number, invite him out for a pint. It's like I'm behind glass, the way he doesn't see me, I can't introduce myself, and I'm right there.

But that guy, I can tell you I met him at a Melvins show in the 80's. I was a guard back then too, and I was in my uniform, a blazer and khakis, like some kind of prep school suit, because that's what the uniform was back then. Now it's all blue. I'd gone to the Melvins show after work.

That guy called himself Rotgut. I get that it's not his name, but that's what he said. He made fun of my uniform, called me a rent-a-cop. Then he offered me weed, to show I wasn't, or to show no hard feelings maybe. That was his thing. I could hardly hear him over the band, but I followed him out of the pit. We headed toward the darkness in the back of the warehouse and ducked under a yellow length of dusty cop tape. We stumbled past a *Do Not Enter* sign meant to cut off a back hall, and took a freight elevator, which was cool, right up until the elevator broke. Stupid. It fell, and we were trapped. We, punk rock drunks, practically bawled for our mommies. I was wasted. It was like I couldn't breathe, like there was no air, except there was air, and there was this space at the top where the elevator didn't line up with the floor. Rotgut said, "Get on my shoulders. I'll hoist you out."

I said, "Shit no." If that elevator dropped again it'd slice a person in half.

I was wasted, but not stupid.

Instead I put my head on the floor and passed out until the

music stopped in the distance. We stayed there forever. It wasn't a controlled environment, not like the galleries, but exactly the opposite: neglected.

"They'll find us," he said, hours later. His breath was smoke and sour beer.

My uniform was trashed, and I didn't even have my lame-ass radio. How did we live before cell phones? Randomly, that's how. We smoked his weed.

So maybe you think if you were trapped for days, you'd drink your own piss, right? That's everybody's last survival secret. But here's what happens. Who packed the pint glasses? Nobody.

It's harder than you'd think to drink your own pee without anything like a cup. It runs out of your palm. It slops on your face. So yeah, we drank pee. Not our own. So what? I thought we'd die there.

There was no natural light, no way to tell how much time had passed, but it all felt like forever.

He was this lanky guy. After what I think was a night and a day and a night, but I don't really know, when we were still trapped, it was like we lived together, it was that intimate. We drank each other's piss. There was nowhere to shit. We fucked. We did. We were grimy, hopeful and forgiving of human body-needs.

We were animals in a cage.

Since then, I can't hear the phrase "man cave" without feeling weird. I'm a straight guy. I am.

In the museum, I can't tell if he still has holes through his lobes. He's in ordinary working shoes, not even toned-down Doc Martins. But I'm glad to see him. I remember him. I rock up on my toes, beam *hello!*

He gives a nod that says, *No worries, guard. Got the kids under control…*

He hasn't seen me yet, has only seen the uniform. I think, *Touch the art!* It'd be reason to make a connection.

He doesn't wear a wedding ring. Maybe those aren't his kids. He's the queer punk rock uncle. He's thicker than I remember, and his skin is ruddier. I venture, "Rotgut?"

He says, "Girls, step back."

I ask, "Remember?"

He looks at me then, with grey eyes.

I say, "The Melvins?" and my voice cracks, like a boy's. I haven't changed. His hair was dyed black in the 80's. Now it's grey. His forehead is broader, going bald. He brings his eyebrows together.

"Elevator F-U-C-K?" I spell, and hope he'll laugh. Those girls are too young to spell.

He says, "Dude. Wrong guy." He holds up his hands in a way that says, *no offense.* But that gesture also says, *back up.*

I don't have the wrong guy. I know his crooked teeth, the curve of his spine.

A voice on my radio: rotate.

Time for me to walk to the next station. Already I hear the soft slap of a colleague's walk down a long, polished hall, ready to relieve me, ready for a change of station.

Rotgut was the one who saved us, risked his life, climbed out postcoitally. He did that. For us. He climbed out that slice of light at the top of the elevator. He got us out of that cage. This is my freedom: lonely.

I take out my notebook, my pen, and want to draw the slope of his shoulders, the tilt of his head. I'd draw the scent of him, if I could. Instead, I write my phone number. My replacement guard is still out of sight, around a corner, but my ears are attuned to the sound of him coming closer.

If I let him go now, he could be gone forever. He's pretending. I want one thing. One moment. I know how it feels to be Stacy now, moving in, and I can't make myself step back. My colleague is getting closer, its time for me to go, Rotgut still wont let on if he remembers me. I trade the security of my security job for a gamble: lace an arm over his shoulder, move in close, mash my lips to his lips, force his mouth open, find his tongue.

When he pushes me away, I fall into a pedestal so hard my hands slap the polished floor. He looks past me, at a woman, frozen, with a coat check tag in her fist. He shakes his head, gulps air. His red face is deeper red. The tallest of his girls reaches for his fingers. His forehead wrinkles, his chin shakes. He's about to cry?

Then an invisible hand pulls the wires, snaps Rotgut's transformation mask closed: His face hardens and ages. *Is it even him?*

We were so fucking intimate. How can I not tell if it's even the same man? I can't. The other security guard, my colleague, is on his radio, pushing the side button, calling for backup. I am his backup! I should be.

I don't know how to save myself, put on a mask and transform. Except then I see the flap of my blazer, hanging open in my fall, and inside, on the white label, in a child's scrawl of Sharpie it says **STACY.**

NEIGHBORHOOD NOTES: SING-A-LONG

You're still steeped in the scent of morning coffee brewing when a child's voice climbs through the apartment windows. "But mama, he died! He's dead," the child wails. Her ghostly little voice passes through walls, through glass. Her words are broken but you can put them together. "He's dead, dead, dead!" She could mean anybody or anything, an extinct animal, a pet, her father.

Her voice is litter blowing down the street. It's like the jasmine, pretty and blooming, so inescapable and strong. As backup singers, the neighbor's chickens rehearse a version of the theme song from *Elmo's World.* They get the first bars right, then stop and start again.

The mother's voice is barely there, a murmur, rolling words untranslatable as thunder but you know what they say: *I'm sorry I'm so happy that my love brought you to this fleeting, mortal scene, baby.* Because love and life and death are knotted together in every parent-child puzzle, tied like a kid's shoe, a burr clinging to a sock on the way to school.

The chickens start their song again, stuck on the first bars of the first verse, hopeful, dedicated performers.

HELP WANTED

Mack's first day out of the big loony bin on the hill, I agreed to meet him at the Marathon Taverna. I should've said no. It was a bad plan. But I went along with it, because why? We'd been kids together out in the dirt at the ragged edge of the suburbs. Now we both lived in the city. Over the phone he said, "I need to get out, see people. Get back in the swing."

The swing of what? I said, "The only people you'll see at the Marathon are drunks."

He said, "I need to see you, Vanessa."

He owned the house I was living in, one of the last splintering shacks still standing in Portland's central industrial zone. I didn't want to meet up with him there at the house—his house—because if I let him in, he'd never leave. He'd pick through my things looking for his things, looking for any sign of him and me together, like playing husband and wife or some other fairy tale.

There was a time when all I wanted was to know Mack would stick around. Then there were the years apart, when I traveled, and tested myself. To come back to him was like Christmas. But that was a long time ago, and so much had gone between us. We weren't dating anymore.

The plan had been that I'd use the house until he got out—out of detox, then out of jail, then out of the Mental Motel that was part of his sentence. He was slated to live in transitional housing until a case worker said he was ready for the real world, and that's where he'd just landed. It sounded like a long enough list that I bothered to unpack. I scrubbed mold off the walls of Mack's house with white vinegar. I hung a framed picture of my sister, Lulu, in the small, warped kitchen. The truth is, I hadn't expected him back for a long time. I thought he'd screw up. Good behavior isn't exactly his bag.

I took a bus to the bar then walked the last blocks. Overhead was a gray sky. My raincoat flapped against the wind like a dying bird, and slapped my knee with each step. Traffic lined the street thick as a parking lot.

A guy in a pickup held back at a green light to let me cross. When I got to the other side I smiled and waggled my fingers in the air by way of a thanks. The man smiled too. He was still looking my way when he stepped on the gas and T-boned an idling Smart Car wedged in the intersection. There was the crunch of metal, a broken headlight, something swimming pool blue that skidded over the macadam. I pretended not to notice, didn't want to embarrass him. We all have troubles.

Inside the Marathon, I found a table and peeled off my coat, then put down my pocketbook. The murky tavern air was thick with sweat, beer and smoke, but so much warmer than outside. It was dark in the bar too, like instant night in the middle of day, and I relaxed into the calm weight of darkness. That bar gave out free popcorn. Scattered popcorn decorated the carpet with a yellow glow like planetarium stars. I looked for the North Star, some guiding light in all that mess. Mack, now sober, crazy and adjusting to antipsychotics, felt like a new world. I had no idea how to navigate.

The thing is, in the place where we grew up, Mack and me, it'd started out as the country and every year they poured more cement. It was like somebody was pouring concrete over childhood. At least that's how it felt to me. I don't think that did us any good.

Taki, the Greek who ran the place, dropped his rag. He said, "Ah, Vanessa, my beauty. What can I do for you?" He wiped his hands on his pants.

He always said, *my beauty.* I ordered a beer and a Snappy Toms. In that bar, beer meant Budweiser.

Taki said, "You're alone?"

"Not alone. With you," I offered, smiling. My hair was thick and hung heavy over one eye. I shook it out of the way, but it fell back again. One of these days I'd pay for a real haircut.

He brought the beer to my table. "If I wasn't working, I'd take you someplace better than this. Have you ever been to Greece?"

I'd traveled through Central America but not Europe. I was about to say as much. An old guy knocked his empty glass against the bartop, calling Taki back to the taps. The old men who lived in tiny rooms upstairs were the bar's mainstay. When I started going there, I'd lived down the street in an apartment with a guy named Ray.

The door opened to let in a big slice of midday sun, traffic and exhaust. Mack's shadow joined the dark with the rest of us. "Hello, my wildness," I called from the dark corner.

He carried with him, in his muscles and his tousled hair, the old days of fields and endless land and all that new cement, back when our world was still at the beginning of being eclipsed by *For Lease* signs. Those signs, posted in the windows of new commercial buildings, showed the buildings had no dreams or purpose of their own. He saw my red beer. "Shaking off a hangover, Angel?"

I said, "I wish I had a hangover angel. Somebody to come rub the aches away." This time it wasn't a hangover I wanted to shake but a life of mistakes, wrong men, places like this dive I wandered into over and over again.

His black hair curled and spiked up in front. His jeans were stained with cement mix from the rock wall he'd been building before he got picked up. That cement called back the days of hanging out with Sanjiv and fist fights, when sheetrock dust coated Mack's dark hair and the apartment building was trashed around them. Now, instead of his usual work boots Mack was wearing Sketchers, like right out of Payless Shoes. They looked so feeble and thin. They were like bedroom slippers on his big feet.

He was thinner now too, but still beautiful, wiry and strong, an olive-skinned James Dean. He was muscled in a comic-book sort of way; the lines of arms were well defined. I stood to let him pull me close. He lifted me off my feet, squeezed my ribs, tipped me out of my high heels. I lay my arms over his shoulders. "You smell like a man on parole," I said. It was all soap and shaving cream, like a guy trying to do things right. When he finally let go I said, "But nobody washed your clothes in that place?"

He said, "Maybe they did. Just didn't come out."

"Maybe nothing changes," I said.

He offered, "I changed." He laced his fingers around my wrist like handcuffs. There were so many times in the past when he'd helped me out, given me rides, fixed my car when he was really just a kid too really. Times when I'd put my trust in him. But his hands around my wrist? It was unsettling. The orange beer lights behind the counter reflected in the darkness of his eyes.

He said, "Mourning and celebrating, same time. I'd give my left nut for a beer." His eyes roamed to the taps.

"What're you mourning now?" I asked. Before he went in the hospital, Mack hadn't been sleeping. He hadn't even been drinking in those last days either. He was too busy talking to strangers in combinations of sounds that weren't real words. That's against some kind of law, apparently, because cops knocked him flat on the sidewalk, tased him in the bus mall, did what they called "subdued" him. Now he was free again, or close to it.

"That I can't drink," he said.

Between the rash of razor burn and a scar on his forehead where he'd hit the sidewalk, he had the face of a baby and an old man at the same time. Time compressed, all the years we'd known each other and the years up ahead and the future and the past were the same thing, marked by booze, high hopes and missteps. He reached and pulled a flyer out of his back pocket. It was information for a program, How to Stop Drinking: Support For Our Native American Community.

I'd known Mack forever. I said, "Are you Native American?" I had no idea, if he was. That could maybe explain the deep brown of his skin, his dark hair, dark eyes. I started to build a story working backwards.

"No," he said. "Not at all. I think that's somebody's racism, telling me I drink like their idea of an Indian. County's projecting a little bias."

Ah.

Least he wasn't wide-eyed and wired, ready to crack somebody's jaw. He didn't look so electric, anymore. He said, "Feels like I been gone for years." His voice was shaky.

There was a smudge of something on the side of his jaw. I wiped it away with my thumb, in a move like a mother, and as I made that gesture, I remembered all the bus drivers who parented him in their way. I was his mom figure, now. "You can have a good life, you just have to make it," I said.

He looked at me to see if I was joking.

I said, "You're still pure potential. Stay off the sauce, you're golden."

He turned to squint at the soundless TV in the corner, as he said, "Got a bracelet." He hitched up the leg of his jeans. I'd never seen him wear shoes without socks before. His calve was wrapped in a brown plastic band with two boxes, one on either side. "Transdermal, they call it. Scram."

"Scram?" I thought he wanted me to leave. I was more than ready, really. I was nervous around this new, unstable version of who he'd been. I pulled my pocketbook to my lap, packing up.

"Secure Continuous Remote Alcohol Monitor," he said. "SCRAM. Reads your alcohol through your sweat. Five percent of everything you drink comes out your skin. They made me take a class about it." He said, "If I don't drink, they won't know I've been in here, right?"

I said, "Booze leaches through the walls in this place. It's in the air." I sipped my red beer. I ran my fingers over my forehead and across my neck. My hands were cold and wet from condensation on the beer glass.

Alcohol-induced psychosis. That was the theory doctors offered for Mack's tripped-up month, like he drank more than anyone else. He didn't drink more than the men who lined the counter, those old sea gulls on their posts. The diagnosis didn't clear up anything. He was crazy. Drinking made him crazier.

I turned a clean amber ashtray over in my palm to feel its weight and sharp edges. Nothing else felt so solid as that heavy, beveled glass. The ashtray was such a sure thing in my hands, hard and potentially punishing really, I slipped it in my purse. Mack rolled a cigarette. I shifted one end of the tavern's orange curtain to see the street outside and knocked a curled and faded Help Wanted sign from the window. There was no one outside except the traffic of people sealed in cars.

Mack took me by one wrist again, and this time held on. I used my other hand to push against the rock of his forearm. His skin was a thin cover over muscle, holding his body together. "I want to drink my drink," I said.

He pulled me closer until the edge of the table bit into my ribs. My hand grew hot; a candle burned in a red glass globe on the table. Mack whispered, "When I was crucified by those cops, you were the voice in my ear. You were laughing, but you had my back." He let go. I knocked my elbow into the table and sloshed my beer.

Taki said, "Don't break anything."

"Like my arm," I murmured.

Taki put the Help Wanted sign back in the window. I needed my own Help Wanted sign, to wear on my back. Every day.

Mack's cigarette burned in the ashtray, a long ash off the end. I said, "If you're going to smoke, smoke. Don't just burn 'em like incense."

Mack said, "So when do I move back into my place?"

I knew it'd come around to that.

"He said I got temporary housing, until I can prove I'm okay on my own. When I come back, you could still stay on." His eyes got soft in a way that made me want to head for the door fast. We'd had our years, and now he was my beautiful, walking broken heart, my sweet hockey player dropout. All the other guys he used to hang out with? They died. Every last one. Sanjiv drove through an intersection in a Fiero. He t-boned a moving van. Turns out in a Fiero, the driver's pretty much sitting on the gas tank, and it exploded on impact, caught on fire. Kevin was still around, with a few head injuries that weren't helped by his compulsion to self medicate.

I found a lipstick and compact in my purse, and painted my lips red. "You and me, a happy home?"

He nodded. I rolled the lipstick back down into the case. I clipped the lid back on, and signaled Taki for another drink. "I love you, but that's not going to happen."

Where we grew up, we didn't learn how to live. We learned how to bury the land, seal life off. There was an unacknowledged backdrop to being a kid on land that was fast turning into strip malls, when you loved trees and a silent corporate presence kept showing up to knock the trees down. It was the helpless sense that everything you ever loved could be destroyed, without debate.

Tino came in the alley door. He went up to the bar without looking our way. He held the pocket of his Levi's down from the outside with one hand and pulled money out from inside the pocket with his other. He bought a six pack of cans to go. His hands didn't even shake when he counted out his change. That only meant he'd been drinking already. Tino worked as a high school narc, catching delinquents, patting down for weapons and drugs. On the side, he'd confiscate drugs and sell back to the janitors. Janitors were selling the same score back to the kids, so they had their own robust economy, circulating money and dope.

Mack's neck was stiff. He had to turn his whole body in his chair to follow my glance. Tendons rose to the surface. His foot hit the base of the table. Maybe he kicked it on purpose, but those Sketchers softened his swing. "Ah. Your boyfriend's here now."

I caught the table to stop it from rocking. "He's not my boyfriend."

If Mack hadn't been there, just out of the psych ward, working hard to not drink and keep his head together, I would've walked over and reached for Tino, pulled him close. Maybe I would've called him a boyfriend. I might've called him mine.

Mack shouted, "When do I get my boots back?"

Tino looked so tired when he turned, his eyes ringed with circles, lips chapped and cracking. Mack had lost his Doc Martins to Tino in a minor drug deal on a day he'd been otherwise broke. I said, "Not the shoes again." It never was a good conversation.

Tino said, "I'm not a hockshop. I use 'em." He lifted a foot, showed us the boots there in the near-dark, and my heart sunk. We were not on good ground.

I said, "Mack's fresh out of the mental motel. Give him the shoes back. Why you don't you swap with him."

But Tino only glanced at the Sketchers, then asked, "You were down here, or up on the hill?" like the address of the psych ward helped anything.

"I was up on the hill," Mack said, so quietly his mouth barely moved. He shook his head, like he didn't understand what had happened himself.

Tino said, "I'm headed to the hospital down here. Good Sam."

"You going nuts, too?" Mack asked. He actually sounded a little hopeful, maybe so he wouldn't be in it all alone.

"Going to see Eileen," Tino said. He swung a chair backward, sat on it that way, then lit a smoke. "She had an aneurysm in her brain." When he pointed, with the orange tip of his cigarette, his thumb aimed at the ceiling, his hand was like a gun aimed at his own head.

I said, "No way."

Mack asked, "Whose Eileen?"

She was nobody. A friend, an enemy. "A waitress, works at Chang's, dyes her hair?"

Tino said, "Living with Ray Madrigal."

There it was, the part I didn't want to say and didn't want to hear—Eileen and Ray. Ray, who I'd lived with before. I pulled the ashtray out of my purse and put it back on the table. I didn't need it, why weigh myself down, with that weight in my bag? But I couldn't let it go. I moved to put it in my purse again.

Tino said, "They cut her head open and clamped a vein or something shut. She's fine, but she's bald."

I slid a salt shaker in my purse and said, "No shit?" Ray's new girl, maybe twenty-three years old, already with hardware in her head.

The bathroom at the Marathon was down a glowing turquoise hall like a pool drained of water. It smelled from mildew. It was the hallway to rooms for rent upstairs, too. Just outside the women's bathroom somebody had written in black marker: MEN WHO FATHER CHILDREN LIVE HERE. I read those words every time I turned the corner. I'd memorized the writing, all capital letters and jagged angles. The sentence seemed wrong and reversed, blaming the men for where they lived instead of anything they did, maybe even asking for sympathy or renovation on the building. MEN WHO LIVE HERE FATHER CHILDREN, it could say. Or MEN WHO LIVE HERE ARE BAD—but the men in the building weren't necessarily bad, only lost and lazy, broke and broken drunks in single-resident rooms. Men who father children live everywhere.

Tino found me in the hall, and we went out back together, to the alley between buildings, beside the Dumpster. He pulled a pipe from his coat pocket. Pot smells so right out in the cold. There's the density of that soft, skunky sweet smoke. I'd like to find that same edge in something solid enough to hold onto. He passed the pipe. I didn't reach for it. "You shake down a freshman for that herb?"

"Maybe." He was still holding smoke in his lungs. "What're you doing with Mack?"

"Helping him out," I shrugged. "He's important to me."

Tino said, "Watch him close. I don't want to lose more teeth."

"That was a long time ago," I said. "It's the way he was raised. Fighting. But I've never been a good referee." Nobody could understand where we'd come from. There'd been some hard living. I said, "He thinks of you as a brother." I remembered how Mack and Kevin used to pound on each other, lock their limbs and take down the furniture under their weight.

"Teeth don't come back." Tino pulled his lips back into a fake smile to show a gap at the side near the front. His eyetooth, a dog-tooth. A fist, a party. I pressed my lips to his, kissed that gap-toothed smile, breathed secondhand pot smoke and leaned in to hold on to the fake sheepskin of his corduroy coat. His skinny body blocked the wind. He was a frail guy.

One time, when he was still underage, Tino got in some kind of trouble and his folks sent him off to boot camp in Idaho. He broke out, hitched home and hid in the woods at night until he made his way back. Then he hooked up with me for awhile, until he turned eighteen. It'd been over five years, maybe seven. I don't know what happened to him out in Idaho. All I knew was that he'd never left this neighborhood again. He said he'd never go anywhere he couldn't walk home from. That was one thing I'd come to count on, with him. I could travel the world, and knew he'd always be there at home when I got back. The scent of his skin was good as home, to me. He was mine. Mack and Tino, they were my guys. I loved them both. I took the pipe from him and sucked that sweet smoke in.

When we went back inside, Mack was working his muscled jaw. Time for more meds?

Someone called my name, *Vanessa,* in a hiss of a whisper. The men at the bar all had their backs to our table. Music rattled under bad speakers. Nobody had said my name. It was just noises, a cloud of tavern sounds.

Tino said, "Come see Eileen. She'd like it."

My hands were light and far away with cold. I rubbed them together. "I'm fine here."

Mack said, "Jesus, Vanessa. She had brain surgery."

I said, "Hospital-land? Can't believe you'd want to go back in a hospital for any reason."

"I sort of started to like it," Mack said, and put his finger in the hot wax of the candle.

"Ray?" I asked. Did anyone want to see him? My ex. He'd be there.

The hospital halls were miles of white, somebody's idea of a sterile heaven, broken by red emergency phones and inset shrines of faded saints. Mack dropped his arm over my shoulders, stooped to bring his face closer to mine. He said, "Where I was, we had big rooms and new carpets. You could still smell the carpet glue. Think we were all getting high off it. It was like the best house I'd ever lived in." His feet swung out, big and out of place, ready to knock things down.

I heard my name again, in a whisper: *Van-ess-a, Van-ess-a*...it was under the swish of clothes and the wheels of carts. It was there when Mack's coat sleeve rustled against my ear. It was my mother talking to me. Not her voice, but her legacy.

The thing is, auditory hallucinations? That was her struggle. To hear my name whispered in the nothingness of ambient sounds vibrated love and terror all the way to my spine. Mom struggled with voices until she died of anaphylactic shock, alone and allergic to new meds.

For me, the voices only came when I was high.

The hospital was a world of its own, made up of clean, creased uniforms, aluminum carts, and Formica. We were a walking cloud of tavern air and beer breath. I laced a finger through Tino's belt loop, pulling him back to me.

Vanessa...

There was my name in the squeak of shoes on linoleum. I heard it again, louder, and this time when I turned it was real. It was Mrs. Petoskey, our old grade school assistant teacher. "Vanessa," she said. She was in scrubs.

Mack, Tino and me, we all stopped together, like one beast.

"How's your mother?" she asked.

I was the middle of the walking animal that had been the three of us. I felt myself flush and my throat tighten. "Mom? She passed away," I said. "You don't teach school?"

She gave me a sad look, either for mom or me, or school, or maybe only for herself. She said, "Well, things change." She waved a hand at her cart, pulled on a papery face mask and pushed through a set of swinging doors. When she said, "Take care," her voice was muffled by the mask and distance.

Tino said, "Didn't she have cancer, before?"

I didn't remember, but she probably did. How were any of us still around?

Eileen was in bed watching TV, same as everyone in every hospital room or dark, dank tavern all over town. Her head was shaved and bandaged. Her face was puffy. She'd put on makeup that sat like paint on her drained skin. I said, "They told me there was a dead hooker in here."

"Not dead yet," Eileen said. "I got years ahead of me. You all look like the walking wounded."

We were ragged, but doing okay.

I gave her a kiss on her pale forehead, because really, I didn't hate her at all. I was only uncomfortable, and sad about Ray, but I'd known Eileen before all that, and what can you do?

"'S good to see you," she said. Her voice came out slow and stuttering. She was the only patient in a room with two beds, wearing a powder-blue hospital gown. She leaned against a luxurious stack of pillows, with her bed cranked up.

Tino pulled a can of beer from his paper bag, like he needed to self-medicate to stay in this place.

Eileen asked, "How 'bout a cig-rette?" There were two *No Smoking* signs, one for each patient's side, both for us now.

Tino pushed the door closed. I sat on the windowsill. Mack leaned against the wall too close beside me. Tino passed around the rest of the six-pack. I ran a hand over Tino's shoulder and said, "You bony armature of a human." He was so skeletal.

Mack took a beer, too. He drank like drinking was breathing, like he'd been held under water and here was a can of air.

I said, "What about the bracelet?"

"I'll try not to sweat." He tipped the empty can for the last drops.

"Mack just got out of the psych ward on the hill," Tino said.

"No kiddin'?" Eileen lit a cigarette, keeping an eye on the door. "Haven't 'moked all day."

"The alarm'll go off," I said.

"What'll dey do if they catch me—frow me out?" This was the lisp of her stroke. Her brain stutter was like a car with sugar in the tank.

I sat on the empty bed and tightened my coat around me, with one eye on the fire alarm's sprinkler system overhead. "What happened to you?"

Eileen said, "Went out for drinks after work…hands started feeling weird."

Tino said, "Must've felt pretty seriously weird, if they brought you to the E.R."

I felt my own hands, imagining my head as light, losing blood and circulation. I looked for Ray at the door, waited for an alarm to scream my name. The dark circles under Eileen's eyes made her beautiful, like a face-lift patient or a drug addict in treatment. She was being take care of, and that meant cared for. To be taken care of was as luxurious as anything I could imagine. The blue hospital robe rested against her skin at her clavicle in a way that said fragile yet still living, so there was a strength to that. Who would've guessed light blue and bandage white could be so dreamy? I said, "You're gorgeous." No rivalry, here, on this earth. Only envy.

She patted the bed beside her. I rolled the food tray aside, then lay down, working my way carefully around her I.V. tubes. She said, "Ray doesn't talk about you at all."

"Music to my ears." I sipped my drink, tapped the can.

Tino and Mack had the TV on and they were flipping through channels, watching TV like it mattered.

She said, "He's doing it on purpose. Like, I think if he said your name it'd all come back…"

My nail polish was chipped blood red. I dropped flakes of it on Eileen's white sheets.

She whispered, "If you wanted him back, you could do it."

I said, "Don't worry. I don't take anything that doesn't belong to me."

"Since when?" she asked.

My purse was bulging with the ashtray, salt shakers, old spoons, a shot glass. Mack crumpled his empty can, smashed it until it was small enough to put in his coat pocket. Tino hit the remote, changed the channel.

Mack said, "Hey, asshole?"

Tino waved the remote, raising his hand. He said, "Asshole. Check. Present and accounted for."

The starting gun, I thought. Boom. A fight.

Except Mack let the TV be his pacifier. He eased into the new channel. Then Tino changed it again. He was doing it because he could, in a quiet power struggle. "Knock it off," I said, and reached for the remote. From behind me, Mack laced his fingers through my hair. He held on, then gave a gentle tug. When he pulled my head back, my neck had no choice but to give in easily. I said, "Hey."

He let go.

I was done there.

It was time to go home, pack, get out of Mack's shack in the warehouse district. I said, "You need to manage yourself." When they cracked a second round of beers, I headed out, said I was going to find a restroom as an excuse to leave.

Eileen offered, "Use mine." She pointed to a door off the side of her room.

Her bathroom was small as a restroom on a Greyhound bus, only it was clean in all its stainless steel and pressed board nooks and crannies. It felt disarming, like there could be a hidden camera in the walls or ceiling.

A second door on the opposite side of the space meant a nurse or another patient could walk in, and I was afraid I'd touch something meant to stay clean. I wasn't drunk, but I was on my way and drunk was how I'd rather be.

When I stood to flush, I saw I'd let my warm pee fall into an aluminum pan meant to catch a urine sample, hung just inside the lip of the toilet bowl. I'd peed in Eileen's collection cup? For all I knew, her urine was there too. I hadn't looked. Her piss and mine would go to the lab together, like one person.

There was a knock on the door outside Eileen's room. A voice said, "Eileen, baby? I'm here." I froze, and listened. That was Ray, in the hall.

Tino yelled back, "Baby, we're all here."

I listened for my own name, Vanessa, but didn't hear it now at all—not in the sounds of the hallway, or in anyone's voice. MEN WHO FATHER CHILDREN ARE HERE. I read the words across the bathroom's blank wall, saw those lines and jagged angles. The last time I'd seen Ray, he'd given me three hundred bucks and walked me to a clinic. What I didn't tell him back then was, I'd already lost the baby. He left me out on the corner bleeding in ways he didn't know anything about, with a pocketful of cash.

I tipped my beer can upside down over the urine collection tray, skipping the middle man, that biological system of the body. I poured beer into the sample like pre-made piss.

On the other side of the door, Ray said, "Bushmills."

Eileen laughed and said, "Bwood thinners and pain kiwwers," working out the words awkwardly. Blood thinners. Pain killers.

Mack was a soft murmur at the far wall, saying things I couldn't hear.

I turned the handle on the second door, making my getaway.

The hallway was right there. I could walk and keep going. I had my coat. We hadn't gone so far that I couldn't walk home.

I leaned into the mirror, fixed my lipstick. Mack, in the other room, was working himself into a fight. He said, "Think you're some kind of comedian?"

Then Ray was the placating murmur I could barely hear. If Mack was drinking Bushmills, let them be Christ crucified. I wouldn't go back.

The ashtray in my purse was like brass knuckles. Solid, hard, beveled. I touched it, for confidence.

There was nothing in the bathroom worth taking, unless I needed a plastic yellow pitcher or a roll of toilet paper. I wanted a powder blue robe. A souvenir. A robe would be soft and sweet as pot smoke in cool air.

I found a place where the counter opened from the top, and I opened it. Inside was a dark hamper. Linens. There was a peeping corner of a robe that called to me silently. I reached in.

On the other side of the wall, Tino said, "Where'd Nessa go?" There was my name, the sound I'd been waiting to hear. Then, I wanted to run.

"She's here?" Ray asked.

I couldn't tell if he was hopeful, nervous, or neither. Didn't matter. I was out of there. I closed my fingers on my souvenir robe. When I lifted it, the soft baby blue fabric was covered in the watery mark of rinsed bloodstains. Everything inside the hamper was a pile of bloodstained sheets, towels and old robes twisted and tangled into one mass, thick as bodies intertwined. It was an orgy of bloody hospital cotton sheets and robes.

I dropped the one I'd held. Was that Eileen's blood? I washed my hands and went back into her room. "Hey, Ray," I said, all casual, holding my voice steady.

Ray looked me up and down. He took me in with his eyes. It

felt like he was stealing something from me, just by looking so freely. I reached for Tino, to let his slim frame block me the way he'd blocked the wind. I gave him the longest, deepest kiss I could, a kiss of love and gratitude. I ran a hand over his hair, breathed in Tino, drank his sweat and salt and alcohol. He rested a hand on the curve of the small of my back, and we fit together. I was in, for the comfort of skin and love.

I had barely pulled away though before there was the crack of Mack's fist. Tino fell backward. His head knocked against a counter on the way down. It was that car wreck all over again, like metal on metal. Eileen screamed. She flung an arm out so fast, her IV pulled out. It was still held by the tape, but a fast bruise bloomed around the port.

Mack's face went white. His knuckles were red. He pulled back, into himself. He'd lost it. He knew he'd lost it. He'd end up back on the hill if he acted like that.

Tino moved but didn't get up when I kneeled and called his name. Ray was too stoned to move fast, and too high to stick around. He edged out toward the door. Eileen hit the buzzer on her wall beside her bed. Tino dripped a slow, slight leak of blood from the back of his head through my fingers onto the hard white floor.

When the cops got there, hospital staff had already cleared most of us out of the room. Tino had already been taken to Emergency. Eileen had gone back into testing, to check her blood pressure and her busted veins. Only Mack and I waited in the hallway to answer questions.

A cop asked, "What's the victim's name?"

"Tino Pepperino."

He said, "Tino Pepperino?" This cop was a skeptic.

I blinked. He was still waiting. I said, "That's the only name I know him by."

We were poor witnesses. We didn't know what happened. At least, that's what we said. Tino fell, Eileen freaked out, we said. After a few more questions and no answers that made anybody happy, eventually they left Mack and me standing outside what had been Eileen's room. When we were alone, I whispered, "Tino's a good man."

Mack's breath was laced with whiskey. He said, "You always have been an idealist."

"What do you mean?" I asked.

He shrugged. "A good man? What's that."

Who was I to argue. I said, "This is terrible. We're all dying. We're killing ourselves and each other."

He said, "I shouldn't have done it. I'm sorry." He put a big mitt to the back of my neck. I could feel the heat of his body, relaxing my tense muscles just enough to let me know how tight I'd been holding my shoulders. He added, "A hospital is one of the best places to be cold-cocked. They'll bring him back."

"What are the other good places?"

He didn't answer that. I hoped Mack was right. Mrs. Petosky, my mom's old friend, the nurse, our former teaching assistant, was far down the hall pushing a cart. From the curve of her back even from that distance I could tell she was ready for her cigarette break. Like, maybe that break was years overdue?

I said, "It's you and me, for now." It was always him and me. This was like the old days after hockey, in apartments, those divorce caves, walking together out of high school. I touched the curve of his cheek, moved his hair off his forehead. I said, "We'll check on them in the morning. Maybe we can get somebody home."

He caught my hand and held it. He compressed my fingers, under his strength.

I said, "Tino's not a fighter. We need to take care of him." I loved them all, my fallen, broken men. I wanted them with me, close and cared for. I couldn't take care of anybody.

He said, "I shouldn't be around humans." He had me in his grip.

Truer words were never spoken?

He said, "I think hockey damaged my brain. Damaged impulse control."

"Come with me, Mack," I said. "Back to my place." I tried to pull my hand back. Our fingers were intertwined like those bloody hospital robes. I didn't mind, even when he scared me a little. The blood that kept us alive was trapped just under our skin, racing through veins. All those cells inside and out were fighting for a way to move closer together, beyond the trap of skin, dependent on breath.

THE FOLLY OF LOVING LIFE

Seeing that girl in the hospital, grown now. Damn. I remembered days with her mom. The best days, maybe. Back before we got old? Or I got old, and Baysie disappeared, and now I hear she's dead.

Not great. But okay, life.

There's one day that girl's mom and I hung out that stays with me like it was a holiday. It was an ordinary day, at the time. I'd come across Baysie out in the Park Blocks, not far from Portland State, downtown. Her hair! It was the first time in a long time that I saw her hair when it wasn't covered with a black velvet hat. That day, her hair seemed like a sign of spring. It was like finding the first crocus, to see it blowing free. When I got a little closer to her I saw her ear, red and cold in the wind, between tangles and tinsel lines of new grey hair growing in. She was just starting to go grey, but it showed up fast because her hair was so naturally dark. She was maybe twenty-five? Not married yet. No kids. I was on my bike and freezing, ignoring the sky's single covering cloud. Baysie was in the park sitting on a bench, working with something on the bench beside where she sat, with her back to me.

I rode up and said, "Baysie, where's your hat?" I loved the way she wore the same thing every day. She always looked fine. I tried to vary my own clothes every three days or so, but not because I cared—only a modified habit left over from the years of having an office job. When we met it'd been summer and Baysie'd worn one pair of homemade cotton Gauguin-print pants until the cotton faded white, turned into threads and gave way. Now it was always black wool pants and a black jacket that she put her coat on over. Red lipstick. And there'd always been the hat.

She looked up and said, "Hey! It's gone. Lost it. But hey—I got these for nearly nothing."

She was stacking baseball cards in piles inside a shoebox. Her hands were thin and marked with the eczema that she claimed came from beer, yeast and sugar creating a habitat.

"Check it out," she said, and held up a card. "Hank Aaron signature. Mint shape."

I took the card carefully, knowing enough to not fray the edges, bend the corners. I said, "That's not a real autograph. Just printed on."

She reached for the card. "It's a signature, something people want. Especially a Hank Aaron." She had a cluster of sandwich bags rubber-banded together and was putting the cards in bags, then putting them back in the shoebox. "I returned my cereal to buy these cards. They're worth more than a box of Wheaties."

What I had was a pocket full of food stamps that I didn't even try to qualify for but bought from a man in my building for thirty cents on the dollar. I pulled out a handful now and held them up, fanning them like money.

I said, "We can always get more Wheaties. No problem."

I had my system down, trading cash for food stamps and then turning the food stamps back into money again, eighty-five cents at a time, tripling my income to stretch out the last of the unemployment. That was back when we still had actual food stamps, before Oregon switched to the Oregon Trail card, with that name like the hungry and broke were all pioneers on the way to somewhere. The trick was buying small things—a single banana, a piece of licorice. Baysie put her shoebox under her arm and walked with me, me pushing my bike, to find a grocery.

Elias's Market was closest but we couldn't take food stamps there because Elias, behind the counter, knew me. He'd known me since I was a girl in the alley waiting for somebody else to buy my friends and I beer, in the days I took an interest in drinking, before I moved away, and before I came back. Now he'd sell me anything, give it on credit even, but he'd ask, "What's wrong with you girls? Why you have no money?"

I couldn't stand the thought of finding work again. I would—I'd go on to every support spot in every town: teaching assistant, office assistant, nursing assistant. But on this day, I was free. We passed in front of Elias's. I waved and we kept walking. I lost the rhythm of my step and the bike pedal's sharp teeth hit my shin.

When I was working, I'd owned a Dodge Dart that I drove until the odometer almost hit two hundred thousand miles, most of them not mine. The motor finally blew up, pouring oil over asphalt. After that I bought a solid Schwinn one-speed with a bent crank for six dollars.

"I don't think this guy knew what he had," Baysie said, still talking about her cards.

I asked, "Who ever does?"

We walked through the Park Blocks to the main street, to the small stretch of grocery stores full of nothing more than potato chips, wine, old apples, and dirty magazines. I bought a five-cent piece of gum and put the ninety-five cents in my left pocket, keeping the paper bills in my right. I slipped Baysie a food stamp dollar and she bought a tootsie roll.

The Vietnamese woman behind the counter said, "Nice earrings. Pretty." She put her hand to her own earlobe, smiling.

"I have more," Baysie said, and pulled a thin scarf from her coat pocket. She unrolled the scarf on the counter. The earrings were laid out in rows, each one attached to the scarf the way it would be through an ear. Baysie made the earrings out of magazine pictures with a laminating machine. I'd been with her when she found the machine at the Goodwill, when it was missing a part that turned up in the bins. Now all she needed, she said, was an agent, a gallery, a place to sell. Walking, she'd find houses close to the street and say, "I could rent that, have my own gallery."

I pointed to a pair of earrings made out of a small, laminated collage. Baysie had laid images of a dark-haired woman's face over a green apple, a simple contrast. I said, "These are beautiful."

Baysie said, "Five dollars." She spread her cracked, eczema-covered fingers to show, *five.*

The woman behind the counter touched a few earrings gently, but didn't buy anything.

Outside the air was cool and dry despite the clouds. I felt it could be fall, if we were in another part of the country where it grew colder, or it could be spring coming on with the rains slowing. Either way it was Sunday, and the deserted downtown was Baysie's and mine. I saw something shine in the road ahead and swerved, pushing my bike toward it. I walked in the street. It was a trailer hitch fallen from an old truck, a solid sphere of steel. I picked the trailer hitch up and turned it over in my hand. The metal was cold and heavier than seemed possible, a weight that made my arm feel like fishline and the trailer hitch a fishing weight, when I'd go out with my dad as a kid. Now I put the trailer hitch in my bike basket.

"What'll you do with that?" Baysie asked.

I shrugged. She made everything into something saleable. I just collected: metal-flattened nails, the handle off an antique bathtub, the insignia from the side of a Rambler American, my own license plates. I liked the integrity of cast metal worn from the road. I lined the pieces along my window sills.

A boy sitting on a park bench had acne-marked skin, too big of feet, and a backpack. His jeans were dark, new and stiff. He was sitting with his chin in his hands, his elbows on his knees, looking as though he'd rather be lost in ideas but was in fact just lost in adolescence—aimless and troubled.

Deep depression, I thought as we passed, judging the curve of his back, the tilt of his head. Despair. I'd been told I suffered from it too. The thing was, I never sensed myself in despair, but rather, in love with something I felt closest to only when walking or riding my bike in the city. I felt it when I kept my windows open all night, or sitting on the rickety wood of the porch my landlord called a fire escape, peeled paint flaking under my hands and feet, looking over the empty lot. It had to do with a texture, with the moon and a stray white cat I'd been feeding, a cat that saw me as home now. I couldn't stand office air, couldn't take the way florescent lights sucked energy only thinly replaced through the false hope of chocolate piled in candy dishes on every desk. I once spent two weeks in front of a computer monitor that whistled in a way only I could hear. I couldn't think in the dust of factories, the noise inside a warehouse.

I breathed in the cold air and stepped on matted leaves and Baysie and I turned down a street that was more of an alley, the pavement broken and opening onto the loading docks of warehouses. We passed behind a Laundromat, the sweet, steamy cloud like a perfumed coat from somebody else's party. Gross.

Baysie said, "It smells delicious, doesn't it?" When she turned and smiled, her teeth crooked, I felt inclined to see it her way.

She said, "The one good thing about being a secretary was that in that sensory-deprived space, the offices, where everything was all beige and cream and grey, I'd have these full-body memories." She said, "I'd eat an apple at lunch break, and it'd bring back a complete dream—sun against the hot wooden siding, some afternoon in the grass eating apples, dirt against my elbows. I'd forget where I was."

She knew what it meant to be alive.

We passed a piece of metal. A car's brake shoe. It was good metal, solid and worn, but also asbestos-lined. Pure cancer. I didn't touch it.

In the next grocery we bought lollipops for fifteen cents each. I gave mine to a kid who'd been turning the key on the gum machine. My left pocket was deep and grew heavy with change that hit against my thigh. Baysie had a beaded coin purse and she put her collection in the purse, then put the purse in her coat pocket again.

Outside the dollar theater, I read the names of movies we'd already watched. When I looked down again I saw a matted dark spot like a run-over animal, a soft and squished pool of black. I said, "That's your hat." It didn't really look like her hat, it looked small and soaked and matted, but it had the right color, had a hatness about it.

Baysie reached into the oily puddle alongside the curb. She picked it up and shook it off. "It is my hat," she said.

She worked it with her hands and I saw the shape come back, the roundness with the flat top, the limp bow to the side. Washed and dried, it would be good as new. We spread the hat out in the basket on my bike, held down with the trailer hitch. It dripped against my front tire in it's own black cloud burst.

By the time we had close to ten dollars it was starting to get dark out, and cold. We weren't far from Tino's. The place wasn't really called Tino's, but we called it that because Tino was always there, behind the bar or out on the floor, wiping down tables, folding up rags. He was trading time for money and smoking during the slow spells.

Tino's was a diner in the front half, but melted fast into a bar in back. In between was a round, gas-powered fireplace. The booths were orange, pointing to the best part about winter, being cold then warm again.

The place was nearly empty. There were three men at the bar and nobody at the tables. We sat at the bar. Tino was watching TV and didn't move except to nod from where he leaned against the stainless-steel counter of a prep station, near a vat of sliced tomatoes, another of lettuce. A handwritten sign taped to the station said, "Don't leave tongs in the bin. It turns lettuce brown." Baysie put her shoebox of cards on the counter, and took the lid off it. She put her scarf covered with earrings to her left, and her coat over her stool. You can't sell in a bar, but it's no crime if someone looks. She opened her purse and turned it upside-down and let the money fall out, rolling and rattling loud against the wood. Her arms were skinny without her coat on. She stuck her elbows out and started stacking change.

I said, "Where is everybody?"

Tino smiled and said, "Home, I'd guess. What'll you have?"

I said, "What's your special?"

He asked, "Dinner special, or drink special?"

Baysie said, "Everything is so special here."

I laughed out loud, because it couldn't have been less special! I liked it that way, a bar, a place. Nowhere. I said, "How about soup."

His soup of the day was chili. We ordered glasses of draft beer and my chili came with crackers and the fireplace was turned up high. My favorite thing about Tino's was that he had the best version of Lou Reed's "Sweet Jane." I took some of our change to play music.

A sign tacked on the door of the hall that led to the bathrooms said, "Leaving without paying is a crime—really."

When I got back to the bar, Baysie was showing the cards to the three men in a row beside her. "They didn't print many of these," she said, flashing a card pulled randomly. "This guy was a big deal." She said, "I don't know if I'd ever sell these cards. You don't find a collection like this easy." The man at the far end of the line got up and walked over, taking a closer look.

The counter had a varnish over the wood so thick it seemed indestructible. I ran my hand along it, wondering why more things weren't covered that way. Outside, it had started to rain, hard. That question the clouds had been waiting to answer all day fell in a steady downpour. Drops danced under the streetlight. Rivulets ran along the gutters. It'd soak Baysie's hat that we'd left to dry in the basket. The day was just about over, moving into night, and I was where I wanted be, watching the rain fall from inside a warm bar; there was nothing wrong with that. Moving her graceful, weathered hands quickly, Baysie played some kind of solitaire. She turned over cards and organized stacks, each baseball card like a headstone for a player not necessarily dead but out of the game, done racking points.

I memorized the completeness of the moment, stored in my body for later the smoke smell of Tino's, bleach on rags and glasses, the way all of us from time to time looked out the window, not saying anything, and my chili sat in its rising steam in the bowl on a plate on the counter.

Baysie said, "What do you say that Hank Aaron signature's worth?"

And I had to laugh. I didn't know. My answer would've been to take what you can get—a day off, a week, a year if you can make it. But she was planning to sell the card; any money she made here would be somebody else's time spent, earning it somewhere else. We were all locked into this system. The safest place to be, when it came to money, was the fringes, where you sold the least of your life away.

The man beside me looked out at the rain, too. He said, "I got fired from Hanford, fired from Trojan, and I'm probably going to be fired again."

Hanford and Trojan, both nuclear reactors.

I asked, "Why'd you get fired?"

He said, "Drunk on the job. And late." Then, "Drunk and late, I guess. Now I'm an asbestos remover. Commercial property mostly."

Life is short and finite. Those places he'd spent time in? They guaranteed an accelerated route to death. All three. Somebody had made up the whole system, selling time to earn money and never enough of it. I said, "You're better off without the work."

There was another guy at the bar—tall, thin. He seemed to be alone, drinking a pint. I was the one who called over to him. I said, "What do you do?"

He said, "Science." He had the pale cool-blue eyes. He added. "Forensic science. I solve people's problems."

Baysie lit up when he said that, flashing the white of her teeth, her red lipstick. She said, "I have a few problems." She had a huge capacity for an easy happiness. He grinned back, and they fit together like puzzle pieces, meant to click.

We didn't know how much was up ahead—marriage, the two girls. Her whole life was tied to that man.

Outside the window, one lone car passed and threw a violent blast of rainwater over the sidewalk. It was a storm, by now. Looking at that rain, I was falling deeply in love with our warm bar. What could you do, with a world like that? I was in love with every minute of being alive even as I floundered.

"Good luck," I said, to the unemployed nuclear reactor alcoholic, and meant it. Baysie shuffled her cards. She couldn't stop smiling, and glanced at the scientist down the bar.

Baysie and me, we were both in love with life.

The man beside me said, "Hell, I'll take another." He gestured at his beer bottle, his own prescription medicine, calling the bartender. I raised my glass, welcoming him to unemployment. He raised his too, knowingly or not, but, cheering the beauty of his upcoming loss.

MODELS I KNOW

My primary concern, when I dragged a bag of clothes, a toothbrush and one lip-liner into the shelter, was to get myself together. It was summer. I had this plan to sit in the sun until I could blend the line between my sunburned shins and where my socks had been.

It's good to have goals.

I can still trace the lines of the word Fry-O-Lator written backward on my arm, like reading my old high school diary. I've tried to minimize scarring since, inside and out. When I wasn't any good at minimizing it, I got tattoos over the burns, trying to make it my own.

Mary's House doesn't call itself a shelter. It's a home for "Women in Transition." I hoped it could be a refuge, like the land I'd grown up on, that place my crazy mom thought could somehow save us.

If I'd known mom, before her breakdown? If I'd been older in those days I've seen in photos, before she grew so puffy with medication, I thought maybe I'd be living differently. I'd be a different person.

At Mary's, they won't take you if they think you'll need to be there more than once. I could feel the finite edges of their offer as a resource, and already I wanted more in the way of help. I wanted to be held, to move in and stay forever. They want to be the stair-step, the ladder for women climbing their way to a better life. I promised I was making changes. I told them ten days. In ten days? I'd be fine!

During the day I sit on the cement steps in the backyard and put baby oil on my feet and ankles. I bring a stack of magazines with me and put my feet in the sun. The magazines are mostly outdated, but the date doesn't matter at all.

The thing about the magazines is that I can never tell where or when those people in the magazines are supposed to be living. Even the people you don't see, the ones who write letters in, I can't picture them any place I know.

One magazine tells you how to put together seven outfits for under one hundred dollars each. The women are only wearing T-shirts and jeans, wide black belts and shoes that slip on. On the weekends they wear the same jeans with brown belts. Then they wear brown shoes like boots, but with lightweight soles, not boots for hiking or work boots.

I don't understand dating. The dresses the girls wear for dating, I don't know where they're going. These girls are younger than me and older at the same time. They're going somewhere nice enough to wear strapless dresses, but safe and clean, without pregnancy and diseases you can catch. Where these women live they have telephones beside the bed and closets as big as public bathrooms.

I don't understand how to build a life. If dad was still alive, I'd ask him about evidence. I'd ask where I wandered down the wrong trail of inquiry.

My arms are covered in tattoos. For a while, yes, maybe I thought that if I had tattoos I'd grow into the kid of person who had tattoos, in a round-about way. I hoped each one would tell the story of my life back to me. I'd hoped that being strong would make me better at being alone.

At Mary's House, my room is in the basement with two other women. We have three narrow beds in a row. Every wall has a poster with an inspirational saying.

"My life begins with me."

"Only I can affect change."

"I am not responsible for the acts of others. I am only responsible for my own reaction."

My father would have said, "Evidence is not intimidated," reminding me to trust myself and trust in the material world.

According to Carolyn, we are here, in this house, to rethink our stories. She says, "Who do you let deliver your narrative? It's up to you to tell the story of your life."

Nobody is allowed to drink, not even beer. Carolyn burns incense at night and plays meditation tapes. Evenings, we're invited to join her in the living room, closing our eyes and thinking positive thoughts. If we don't want to join her we can sit in the kitchen and talk. Then mostly we talk about how bad things were, or how bad things are, for the ones who think it's bad now being in a shelter.

The third day at Mary's was the only day I thought was bad, besides the first day when I walked all day and got the burn on my legs. The third day I found bones on my car, between the windshield and the windshield wiper. I didn't even see the bones until I was in the car, behind the wheel, behind the glass with the bones in front of me.

It was a whole chicken that had been boiled and only had a little skin still on the bones, a few pin feathers on the skin on the wing. The legs and the wings were held together by cartilage and tendons.

Carolyn was on the porch, waving goodbye. I was going into town to file for a restraining order, and she knew I didn't want to go. She saw the bones when I saw them, and she stepped over to my car and lifted the windshield wiper with one hand and the bones with the other and she threw the bones into the trash can by the side of the house.

She said, "Wait, Lucille," and she used my full name, like a mother or an interviewer at a job I wouldn't get. She said, "I'll clean your windshield." She brought glass cleaner out of the house and cleaned the glass and acted like it was that easy and not a bad sign at all.

I said, "Travis knows where I am. He knows. He's seen my car." I loved him, but his problems were bigger than anything I could fix. He lived through his own endless, internal war.

Instead of the Justice Center, I went to a park on the river with a boat dock. I rolled up the bottoms of my pants and put my feet in the water off the side of the dock, then put my feet in the sun. I read a magazine I'd brought. Restraining orders don't work anyway.

The backyard at Mary's has a fence that is wooden and over seven feet high. Nobody can see over the fence. There's a picnic table and a sandbox for the children of the women who have children and stay at Mary's. I paint my fingernails at the picnic table.

By the fourth day I have a burn on my feet, but not one to match the burn on my legs. The burn on my feet is spotted, red on the top and white on the ankles. I put sunblock on the red spots and baby oil on the white places and keep my feet in the sun. There is only one other white girl in the shelter and she doesn't even look white. Not white like I'm white. They laugh at the way I burn.

A model in the magazines is the same age as me. When we turned twelve, when I started reading magazines, she was in a movie. When this model went to college the magazine had a full article about the clothes she packed. The article listed what the model used to wash her face, and how she packed shampoo in plastic containers so it wouldn't spill and toothpaste in a plastic container so it wouldn't break open in the luggage on the airplane.

This model, before she went to college, taught me how to cut my own hair. In the magazine there was a photo of each step as she combed her hair forward over her head, collected her hair together in front, and cut her hair into a long, angled bob. Now her hair is short, up over her ears, and sleek on the back of her neck. In an interview, she says she's not as ambitious now that she is older. She enjoys doing the laundry. Her favorite part, she says, is cleaning the lint filter.

At night, awake in my bed in the basement, I hear the noises of the gangs in the empty lot next door. In the day they use hand signals. At night they whistle. I listen carefully, trying to identify the whistles.

One night I heard the whistles, and I heard voices. A car passed the house driving slow, then faster. When I heard footsteps upstairs, I went up. Carolyn was in the living room, wearing only a buttoned-up shirt, pulling back the curtains to look at the street.

"They went through the yard," she said. "But they're gone now."

They weren't gone far. Two cars in the street were stopped, driver's side window to driver's side window, facing opposite directions, with only their yellow lights on.

I said, "We should call the police."

Carolyn opened a drawer on a desk near the front door and took out a box of incense. She put two sticks of incense in a brass incense burner and lit them with a wooden match.

She sat on the couch and said, "Sit with me. Participate. Let's build a circle of safety." She crossed her bare legs underneath herself, closed her eyes, and tipped her head back. She said, "We will bless this house and keep ourselves free of harm."

It's Carolyn's neighborhood, not mine. I like to think she knows what she's doing. When I talk with Carolyn, I try to believe as much as I can. In the shelter, every day I ask her the same questions. I tell her about Travis, who I'd been living with—the good and the bad, and how there was plenty of both. I like to hear her answers, and she always answers the same.

"Remember," she tells me, "it's not your job to be a teacher. It's your responsibility to decide what you are willing to accept. It's your life that's important." Carolyn says, "Protect yourself. Follow your own path."

Men come to the shelter. They stand on the porch and ring the doorbell or open the screen door and knock. They yell when they don't think we'll answer.

"I know she's in there," they yell.

"Louise, I love you," a man yells at the door or at the fence in the backyard. "I need you. It's not going to happen again. It'll get better, it really will."

We sit in the house or in the backyard and listen. Some women go home. It's their choice.

My feet are still white with red patches and my legs are burned. My fingernails are starting to grow long and I shape them with an emery board. I'm in the kitchen shaping my fingernails at the table the day I hear Travis's voice.

"I just want to talk to her," he's saying. "I know she's here. I know she's here, I want to talk."

Without seeing him I can imagine the look on his face. He's pleading, not yelling. He's learning from mistakes. I almost walk out to meet him, to go home. It would be easy. It's been easy before.

I wonder how my sister would manage this. I wonder where she is. Our parents are gone. The place we grew up? It was a Bi-Mart now.

"I'm sorry," I hear Carolyn say, "this is my house. You have to leave."

My nails are smooth. Carolyn closes the door. She comes in the kitchen and tells me he isn't going away. He's standing on the porch knocking on the door. He's walking in the front yard trying to see through the windows. He's sitting on the hood of my car.

"Should we call the police?" I ask, wanting more than anything, Carolyn's advice.

She says, "You are responsible for your own decisions. You initiate change."

I don't leave the house the rest of the day. The next day he's gone, and it's the first time I've made it this far. I go into the backyard, behind the seven-foot fence, and rub baby oil into my ankles.

The model in the magazine would never burn the way I've burned. I hold the magazine close to my face and look at her skin and it's flawless.

A woman across the street from Mary's takes care of her grandkids, and any other kids that come by. I wave at her from the porch. The two oldest kids ride Big Wheels up the sidewalk. I talk to her about her grandkids and her own kids, who are always gone.

"You ever heard of someone having chicken bones left on their windshield?" I ask her.

She shakes her head. "No. Can't say I have. You heard of that? That happen over there?" She points at the house she knows is a shelter, Mary's House, my house for now.

"Happened to me," I say. "On my car."

"To you? Well, can't be too good. That's what I say, can't be too good." She's bouncing a baby against her shoulder and watching the girl on the Big Wheel. She says, "Chicken bones?"

I tell her, "A whole carcass. Boiled."

"Never heard of such a thing. Not in this neighborhood."

That night in the basement I heard the cars again, driving slow and fast, circling the block, one with its engine too loud and the muffler dragging. I heard voices. When I went upstairs, Carolyn was already up and in the living room. She was wearing a T-shirt that didn't reach past her hips. Carolyn says nudity is nothing to be ashamed of, and that it's not my job to take on shame anyway. Still, I didn't know where to look.

She put a meditation tape on the stereo and said, "Join me in a guided visualization." She sat on the couch and made a circle with her fingers, touching the first and second fingers on each hand to the tips of her thumbs.

I sat on a chair, but didn't close my eyes and didn't make the circles. There was a noise upstairs in the attic, like something falling to the floor, and two footsteps. I stood up fast.

We heard it again, then Carolyn, without saying anything, turned off her meditation and called the police.

When they got there she still wasn't dressed. Carolyn opened the door and let two officers in and she stood there with her arms folded in front of her to keep off the cold that snuck in the open door. When she moved, you could see her dark brown patch of hair just below the faded-out T-shirt. One officer had his notebook out and asked exactly what the problem was while the second one looked around the house at the posters with all the inspirational phrases on the walls. The second one was smiling, but didn't want to be caught smiling.

Carolyn showed the officers where there was a closet you could open that had stairs leading to the attic. They got out their flashlights and their guns and they went up, one behind the other.

While they were up there, I asked, "You don't want to put something on?"

What the police found was a cat. They brought it down, a skinny thing that was always prowling the neighborhood.

"You know there's no glass on that window up there?" the first officer asked. "The board's been taken off. You'll lose all your heat that way," he said, and he laughed. He handed the cat to Carolyn. She held it, rubbing its ears.

"Thanks for coming," she said. "Thank you. Bless you both."

I don't know when I quit trusting police. When they walked to the car anybody could tell they were ready to talk and to laugh about the woman with the cat in the attic who didn't even bother to put on enough clothes when she called the police to her house. They'd tell the story, talk about the woman, talk about Carolyn like she was crazy.

Maybe she was crazy. I couldn't believe we had a window that wasn't even closed with a board or glass. Anybody could climb through that window. It's only a one-story house with an attic. The truth is, I didn't understand what Carolyn meant by some of the things she said. *Circle of safety?* A week in her house and Carolyn was as good as one of the women in the magazines, living in a way I couldn't make sense of.

I wanted to pull her up close, look at the details, study her pores, like a picture in a magazine. The house I grew up in? It was the loneliest place on earth.

I took the cat and went out the sliding glass door into the backyard. The streets were silent, with no cars and no gang whistles, just a full moon and a neighbor's backyard floodlight. The Rottweiler on the other side of the fence started barking. The Doberman in the next yard over joined. That made all the dogs bark, close to the house and farther off. Once they start they keep each other going. My magazines were on the table and I opened one, looking for the model I'd known since I was twelve. Other models, in their clothes, with the ages I couldn't place, were running up steps and turning their heads in cities I'd never seen.

From the parking lot on the other side of the fence I heard one whistle. I listened for a response, but only heard the same call again. I moved my own tongue and mouth but didn't dare make the sound. Like bird calls, one set of notes whistled says, "I'm on your side." Another tells, "I'm your enemy." The places I've lived, nothing has been that clear.

NEIGHBORHOOD NOTES: REVERSE MORTGAGE

The old women on our block never die. They only stop coming out to feed their cats. Ask their children, who aren't really children anymore but all adults who still live at home. Say, "How's your mom?" Try not to let anything at all seep into the lift or drop of your voice. No insinuation! And no mention of an institution, none.

"Fine," they say. "Mom is doing fine."

Thank God. But the cats are thin and yowling. One has lost its hair in patches. The best way to disguise the cat-piss scent of a meth lab is to bury a house in stray cats. "That one doesn't look well," you might say, pointing to a white cat whose pink skin is more visible than it should be, the hair gone thin everywhere.

"Needs cortisone shots," one grown daughter offers. She's in shorts, out at her car. Her calves are strung with muscle. Her wrists are pocked with chemical burns.

Cortisone. Right. You nod, like a question has actually been answered.

It's been months since you've seen the older generation of mothers on the block. How fine can those mothers be, never let loose of their little houses?

The thing is, each one of their houses is on a reverse mortgage, like a clock counting backward, a banker's wager. A reverse mortgage is the bank's offer to senior citizens: they say, sell us your house now, we'll pay you a little bit out of the equity every month. It's a check coming in instead of money going out! All money, no bills. There's always a catch. This time, the deal is that when the older generation dies, the house belongs to the bank exactly forty-five days after the date of death. The mothers on our block? They've sold their houses to the bank in installments.

The adult daughter's teenage son comes to the door, saying, "Mom? We're out of Yoohoo." He's got a baby on his hip, what he calls his girlfriend's kid, though it looks just like him. Four generations pile up between the street and the back bedroom where we're told the mother lies in bed.

If she dies? Forty-five days later the bank will kick out the adult children. The children of the children will be out, all the way down to the littlest, and the generations will unspool.

It's a reverse bounty.

If the mothers can hold on forever, the bank pays forever. There's no incentive to tell anyone if the old mothers are dead. I'm watching the families, worried about the mothers, and quietly writing the screenplay for a horror movie. *Reverse Mortgage* would be a thriller about the opposite of murder. It's about keeping people alive, propping up dead bodies, the crush of time against age. The value of a broke old woman's body is in supporting all the babies born, forever.

The bank and the next generation, they're duking it out.

The bank is betting on death, but we live in a neighborhood of off-the-books transactions, babies having babies and all those secret backyard bones.

NEIGHBORHOOD NOTES: REWIND

The diabetic alcoholic across the street had lost all limbs by now. He only came out anymore for Medi-Van transport to dialysis. It took two strong men to hoist him and his wheelchair down the splintered wooden front stairs. He lived alone with his aging mother, who never came out to wave goodbye. That mother? I'd guess she was about a hundred and fourteen by now.

She was on a reverse mortgage, hidden away.

The diabetic had gone to dialysis. It was a blasting hot spring day. I was staring out the window, enjoying the calm. A Cutlass pulled up in a rush of shaking bass blasting from rattling speakers. A girl ran out of the diabetic's tiny, old house toward the street. She ran like an escapee, and moved like a track star, fast and smooth. The sun flashed against a long silver blade in her hand, making her gleam like a goddess. She clutched a butcher knife. She slammed against the Cutlass and yelled, "Get out of here or I will kill you." Every word carried the force of her full conviction.

A flood of people poured out of the house behind her. So maybe the diabetic didn't live alone with his mother? Except, who were all the rest of those people, and when had they ever gone in the house? I had never seen any of them arrive. I'd never seen them knock, or leave, or hang out on the porch. It was like they were born inside the house and never emerged until now, as far as I could tell. Some were barefoot. They were all in lounge wear, pajamas and slips. One kid, maybe ten years old, came out still holding a box of Fruit Loops, spilling as he trailed behind.

They yelled, "Don't do it!" The voice of reason came as a chorus. They yelled, "You're only wrecking your own life."

A man pushed his way ahead of the pack and caught the raging girl by her elbows. He pulled her backward. She stabbed the knife in the air toward the car, but she let herself be dragged. In his arms, she walked backward down the sidewalk, over the yard, up the stairs, into the house. The car peeled out backward. Everything had gone into rewind.

When the street was quiet the MediVan brought the diabetic home, back to home sweet home, to recover.

Late that night, I was still up when the doorbell rang. It was a drunk who climbed onto our porch, who rang the bell just after midnight. Our front door was open to bring in the cool night air, the security door we call a screen door there to hold the world out.

He said, "I love you! I've always loved you. I will love you forever." Those words traveled like the worst kind of threat, the wrong kind of love, a rusted razor of high hopes.

I offered back, "You have the wrong house." Wrong person, wrong time, wrong season, wrong promise.

He said, "I love you! Only you!"

It was too late to close the door without moving close to this man, where his fingers were laced through the grating. From my dark corner, I said, "Good night."

He said, "But I love you." His voice cracked with his truth.

I didn't call for help and he didn't make any threats except eternal love, a non-threat that seemed able to sustain itself forever.

I said, "I don't know you."

He said, "Only you." I was alone and he was alone and we had nothing in common short of being human at night. The moon loomed over his shoulder, white and bald.

"You have to go," I said, Juliet to his Romeo.

Finally, he turned around. He wobbled down the stairs. He tipped to the right toward the roses, then he tipped to the left, and held the old metal railing to keep steady. "Goodbye," I whispered, just loud enough that he might hear.

He turned back to me then. He said, "I never loved you. Not at all. I never did." He took his cloud of sweat and love and left me only the moon, alone.

S.T.D. DEMON

I'm no fan of summer—that big ball of fire hanging over all our heads, edging a little closer? It brings the slowest of deaths, skin cancer, drought, famine, dehydration. Plus, wrinkles!—but I was sweating my way home late-afternoon and saw a guy downtown whose body advertised summer sports in a way that even I could imagine paradise as involving an unfiltered sun. He was a natural sunshine model. Decades of catalogue-perfect camping-swimming-fishing-canoeing trips glowed in the tone of the way this man's muscles slid beneath his skin. He hoisted a mountain bike onto the top of a beachcomber's van. A downy pinfeather fell from where it'd gathered on his clothes, and then a bit of cedar's greens, like he'd been sleeping in the woods. Sun rippled over his surf-fried curls. Golden. Timeless. Precious.

A bit of nature in the city reminded me of the place I'd grown up, covered in trees. Where did this guy come from?

I stopped in my tracks, stayed in the deep shade and cool air trapped under the freeway's overpass. I lurked, a pale troll beneath the bridge. Homeless people slept in that spot at night. There was a twisted blue sleeping bag in the bushes. The air was ripe with piss, true. Still that heavy shade overhead was a gift. Sun cut a hot, bright line across the pavement, daring me to cross if I wanted to get home. Ugh. Sunshine! Such a fake friend. Can't live under it, can't grow pot without it, unless you've got a good grow light system, as the late-night infomercials always said.

Oregon is a rainforest. It used to pour down nine months out of the year. Now Death Valley had moved in, carting along a crushing heatwave. While I paused in that dark, dank corner of the city, a dog ran through the brush of public shrubs. This beautiful, dirty thing, fur flying, danced around me with an open mouth. Its pink tongue trailed like a parade banner. "Hello, Gorgeous," I murmured. "Come here often?"

The dog seemed happy, or scared or maybe rabid. Who am I to judge? I'm no veterinarian. It was alone, and so was I. "Come here, sweets!" I called, hoping it might follow me home. I clapped down low, careful not to chase it into traffic. We were surrounded by high-traffic streets there near a freeway entrance just beyond the overpass's shade. "Little lost soul," I crooned, making my voice go gentle. "You're so sexy, baby."

It was sexy, with its muscles and energy. I'm a terrible flirt—by that, I mean, I'm bad at it, not that I do it compulsively. The opposite: I don't even know how. But I was doing my best to flirt with that dog, practicing social skills. All those Social Studies classes back in school? They should teach a kid how to flirt. That'd be the ultimate *Social* Studies, a game changer for some of us.

Beneath the overpass, the freeway rushing overhead roared like a crazy river, like the sound of the Sandy or the Washougal, so rocky, clear and cold, and I could forget just how dry and strangled Oregon had become. I had a slice of Bundt cake crumbling in my backpack, and swung my pack off my shoulders, thinking to lure the animal. It came over so willingly, I didn't have to. I ran my fingers through its matted coat, saw my hands in the sea of its pelt, found comfort in pressing my face to the shorter fur of its ears. Why is the fur on a dog's ears always so silky and inviting? What evolutionary success is that? The dog left rusty red dirt smudged on my white cotton shirt.

I was just off work as the day-shift cake cutter at House of Cake, downtown. I'm fast with a hot knife and a cool plate. This was the new Portland—a constant, throbbing sweet tooth. There were endless lines for ice cream, cake, beer and breakfast. Everybody was carbo-loading for the marathons. In the old Portland, the rainy, broke, working class city, where I migrated as soon as I left the Arboretum? The masses had been more into heroin than doughnuts.

I had a break, a day-and-a-half between workdays, almost a whole weekend mid-week. I'd work at home. Not cake cutting, but writing a book, my magnum opus! *Moby Vagina.*

That dog needed a bath and a meal. It licked my face. I let it, despite its breath. Yes, I wanted love to come by chance—fated and romantic—even if it was only in the form of a dog.

Out in the sun, the man jerked his bike forward then back, fitting it into place. His surfer's hair shimmered and skimmed the neck of his old t-shirt. His body held a space between the discipline of a working man and the luxury of indulgences, hard and soft, physical and relaxed. The van was primer-grey. The man's shirt was thin, marked with holes. His jeans hung rugged and weathered, like he'd been somewhere out on the road, dusty and traveling. I thought, *Oh, you pretty, briny mass of cloth-draped flesh! You sunbaked stoner, you late night pizza!* I have no flirting skills but I have enthusiasm.

Eight hours of cutting cake leaves me buzzed. Sugar seems to seep into my blood. It's in the air and leaves me high and shaky. The whole time I'm cutting giant layers of merengue, fresh fruit, mascarpone and flourless chocolate rounds ready to melt I keep a dizzingly tight focus. My world shrinks down to the counter, knives and cake. No matter what music's on, I hear Miles Davis's

"Bitches Brew" wailing in my head, alongside the endless string of orders. I turn left and right on my little black mat, behind the gleaming cake counter, dropping whipped cream and berries in a particular kind of sweet hell.

I took out my phone, snapped a photo of the dog to send to Jenna, who rented the tiny place next to my own tiny house. Hers was a garden shed turned into a shack. Mine was an ancient barn with an IKEA kitchen wedged inside. We lived in Accessory Dwelling Units. The big house had been sold off, replaced with a triplex of skinny houses on the other side of a fence, so now we were accessories to nothing. It was like being accessories to a crime, only the crime was all around us in overcrowding, corporate landlords, stock market investments in market rents, all strangling renters! For real. I was in the slow grip. Big houses spawned small houses out of converted outbuildings. Rental units were cut in half, then quartered. It was Zeno's paradox in action, slicing the smallest halves into halves again, for the have-nots, which was us. These new clusters of micro homes were hipster Hoovervilles. But we could house a dog. I wrote, "Should I bring him home?"

The dog was a blur in the photo. "Nothing to risk but fleas," I typed, wanting Jenna to welcome the dog to our shared yard, maybe even co-pet-parent. My phone rang right then—Jenna, calling to say yes? But no, it was a guy I knew, a one-nighter, and I'd already cut ties. This man and me, we'd said goodbye, scorched that ground. What did he want? Mostly he was into money, making lots of it, which was fine for him but dull! I took another photo without answering the call.

The man at the van moved like mercury. He blinked in the four o'clock sun, in a gleaming halo. His hair was in conversation with the sun! It was there in the way light bounced back, like birds calling to each other, voices echoing, and he was his own bright burning star. When he turned, I saw his ripped T-shirt read "Satan's Pilgrims."

If he was any kind of Pilgrim, it wasn't one of the Puritans that stepped off the Mayflower, but more a man on a pilgrimage, a traveler seeking who knows what with only the clothes on his back.

Beardless.

Yeeee-ow! Portland was choking in beards like an old hippy's bathtub drain. Women like Jenna spent their paychecks to wax every last hair off their cooch just so they could date a guy sporting a crazy beard like he'd never had a job in his life, acting out some entitlement parade. Why was it that the whole stripper look had come into style at the exact same time as a resurgence of beards? Why was hair so gender binary? Except, when those guys did work, because the guys we knew really mostly did, in kitchens and brew pubs, they had to tie on industrial nets like facial Kotex, so there wasn't much entitlement to it.

But this guy? It was fine to see the lines of a man's jaw again.

I snapped a surreptitious photo and sent that to Jenna too with the same question: "Bring him home?" As I took the picture, the guy peered into the shadows, where I was pale and curled into the shade. He flashed a smile and a low peace sign. Beautiful!

"Intestinal parasites," Jenna shot back, with a frownie-face emoji.

Parasites? I wrote, "He's the picture of health!" I text in complete sentences. I like to think that's grad school, but maybe it's age? I'm almost ten years older than Jenna.

"D K9," she texted. "But MayB him 2?"

Her life was a tribute to optimal gut health. Your gut controls your mind, she always said. And from the workings of her mind? Her gut was insane. Her gut was an all night party of weird food. Her tiny house was a lab in pursuit of micro-organisms, through home-brewed kombucha. She was big on fermentation, making kimchee and yogurt cultures. Plastic garbage cans ringed the shed where she lived, full of deep brown fermenting broth. Soy floated in them like bloated sponges.

Jenna spent her free-time working on a project she called *The Game of Lice.* She hoped to patent a board game based on parasites. From what I'd seen, the game went like this: *Contract lice, move back three squares!* Then there was: *Allergic to RID. Should've used neem oil! Pay $1,000 to the bank.*

The van was parked haphazardly, hindquarters out in the street. With a hand on the stray collie, I called over, "They'll ticket you if you leave it like that." I was doing him a favor. It was probably this man's dog beneath my palm. Maybe he had a family, kids. One child, or two? Or seven or seventeen. A pack. He looked like a spawner. They'd be in the back of that van, golden and beaming. A white plastic skull, like a mask, was wired onto the front bumper, wires drawn through the skull's eye sockets. That, I thought, was a pirate touch meant to charm the children.

I was a pale ghoul, calling from the shadows, holding his own dog back in my dark piss-scented lair! I knew what I looked like.

Mr. Sunshine, Satan's Pilgrim, captain of his pirate van, walked closer to hear over the rush of freeway above. His skin was more weathered than I thought from a distance. His hair had been let go, singing its song of beach sand and saltwater. Maybe he walked closer to get his dog. No children climbed like intestinal parasites out of the guts of the van, though. It was just him and me. I reached for the dog's neck to check for tags. The collie gave a yipe, crouched and took off. It ran right for home, made a bee-line to the beach bum! If you love something, let it go. I always follow the advice of brainwashy old basement posters from the county health clinic.

Satan's Pilgrim stretched, raising his arms, and flashed a slice of abs. He shimmered in sun so bright I could barely see. I had to shield my eyes. The way that man stretched, it was like we'd woken up together right there on the sidewalk. He was on the sunny side of our sidewalk bed. I gave him a salute. "Nice dog!" I called, by way of goodbye and goodwill.

That Pilgrim's voice floated toward me through that brilliant light. "Thought he was with you."

The dog zigzagged and veered, heading for traffic. It wasn't his? I yelled, "Catch it!"

It ran, then turned back—looking out for me! Lassie, my Lassie, telling me to go, follow, get out of there? It leapt into traffic, cars passing in a sea of honking horns. It was across, gone for real this time.

"I don't think he trusts you," Satan's Pilgrim drawled. "He took his chances."

Me? The dog didn't run from me. I said, "It came when I called."

One of us was sketch, in that animal's mind. He walked in fits and starts, ambling closer until he found his way to where I lingered near the giant concrete legs of the overpass and the locked gates of an under-the-freeway U-Store-It. He brought his golden boy heat into the shade. The closer her got, the more unnerving his presence became. His eyes were an unstable watery green. His nose had been broken and healed on it its own, maybe more than once. A truck put on its brakes on the freeway above, screaming. Maybe I should I have been screaming?

But I was single, and this guy was hot. Both were true: unnerving and hot. He said, "Go after it?" Even as he said it, he stood in my way.

"You have to trust an animal's instincts," I near-whispered, and wished for the best. That dog was gone.

Satan's Pilgrim's voice lost pieces of words under the sound of traffic, like a fuzzy old cassette recording. He said, "...just got to town, trying to find a place."

He had a haunted look in his unstable eyes.

"To live?" I asked, and he nodded.

So he was a transplant, a new arrival to our crowded city, where we'd all been reduced to living in boxes, sheds, RV's and storage units. Somebody could be living in that storage facility, in the dark, right behind me. We could knock on a door, see if anyone answered. But if he was new to town, he was alone. I could be his tour guide, his first date. A woman he found under the overpass could be good enough to hang out with for awhile.

He opened his mouth, about to say something deep, possibly painful, from the way he hesitated. I gave in to that pause, curious. His Adam's apple moved as he swallowed his own voice, holding back. He said, "I, uh—" He was either sensitive or psychologically fragile. Sometimes it's hard to know where the line is between the sensitive man and the destroyed, all that potential broken and raw. He said, "I need to park the van somewhere for the night. Sleep in the back."

That wasn't deep or emotional, only needy.

He needed a driveway. We had one, Jenna and me. I couldn't offer it without talking to her first. I wouldn't offer it anyway.

Moby Vagina called me home to get to work, build the life I wanted. My plan was to write all night, alone and cranking out the pages. The book would be so good! It was a re-appropriation questioning the quest, adventure and gender in lit.

Like most of Portland, I was food-service-with-a-Master's-degree. I'd gone back to school after traveling, and after working forever. I finished my undergrad. Then I earned a one-year M.A. in Critical Theory. I was qualified to hold a mirror to the world, not just a knife to the sweets! In terms of writing the book, so far I was wrestling with fundamental questions about form: should *Moby Vagina* be a small, tight delivery, or big, powerful and piercing?

This essential detail was a question of how self-referential reappropriation women's literature might position itself to speak back to the so-called canon. Boom! Bottom line: size mattered. Small, tight books are often women's terrain. I could either fight that vaginal value system paradigm or shine a spotlight right on it.

The rattle of a shopping cart's wheels against ragged asphalt broke against the song of the freeway overhead. A tall, skinny man wrapped in layers, in the heat, with a hood pulled low, came toward us, like a walking free-box of clothes.

Satan's Pilgrim patted his pockets. "You have a dollar, maybe five?"

Like I'd hand over money. Portland was richest in need.

The pockets of my black cotton server's pants were lined with a long, sweaty shift of cake cutting tips. I shook my head, took two steps, a shuffle, on my way toward that hard line drawn by the sun, but then hung back, still damp with my own sweat, not eager to head into the white hot heat.

"I have large denominations," he said. "Traveling funds."

Sure. Big old large denominations...easy talk, in *ten-dollar words,* as Hemingway called the long ones. I had the smallest of denominations.

That fallen angel pulled money from his pocket and peeled a bill off the top. He held that money and waited like it was the ice cream truck on the horizon. Because the rattling shopping cart was slow and jostling, towering with bags on top of bags, finally he lunged forward to meet it. He thrust out a fistful of cash like a street-level philanthropist. His mouth moved but I couldn't hear over the river of traffic overhead. He could be an evangelical preacher, running religious outreach, or a hard-up junky new to town and trying to score. Who would buy drugs from that scrambled brain pushing the cart?

Maybe he was that desperate. I was ready to leave any minute now, sidle past this interaction. He handed over all the money he had in his hands.

The dark hood slid back, showing a badly shaved head, a thin neck, a kid so young, a boy really, poor chump. Then I saw the profile, a small nose, the curve of a woman's lips, blistered and cracked. It was a woman dressed like a boy, a skate punk costume, and not all that young, closer to my own age, in too many sagging layers. She took the bills with jaundiced fingers and tucked the money down her front, into whatever flat bra-turned-money belt wrapped around her emaciated ribs.

Her sallow and bony, chapped fingers reappeared from her clothes, not empty, but full. She'd pulled money out of her bra. Her flat chest seemed even less substantial. Giving the money back, she pressed even more bills into my Pilgrim's hands, forced it on him, wouldn't take it. She was brittle and thin, determined and insane. That fragile, crazy vibe worked in her favor. I saw him try to give the money back. I'm sure he was afraid he'd break her fingers if he forced in into her hands.

She took up with her cart like a woman shopping in a nightmare grocery store. Her head swiveled and bobbed as she scanned high and low on complicated, invisible shelves, like she was looking for the right ingredients to make a life worth living. She started back on her wobbling path. Her voice rang like a chicken's song, mid-range, wordless and garbled.

Satan's Pilgrim, street preacher, sunshine man, trying to be generous and snubbed by a rambling psychotic? His money was no good here, apparently. Oof. My heart gave a twinge on his behalf.

My Pilgrim opened the door to his van, dropped the fistful of bills on the front seat and started organizing clutter. The knobs of his spine showed through this thin t-shirt. His back was long and strong, with broad shoulders. He shook his head, talking to himself. I said, "You can't help a crazy person."

The bills blew about on the seat of the van. He stopped sorting trash and turned like he'd just realized I was still there. He said. "I should've saved her life."

Kind, or delusional?

I said, "The chick's crazy. Maybe wash your hands."

"She was my wife." He paused to fold a paper map, a thing worn on the fold lines until it was falling apart, and he handled it more carefully than he'd handled the cash. He said, "She still is, as far as I'm concerned. She was a genius when I met her," talking low, like he was talking to himself or to history now. His eyes welled up, ready to cry.

Ex-wife?

So it was his wife who haunted him. Words to his wife caught in his throat. She was the reason he'd pulled over, parked there, fast and badly. I'd spoken carelessly, without being kind.

He said, "She's been off the grid. I didn't know she lived here. Just saw her coming, down the road." He looked baffled. His car smelled like apples and black licorice.

He was shaking with emotion, or need. I wanted to put an arm around his shoulders. The papers he held trembled. He saw it too. It was grief, or love. Words found their way through me, riding along on my breath, past the gates of my teeth, over my tongue, uncontrollable: "I have a driveway."

He said, "I need to eat."

The moment felt urgent.

I loped into the sun, moving down the block. "Over here," I said, and slapped my thigh like I was calling a stray dog, really. He slammed the van door and followed. "I'll buy you tacos," I said.

This was taco triage. My goal? To diagnose. I'd pony up six dollars of generosity, buy time and learn what broken, beautiful man I'd invited home to use our driveway.

I told him my name—Vanessa—and he told me his, but to my mind stayed Satan's Pilgrim, close enough.

I lead him to a skinny, narrow place where half the people ate standing up, dropping chopped lettuce and beans over the heads of anyone lucky enough get a table. I always scored a table. I was grandfathered in by the fates, old school Portland-style, from before we even had lines to wait in.

We joined the line and scanned the menu over the counter. The place was air conditioned, and I took that cool air. It smelled heavy with the metallic bite of fresh chopped cilantro. "Tell me what you want, I'll get it." I gestured for Satan's Pilgrim to hold down the single table that'd opened up.

A Happy Customer is a Return Customer, it said on a sign in the back, alongside the stainless steel counters.

Returning, I thought, mentally revising the sentence.

The guy behind the counter was short and broad, built like a bull, with long, pretty eyelashes. He also shaved, so there was that. He and I, once we'd met up down in the madhouse of Portland's Rose Festival along the waterfront where he ran a temporary food cart and I'd been cutting through on my bike. Surrounded by sailors and drunks from the sticks who'd come into town for the festival, we'd bonded over a bottle of tequila and contempt for outsiders, like good locals. We'd snuck behind the floats where they were stored before the parade and swapped spit, meaningless high times.

He wouldn't take my money. I pushed a few bucks across the counter and sang a quiet, private, chirpy little, "Not your taco whore, sweets."

We were friends and basically neighbors, less than a mile apart. As a business man in Portland, owner of the taco shack, he could afford to live in a fine, two-story, swank, tiny converted free-standing garage.

He kept up the dance of his job behind the busy counter even as he smiled and pushed the dollars back—implying that I was his taco whore? I was not. I slid them over again. He hit a button on the register that meant *We're done here,* and moved on to the line behind us. "See you around," he said. He hoisted a dozen or more hot sauce bottles between his outstretched fingers. The muscles in his arms flexed and shifted, meant for more substantial work.

I collected my cash. "Fine," I said. I'd float along in this current of emotional currency that held the city together. It was the current the long-time Oregonians shared, and only the luckiest newcomers would join. Another employee slid over our order, two orange trays of tacos and a bowl of chips.

My Pilgrim, at the table, had missed the quiet drama. I sat with him, and took in the way he moved, his lank, golden hair, every blink. I studied how he unscrewed the cap on the Tapatio: steady.

What was I looking for? The shake of addiction, nonsense obsessions, or even ordinary narcissism running too rich. He splashed Tapatio on the tacos and sipped a paper cup of water. His fingernails were clean and short. His hands showed the pale line of a ring recently removed, like a farmer's tan around that fallen marriage—a divorce tan.

He said he'd grown up down South, in a place where the water tables shifted. Sometimes down by the swamps, in the old graveyards, the earth cracked open, muddy and shaken. He'd seen coffins rise up to the surface. His first job, he said, as a kid, was to stand on those coffins and help the old folks get them buried again.

A woman rattled open the front door of the taqueria. She reached long fingers to find a paper cup and scanned the menu. She was taller than everyone around her, dark-eyed and gorgeous in a way that made me wish that I was her. To be so tall!

Satan's Pilgrim said, "Mud used to get heavy on my boots, when I'd work the coffin back down—"

My phone rang. It was that same guy, ancient history, the man who was heavily into making money, lazy in the sack but probably as decent as they get.

The tall beauty paid for her meal, and that man, behind the counter? My friend from Rose Festival, my parade and tequila date, he slid those dollars back. She pushed them over. They were having their own quiet drama! I thought, her? Wow. He'd scored.

So she and I, we were both his taco whores, drifting in the same current of emotional currency.

I lifted the carton of Bundt cake from my pack, and put it on the table, a beautiful dark cake with a sweet glaze and fresh strawberries on top that stained the recycled cardboard carton red.

The man behind the counter, my one-time date, called over, "We have a policy! No outside food." But I knew how he loved his meals. It was spite, the way he tried to control his territory.

"It's one piece of cake—" I started to say.

The tall beauty looked over, and her face darkened. She yelled, "You!" She threw the word at us like a weapon, a throwing star or a curse. I scanned to see if she had a gun, for real.

Pilgrim only flashed his pretty, white-toothed surfer's smile. "He-ey," he said, in a slow, calm drawl. The woman bore down on us, primed for murder. He pulled out a chair, inviting her to sit.

Jesus.

She was over six feet tall, twitching with fury. I didn't want to be her anymore. She wasn't lovely. I used one foot to push the chair back where it'd come from, and it fell over, hit the floor with a sound like a gunshot. She snarled. I lifted a grilled chicken taco, leaning over my plate, to get on with this meal and pretend all was well. I was cool, we'd be fine. She didn't let me fake it though. Instead, she leaned down until her glossy hair skimmed my tacos. Her perfume was jasmine and Dragon's Blood, from the oils shop. She hissed, "Watch yourself, missy. Bastard doesn't know shit about how to love." I wiped sour cream from the corner of my mouth.

It was through a mouth full of food when I spit out the word, "Love?"

He said, "We can get along—"

She slammed down her paper cup in the middle of our cake, then crushed it under her palm. People were staring. Somebody dropped a few pinto beans and chopped tomato on my head as they moved too fast to get away from us.

My Pilgrim's voice cracked. He said, "What are you doing, honey?"

"Destroying any illusions," she said, and ground that cup into the chocolate and sugar of our sweetness. "God damn mother fucker bastard—".

"Keep it down, keep it clean! This is a family restaurant," the taco guy hollered. It was too bright in that place for this bar fight brewing. The woman snorted and stormed out, a wraith rocking her own fury.

My Pilgrim picked up a crumb of flattened cake, and ate it. "She's very fragile," he offered.

"She didn't seem fragile," I said.

He said, "People are deceptive. But I know her, my ex-wife. Ten years."

Was that ten years together, or ten years apart? Either way, I wasn't buying it. I said, "How is that even possible? You can't use the same line twice." He was a liar. This was a racket. It wasn't the same woman, dressed in normal clothes now. With hair. Without blisters or scabs.

"A different ex-wife," he said. "With anger issues."

"That part? The anger issues? I see it," I said.

The thoughtful, patient way he delivered his words was soothing as a meditation tape, like voices that sometimes poured from Jenna's shed. If anyone could bottle the chemistry of kindness, it'd be an aphrodisiac. It was all I wanted in a man: patience. He and that woman definitely had history. From what I'd caught, this ex-wife appeared to be my one-time-drunken date's other date, that co-taco whore, in a small, swirling eddy of a crowded town.

Those two wives were like coffins coming back to the surface of the earth. They'd been buried! He was divorced. Love and burnt love was the tide that tugged them to the surface.

He picked up a taco again, took a bite.

I pushed the flattened Bundt cake aside in favor of our shared bowl of chips. "How many ex-wives do you have?"

He choked when I asked, dipped his head to swallow, and held up one hand, laying his thumb along his palm, wiggling fingers in the air. Four. He had four ex-wives.

Who gets married four times? A romantic, that's who. Four times he'd turned himself over for love. I'd been to a zillion weddings—I made extra money under the table by slicing wedding cake, professionally—but I'd never been married. Always a cake cutter, never a sucker! Weddings had taken on a sameness, in their details.

He said, "They're all suffering."

That seemed to be a common thread post-wedding in a lot of couples, from what I'd witnessed.

He said, "I have a weakness for unstable women."

"I'm not unstable." As soon as I said the words, I was tripped up by my own bare assumption: He hadn't taken an interest in me. Not necessarily, not yet. "How old are you?"

"Thirty-eight," he said.

Thirty-eight. That golden age of men, when a guy can date twenty-year-olds and still feel okay about it, when they can date fifty year olds and it's not too weird. The high tide of men and sex and love and lust and bones and backs and pilgrimages for God and Satan and maybe himself.

Women lined up to marry this man. Four wives so far? That constitutes a line. I knew what people did all over this city when they found a line: join in. The best brunch spots had long lines. The doughnuts are better the longer the line, the theory goes. House of Cake was all lines, all the time. Right then, I envisioned myself down on one knee in that taco shack, saying make me your fifth, fill out that hand, count your mistakes and me among them.

I said, "Me too." I was thirty-eight. My age? It's different, for a woman. I was supposed to be worried about making babies.

I slid fallen tomatoes around on the restaurant's orange tray and said, "If you're ready, I'm ready."

We took our time walking back to the van, letting the sun drop lower and the day cool off. I don't usually ride with strangers. I checked the locks to make sure I could open them, that they weren't rigged. A skull mask lashed to the front bumper of a primered van seemed more light-hearted when I thought kids were onboard, it's true. Yes, I stayed close to the van door. But he drove slowly. I could step out at any stop sign.

I showed him the driveway. When he pulled in, his van's lights ran over my slouched barn-home. Our giant Atlas cedar waved in the night wind, in its own rustling welcome.

"What's that?" He pointed across the narrow strip of weed-filled grass. Moonlight hit a stain near the broken doorbell, in a shape like a happy cartoon splash, with a long, long drip against the old wood outside of my barn-house. It's easier to see that stain than it is to find the actual numbers of the address, so I use the stain for identification purposes—"Look for the house with the big stain right beside the doorbell."

"Somebody splooged on the siding," I said, and waved it off. We climbed out together.

He was taller than me, and had a way of slouching as though to be closer, when we stood in the dark of the yard. "Splooged?"

I clarified, "Ejaculated. Let loose." I made a gesture. My performance probably wasn't necessary but it was a good pantomime and I liked offering it. "It's a gentrification thing. A protest." Generally I ignored that spoolge the way I ignored ants on my counters or spiders in the corners. My barn was covered in ancient aluminum siding. The siding was covered in paint, and the alkaline sperm as it dried against the paint had eaten through to the silvery shine of old aluminum.

Every neighborhood in Portland I'd lived in had gone from affordable to cost prohibitive. When it did, somebody always splooged on my door.

He ran a hand through his moonlight blonde hair. He tried to nod along then shook his head instead. "I don't think that's about gentrification."

Inside, on my wall near the door was a stain that always seeped through the pale paint. In backwards letters written in blood it said *Heathens.* It was the blood stain of the renter before me, the couple who gave me their place. They were moving out. I spent a few days with them, one of the rough patches with Ray Madrigal, late in the game. Then it turned out I needed to get a place of my own. I'd been in the barn ever since.

Now this Pilgrim came in to use my shower. The space was small, and the shower filled the barn with steam and the scent of mint soap. Out the window I saw the orange tongues of a small fire flickering in the backyard. The pages of my work-in-progress were spread over my one all-purpose side table, and I flipped them over because I'm private like that. Goodnight, *Moby Vagina!* Yes, I felt guilty, shirking my grand literary work!

I slid out of my frosting-marked cake cutter's uniform, into a dress, or maybe it was slip or an old-fashioned nightie. It was something silky. I'd found it at a curb, and didn't concern myself with categories.

Jenna was out back in our shared yard, in the dark with a fire going in an open pit. She held a piece of white soap carved to look about like a potato bug. When she saw me come out to join her, she reached down into the shadows and raised up a Mason jar of clear booze. "Made it myself. How cool is that?" The lid rattled as she unscrewed it. Jenna was younger than me in the day but the fire under her chin brought out every wrinkle and line, a crone in that firelight.

"What's that?" I asked, about the soap.

She polished it with her fingers, smooth as a Netsuke. "I'm designing game pieces for *The Game of Lice,*" she said. "It's a fluke. One possibility. A fluke can live on your liver for twenty-five years."

I could watch the massive Atlas cedar shake all the way to the sky, over the top of the house. It was magnificent. It held up my little world, or at least my spirits.

I tipped her Mason jar to my lips. The strong booze bit back, all the way down my throat. It found my heart and burned. The best hard stuff is always punishing. The moon rested full and pale overhead, shining down on the moonshine jar. The sun had set late that evening. The moon had been out since four, sun and moon both in the sky at once, like our side of the planet was hoarding. We sat by the hot fire in the slowing cooling dark, and passed her booze. She was burning old papers and bills, and had a bag of them at her feet. She dropped another page on the flames, sending orange spark-moths into the blue-black sky.

"I brought him home," I said.

She looked to my house. "The dog?"

I said, "The guy. He's going to stay in his van out in front."

When she lifted an eyebrow, the light of the fire moved in orange light and deep shadows.

I said, "It's love."

She laughed, took a swig off her jug and spit booze across the flame just to see it hiss, crackle and burn mid-air. She said, "For ten minutes, maybe."

An unsettling jostling sound came from the bushes. Our yard was lined with Jenna's plastic garbage cans of fermenting foods. One gave a slosh. A cat leapt onto the lid, letting the lid buckle, then it jumped down and ran off.

I said, "When we reached to put our trays on the stack, at this taco shack, our hands touched. It was electrifying."

She said, "Of course. We're all conductive. Remember the hotdog?"

I did remember. "That's not romantic," I said. What could kill romance faster than a hotdog?

Jenna and I, a few weeks back, had worked together as temps in a trade show at the Coliseum. Our job involved a few hours of handing out leaflets for a metal fabricating biz. Another company called SawStop was showing off their product. They were promoting a table saw with a safety feature: it wouldn't cut off a finger. The inventor was Stephen Gass, a Portland local—because everybody in Portland needs a creative outlet. While I was working on *Moby Vagina* and Jenna was carving parasites out of soap to design *The Game of Lice,* Mr. Gass was working out his creative urges by saving people's limbs. His last name was perfect for a mad scientist: Not solid, or liquid, but gas, with an extra "s", reminding us we're all molecules in transition, taking on new forms. The demo used a hotdog instead of a finger, running it in the way of the spinning blade, because I guess maybe they weren't taking chances? The saw ran a steady electrical current. When the blade hit the hotdog the current was absorbed. A sensor sensed the shift in conductivity, and the saw's mechanism shut down in the smallest fraction of a second. The message? A human finger is exactly as conductive as a hotdog.

We're all hotdogs walking this earth in our human casings.

But I was one walking hotdog in love with another. That was still phenomenal. I said, "It's chemical."

"I've heard this before," my daytime beauty, nighttime crone said, speaking truth, yes, and made her little soap fluke walk on my face. I pushed it away. A blackberry tendril from our overgrown yard found its way into her hair. She put the fluke down, and delicately untangled the vine, moving carefully around it's thorns. A berry dangled ripe on the vine.

I leaned in to help fold the spiked vine back out of the way, and said, "I'm a tactile learner." She'd seen my short-lived loves, one night, one hour. I had to get my hands all over a person to know exactly how much I wanted them to keep on walking. Goodbye! That was my history. This guy? Entirely different. I pulled the berry from the vine and ate it. It was rich and ripe. Blackberries are the best use of sun. They hold the taste of a summer inside their juice. To eat one at night is a cool, nourishing late night sunshine.

I told her about the wives, how we'd seen two and he had four. I told her about his watery green eyes, and his van. I said, "He's heart-broken. You can practically see it, in the molecules of air around him. His world is beautiful and crushed." I'd met a romantic!

"What happened to the dog?" she said.

"It ran."

"It's a shame." She said, "Dogs are so much easier to love than men. They're all limbic resonance, no mind games, no ego."

"This guy's different." I felt good just being alive, near this Pilgrim. His gentle, stoic brokenness was the thing that made me want to bring him home. My heart grew bigger when he said quiet words. His skin was welcoming, energetically compatible. I said, "I'd be a better person with him around."

"Want to be better? Do volunteer work." She slung one leg over the other and folded into herself, slouching over her Mason jar. The moonshine shook and glimmered like a jewel, or maybe it was the booze in my brain making the world pretty and precious. She said, "Two crazy ex's, showed?"

I nodded, all sympathy for his struggles. I wanted to help him find happiness! I could take care of him. "It's soooo sad."

"That's a man with a demon," she said, clear as crystal.

And I laughed. "He's the nicest guy ever. I'll bring him out here—"

"Don't." She said, and took a swig off the jug, then passed it.

"—You'll see. He's fine." He treated those ex's with respect.

In that light her face transformed so entirely that it was almost as though I were speaking to somebody else—a grandmother, a hag, a person from the homeless camp down under the overpass—but she was a beauty, and when she moved into the moonlight, her day-self surfaced again. I swigged her booze. It was like drinking barium, or radium—like if a person had the right camera, you could see that poison cure for daily life draw its way through our veins.

I said, "You'll meet him. He's gentle."

"No," she cut me off. "I don't want to meet him. He has an entity. That's my diagnosis." Done.

"I'm going be wife five—" I murmured.

She coughed on her booze. "Stop saying that! Don't get near him."

A light came on in my tiny barn-house, visible through the gap in the bushes that half-covered the window. Then there he was, a dark silhouette behind sheer curtains. He towel-dried his hair, arms raised, head bent, a lone man-boy-animal.

Jenna and I huddled, and watched. He moved as gracefully as smoke. It was hard to see details. He turned. I admit I was looking: boner? It was either a boner, or the arm of a chair, no way to tell. It was a phenomenal shadow puppet show until he wrapped the towel around his waist. Who was this man to walk naked in my house? It was like I'd lured and trapped a feral animal. "Are you worried?" I asked.

She whispered, "There are entities you can only pass through sexual contact. So no, I'm not worried. Not about me, anyway." Her breath touched my cheek.

Her point was clear: me.

Entity? I whispered back, "You're demonizing sexuality."

"Not all of it," she whispered. "Only with a man with four mentally ill ex-wives. They weren't strong enough containers for his energy."

"You're calling women containers? That's entirely not feminist." It was the opposite of feminist. Then a thought came to mind, containers and energy. "He did say he'd worked burying coffins. Old coffins, that'd resurfaced near his house. As a kid."

Her hair whipped me across the face, she turned around that quickly. "Dead bodies?"

"Yes," I said, and felt a tickle, like a spider crawling along my spine, under the silk of my used slip-dress. I tried to shake it off. The log I perched on rocked, unsteady against the earth. Neighbors in the triplex on the other side of the fence turned out their lights, and the velvet night pressed in around us. Claws scrabbled down a nearby roof, and a fat raccoon dropped then ran along the edge of the fence line, eyes yellow and glowing.

She said, "Why would he tell you that?"

"It came up, in conversation." We'd been talking about work, and the taco stand.

His shadow was shape-shifting against the lights on over in my space, murky, strong and strange.

She said, "Entities reveal themselves. They laugh at humans who don't take the hint. His demon was telling you the truth, right then."

"He makes my heart bigger," I said, in protest. It was a good feeling to not hate all humanity all the time, to not mock every Portland transplant who wandered in and crowded our city. The more people to love, the better my heart rested. I'd welcome him to town.

"Your heart feels larger because an entity is invading. It's testing you," she said.

Her words turned my heart into a bed in a bed store, like a new mattress, everybody climbing on, testing it and leaving again.

The lights went off in my tiny barn house. The screen door out front rattled, creaked open and bounced shut. He was going to his van. Maybe he'd write in a diary. I liked to imagine as much. *Dear diary, tonight I met the woman of my dreams*...Goodnight, Satan's Pilgrim!

Soon he'd be sleeping, naked, sweaty and vulnerable, stretched out in that van, all golden hair, muscles and good energy, that cock that was maybe an erection, or maybe an illusion or—

"If you're thinking about being body fluid bonded, you need to remove that entity first," Jenna said.

That was how she talked about sex—you were either body fluid bonded, or all precautions taken, latex gloves on.

"He's just a guy I let stay out front." I took a swig off the jar, erasing the taste of my own uncertain words.

Jenna said, "The demon will call you out. Next thing, you'll want babies." She swatted invisible gnats in the air. "It's the demon's colonizing urge to expanding human territory. Every new human carrier is a wing on the demon manse. Have your babies, ladies!" she scoffed and flung a hand to the world.

"You think there's a heterosexual demon-spawned recruiting agenda?" I shifted my bones, where I sat, on that upturned stump.

So we weren't just childless by choice. We were demon free! Rock on.

The motive of all pathogens is to reproduce. Same thing with humans, we just have baby showers.

She said, "Entities live near the tailbone." She put a hand on my back, then walked her fingers along my vertebra, following the path of that creeping tickle, the invisible spider.

Her words conjured up my Pilgrim's tailbone: human, vulnerable, hidden in those jeans, under skin and muscle. His body was forever built to be manly, to carry the weight of outdoors, an adventurer's life, in the wake of broken women. It hurt to be him, I could tell. I said, "I don't know if he likes me."

She said, "He followed you home."

"Desperate." I had no illusions.

She twisted a finger in the air. "The demon would be laced around his spinal chord. They hide in the pelvis."

I gripped her arm, and made a sound, like a laugh or a cry, or barking. "Stop saying pelvis." His pelvis? That was private. It was mine. Everything tucked into those jeans was mine. I laid claim.

I said, "You're only articulating another kind of metaphoric gut health, an extreme biome, laced with demon bacteria."

I saw her mouth lift into a smile, the fire accenting every shadow. Jenna whispered words full of sibilance, her tongue against her teeth, against the roof of her mouth. She said, "Make that entity release."

"Don't say release," I said. He'd be stripping down in the van, now. I knew what to do, to bring release.

"Get him to a river or a body of water. Shouldn't be hard tomorrow, in this heat."

Hard. And Body. This was a man who invaded every word. Language was heated, and silence too. I said, "Like a baptism. You sound like a back woods revivalist."

"Take one of these rocks." She tapped the rocks outside her fire pit with her bare toes. A single toe-ring glinted in the light of the flames. "Basalt. River rock. They're all containers. Water inside. They do fine outside the fire, but if you were to push one in—" When she pushed a rock with her foot, it rolled into the flames. "Move back," she said. "Way back."

We stood in the yard and watched the fire until a sudden noise, like a gunshot, rang out. Bam. The rock flew into pieces, throwing shrapnel. "Jesus." It was like being shot at. "Now the cops'll show up."

"What—you didn't do that, as a kid?" She was drunk, booze going to her head, leaking through her bloodshot eyes. "Fire explodes rocks from the water. Not all rocks, but these." Her walk was tipsy. Our yard was uneven, and the combination pointed to all kinds of instability. I reached to take the booze away. When I put it down in the bushes, she said, "That's mine, my cure."

"For what?" It was a question she never answered. Loneliness, I'd come to think. My beautiful, lonely darling.

Her words ran together. "Press your hands against his vertebrae, all the way down his back, until you find his tailbone, then keep going lower."

I pushed the jar further into the bushes, away from her reach. "Lower than his tailbone? Is this an exorcism, or an anal massage."

"Do not offer an anal massage," she said, seriously. "That'd be a mistake." The moon caught on the shiny lid and when she spotted it, she lunged enough to get her fingers around the jar. My drunken witch friend, there burning her secrets in our shared back yard on the hottest day of the year. She said, "You'll need a fertilized egg..."

I said, "You've either been talking to my mom or my gynecologist." My own viable eggs were on the wane.

"You can find one at any house with a rooster. The city outlaws roosters, so there's the rub." She wagged a finger as though it were a plot, City Council against the Wiccans, the shamans, the alt-lives of dark healers. "This city is run by demons," she said. "When you hear about those couples who die within a day of each other? That's demons. They're possessed with mated creatures deep in their bony spines. They were not faithful to each other, those pairs. They were faithfully feeding their mated creature's needs together." She nodded, and narrowed her eyes. "Their whole lives have been spent hosting parasites."

I let her tip her jar of homemade rotgut to her lips one last time, then took it as though I wanted a swig myself. While she wasn't looking, I cut back through the bushes to my shack, that jar under one wing.

"Take a rock!" she yelled, and hurled one that landed like a bird dropped out of the sky. It could've hit me, could've killed me. "For your ceremony!" she said. "Promise you'll do it. Lock your doors, and promise—"

"I promise," I offered, and picked up the rock. She'd forget any promises once she woke up with a pounding headache. She'd begged me to run to Juicy John's instead for fresh carrot-beet juice, her hangover cure. Goodnight, my scared little fallen witch. I saw her soap carving, the fluke game piece, glowing from the grass where it'd fallen.

That night, in bed the barn was sweltering. Laying awake, invisible tentacles laced around my own tailbone, fluid as an octopus, built from Jenna's words and Pilgrim's sweat. I rolled and tossed and sweated it out, holding a cool cloth, in the summer heat.

***

The next morning, hot animal breath skimmed my face before I even opened my eyes, and there she was, leaning over me as I slept. Jenna hissed, "Don't move. I'm trying to spot demodex fucking on your eyelashes."

Demodex. Tiny eyelash mites. "How did they reproduce?" I mumbled.

"They have bodily cavities," she said. "We need a microscope." She studied my skin and lashes.

I rolled away from her. "I'm not your microbial porn channel. I don't have mites anyway."

"Everybody has mites," she said. "Just more, or less. Have you heard of the Great Demodex Defenestration?"

I had not, and groaned.

"Sixty-three monks in a French Abbey threw themselves out windows. Turned out tiny mites were driving them mad! They all had the same distinct patterns of rosacea." She lay down on my bed and said, "Eighty-five percent of Americans are estimated to have pinworms. Sleep beside one of those people and the worms can wriggle out of one anus and into another. You can breathe in their eggs. You can spread parasites just by sleeping side-by-side," and she snuggled alongside me as she said it. "It's not so much a sexually transmitted disease as it is an infestation spread through basic domestic intimacy."

"Get away," I said, and wrapped the blanket around myself.

"It's interesting," she said.

I said, "It's gross."

She brought a hand toward my face. She held an egg so close that when I opened my eyes, I went cross-eyed.

"Got one," she said. Her breath smelled like stale booze. The egg was marked with dirt and bits of hay. "From a hen house!" she cackled.

"Breakfast?" I reached for it. What the hell?

"I candled it already. It's fertilized," she said. "For your ceremony."

Oh, yes. The exorcism. The baptism. "Candled?" I asked, and sat up in bed.

She said, "Candling is like the chicken version of a pregnancy test."

My bed was covered in sheets of paper, most of them blank, some with writing. I'd scrawled a list: *Moby Pussy, Moby Snatch, Moby Sinkhole.*

She lifted the page, asked, "Is this medical?"

I took it back. I was working on the title, because Vagina isn't really the parallel to Dick, now is it? *Moby Pussy* would the story of a deep sea diver in search of the largest, most insatiable sea anemone. It would be the story of defiance, duty and great friendship! "Call me Isabelle," I'd written. So easy! So clear. I needed to work.

But it was going to be another blasting hot day. If it was necessary to go to the river with Mr. Sunshine, Satan's Pilgrim himself—to rest in the sun, with our feet in the water, nearly naked, and get to know him—who was I to argue? I was called to duty.

"Took me all night to find that egg," Jenna said. She moved to my computer, sat on my orange yoga ball and started Googling demons, Googling entities. Her thighs were smooth and tan below her shorts. Her hair was a crazy nest.

I said, "I don't even know if he has normal diseases."

"For that, there are clinics." She leaned forward and gazed into the computer screen like it was her crystal ball. My phone rang.

It was the same guy, that one-night stand. Exhausting! It's always hardest on people to break up when you aren't even together.

"Entities sneak in after soul loss," Jenna said, reading from the screen. "The best way to be resilient is to always nourish your soul. That protects it." Then she spun toward me on the yoga ball, and said, "It doesn't say this here, but I know one clue, how to tell if you've been invaded. If you start thinking you need to write songs about love? That's a symptom. Demons make humans sing sappy lyrics. It's a dominance thing. Bad lyrics are like a demon joke."

She seemed reasonably sober, big-eyed and thrilled with the start of a new day blending into the night before. I asked, "How did you get into all this—were you raised in a cult?" That was my first guess.

She pointed a finger at the ceiling, asking for silence. She said, "Fourth grade, I had lice."

I wasn't impressed, not yet. "Who didn't?" It was the Portland schools way. I'd seen a brick wall in our neighborhood now where somebody had graffiti-ed one word over and over again—*licelicelice*—covering the whole wall with the visual off-gassing of a tortured mind.

Jenna tugged one long, bug-free curl. "My mom wanted to shave my head. I wouldn't let her. She held me out of school for a week until I was cleared. I missed the whole Lewis and Clark Trail unit. I stayed home alone, with maybe too much time to think about the little lives on my head. They were like my sea monkeys, little pets. I thought of them as tiny versions of my dolls—having dinner, going to lice church. Smaller than my Polly Pocket dolls."

I got out of bed and looked for a pair of pants in the bacteria-breeding piles of clothes on my small barn floor.

She said, "I got impetigo right after lice, crusty sores all over my face." She rolled on the exercise ball, her feet digging into the wooden floor, legs strong as a dancer's. "I was like eight years old.

This old doctor told me human skin is covered in invisible life. I could see the pores on his nose, the hair, and felt like I could see bugs. Lice bites broke my skin, and then I missed more school, missed learning the story of Indian slaughter as told to kids by white people."

She nodded, story over. "Tiny, tiny lives control our lives. That old doctor turned me on to the human microbiome," she said. "I was totally a disturbed kid."

I found a t-shirt under my mattress, clean enough to work for the day.

Jenna said, "Ninety percent of the cells in your body aren't even you. They're microbes. How can people feel so alone, when every body is like it's own crowded city?"

She blinked, waiting for an answer. I had no answers. I liked time to myself. "Why didn't you study microbiology?" I asked her, and buttoned my shorts. Jenna and I might not be friends in the big world, but fate brought us to the same piece of ground as neighbors in our shacks, and I'd tolerated her obsessions until I'd started to take an interest in her brand of crazy.

She said, "Lice got me exiled from fourth grade. How would I get through college?"

So she wasn't academically identified. I wasn't either, really. And I'd had my round with tiny creatures. An "intra-cellular parasite" killed my dog, when I was a kid. Tick fever. A tick had attached itself to Muffin's skin and spread a blood-borne disease. I'd wanted another dog ever since. I'd been afraid to take on even a dog. Muffin was the dog love of my life.

She started humming a song. I recognized it—*I got you under my skin...*She said, "That is a song about having heartworm, as far as I can tell."

The fertilized egg rested in the nest of my sheets. I said, "There's a leap from parasites, or even bacteria, to demons."

She printed out a page on exorcism. "It's all parallel lives, visible and invisible. All I know is, we're lonely, and we're not alone. It's a nightmare."

***

By the time I was making coffee in my tiny Mr. Coffee machine tucked on a bookshelf, Jenna had gone out to do Jenna things in the backyard. She was picking up sticks, and checking her Korean fermentation recipes. My Pilgrim was out front in the sun flanked by a wandering dog. It wasn't the stray from the day before, but another dog. Then I saw the long, dark line of a leash. A woman came into view, almost hidden behind the van. She was short and round with a permanently apologetic look etched into the lines of her forehead. She gazed up at my Pilgrim and nodded , holding together a trembling, unsustainable smile.

I carried out a cup of coffee. That Pilgrim introduced me to her by name. "She lives down the block," he said, and laughed like that was crazy! Unbelievable. "She's almost your neighbor."

When she bent to pull a burr from her dog's hair, he mouthed the words to let me know: *ex-wife*...I mouthed back, *No way!*

This short, round, anxious woman? This man and his wives all had each other on short leashes.

If this new ex was unstable it was only made manifest in the way she bit her nails and plucked individual hairs from her scalp. She clicked her teeth while she listened, and tapped her fingers against her thigh, counting under her breath.

When I went back inside, Jenna was there again, this time pouring dried garbanzo beans in my old pepper mill. She said, "I'm making you a little rattle," like that was something I wanted?

"That's a third ex-wife," I said, and pointed to her through my front window. "He's like a polygamist, the way they stick around."

Jenna gave the rattle a shake, then opened it again and poured some beans out in search of the right tone. She said, "We all stick around, until we don't, right?" Shake shake, shake shake.

With that percussion, she sounded ready to break into spoken word. Outside, the sun was slowly rising, to take its murderously hot station overhead. All over town, people put keys in the ignition, started their cars, fueled the petroleum industry, fueled rising temperatures, heading to work they despised. The woman with her dog outside tried out a laugh, but it was the saddest pantomime. Sunlight in my barn-house was alive with the dance of dust motes.

Jenna said, "I read that sperm can actually stick around long enough to alter DNA when it passes through a woman's body."

What was she telling me? "So all his wives have his DNA?"

She nodded, and rattled, and burst into her impromptu poetry slam. "It's possible. A child born to a woman can carry traits of earlier lovers. Fruit flies do it all the time, in their tiny transferrable lives. A fruit fly's brood can be shaped by what a previous mate ate *as a maggot*." Shake shake, shake shake.

I said, "Some days I think humanity is still in the larval, maggot stage."

She said, "We're never close enough to other people, and then we're never far enough away, when we want to be."

"Stuck in relational purgatory," I said. She nodded. This was how we got along, in agreement, on our tiny piece of land in our two houses, separate and together, speaking parallel languages just clearly enough to sometimes hit the same note.

She said, "Demons pull their spawn close. It's his demon keeping those ex-wives around. Every last one is possessed. Clear up his demon, and the wives will be released too."

My phone rang and I flipped it over, to cover the number. Same guy. Whose demon was keeping that man close? I gave him nothing to go on.

It wasn't hard convincing my Pilgrim to go to Dugan Falls, along the Washougal, on that blistering day. He had a van, I had a map. I brought Jenna's rattle and the fertilized egg, carried in a Tupperware container in a cotton bag.

Once we were at the river, I was supposed to bring about the conversation: *Hey, think you might be possessed?*

If I asked too directly, Jenna said the demon would dodge and make this all harder. I was negotiating with a demon, a hostage-holding beast.

I wouldn't do it. I was ready to forget about the demon question, except—

There at the water, under an endless expanse of blue sky, Pilgrim picked up a flat stone. Mid-week, late in the day, the air was filled with the buggy sounds of summer heat. I'd found a stretch of riverbank we had to ourselves. Even the murderous Death Valley imported sun overhead didn't feel so threatening, with that antidote—water—rolling by in luxurious proportions. Pilgrim brought his arm back, then skipped the stone against the current, his hair shimmering in the sun, evoking the boy he'd been and the man he was in his movements and muscles. I could hear the grass sing. Even the sun seemed to bring a sound to our world. It was the most relaxing spot on earth. Jenna's instructions were fading from my mind when my Pilgrim said, in his honeyed, mellow drawl, "I've always been possessed by the life force of water."

And I froze.

Why would he say that? Why *possessed?* Why *water?* Jenna had already called it: fluidity. She said his fluidity was a sign of his aquatic-like demon's octopus ways.

She said fluidity kept him young and detached no matter how many times he entered into marriage.

Demons reveal themselves.

It was impossible, really—his choice of those particular words. Out of all the words in the world, he'd put that set together. He was possessed. He just said it.

I gave in to entertaining the concept of another world alongside the world I knew. I don't believe in the supernatural. I'm not New Age. I don't buy into the charming stories behind the principals of Feng Shui. I'm not even sure I care about the art of de-cluttering. But the thing is? Some philosophies are packages that secretly hold very solid, real-life benefits.

Sometimes, if you de-clutter, your life comes into view. If you utilize Feng Shei, the space feels more welcoming, and all the words used to describe that are only variables.

What would it hurt to do a simple ceremony? People engaged in meaningless ceremony all the time, like ribbon-cuttings, office party birthdays, and at least half the weddings I'd ever been to.

If this Pilgrim didn't need the cure, the ritual would have no effect. It'd be theater. I had all the props. We had the afternoon. I'd tell Jenna I tried.

If it worked? We could shake off those ex's. It'd be serious emotional de-cluttering. We'd get to know each other, alone.

The directions said that he should hold a river rock. I'd run another rock down his vertebra. He'd breathe into my fertile egg. I'd envision my uterus and shake the rattle Jenna made out of garbanzos and my old pepper mill. We'd do yoga breaths together.

I scoured the banks for the right second rock. He rested at the water's edge. His toes were long and graceful. He could've been a male foot model, if there was ever a call for photographs of men's feet. His toenails brought along the right mix of adventure, savoir faire and pedicure.

Soon we'd take a swim. I handed him the first rock. "Hold this?" I hoped to lead him through the ceremony without explaining. Who isn't willing to breathe deeply?

My pale skin reflected the sun in an obstinate, Oregonian way. I generally took my vitamin D in pills, year-round. I opened the Tupperware, lifted out the fertile egg. With that egg tucked in one palm, I found the second rock, also in my bag. I stood behind where he sat. Moving quietly, in a clandestine way, I stepped forward, shortening the gap between us. Gravel shifted and clicked under my feet. My shadow fell over Pilgrim's shoulder. My job was to touch the rock to his head, then bring it along his spine, like a hot stone massage.

Because I had no pockets, I tucked the fertile egg between my cheek and shoulder to carry it while I used both hands to heft the rock. Minnows darted like little shadows in the shallow water near the shore. Two buzzards soared high overhead. Their shadows crossed ours. A spider scrambled over the pale, dry rocks and was gone. A water skimmer darted over the water, into the grasses that grew at the far edge. So many creatures! We were between layers of life, in the air, earth and water. Why not believe in more lives, too small or transparent to be detected?

My Pilgrim tossed the potato-sized river rock I'd given him from hand to hand. He talked about his ex-wives. "I loved them all," he said.

I crept closer, behind him.

He said, "I still do. But they all changed, so fast."

I said, "I never change. I'm the ten-year-old I used to be. Same interests." It was true. I lifted the rock from Jenna's fire pit over his head. I could see myself in shadow, my arms high, the rock between my hands, my head at a strange angle, cocked to hold the fertile egg, one shoulder hunched like a monster.

He said, "The real problem was how much they wanted to change me. I've only ever been myself."

"I wouldn't change you, ever," I said, and tried not to feel guilty about the whole exorcism proposition. A small change: lose the demon? Lose the life force that is you...Yes, I felt guilty. I started to bring the rock down to touch the crown of his head, then stumbled on a loose rock. He turned at the sound, just as I brought my arms down, that rock over his head. I slid it to the side.

I was not going to hit him! How to explain?

I threw the rock over him into the water as though I were only sending it out to sink all along. But as I threw it, my shoulder moved. The egg slipped. It tumbled. I danced fast to catch it, hitting the egg with my palm each time, instead of grasping it, sending it in another arc. Sharp edges of granite ate my feet as I danced, until I caught the egg in one hand. Saved.

My phone vibrated in the bag. I took a quick look. Jenna had texted, "Is it done?" She made it sound like a murder. I was her hitman.

Maybe I was the one possessed? Maybe Jenna was the demon.

I put the fertile egg down in its open Tupperware bowl, then sent back a challenge. "Why would a demon make him get married?" For him, it'd gone beyond being body fluid bonded all the way to the chapel, the church or courthouse, or wherever he'd tied all those knots.

She replied, "Marriage is a byproduct. Demons create a sense of affinity...."

I dropped the phone back in my bag, and asked him, "Why did you get married, all those times?" I stepped lightly over the jagged, hot rocks of the embankment.

He stared into the deep green river water as it slogged past, as though searching his own murky history. He was a beautiful, moody romantic. He said, "I don't know." He ran his fingers over the hot stone I'd given him to hold. "It felt right. I felt a complete...affinity," he said, as though the words were new, and his, and perfect.

Affinity.

That word had once, back in the Middle Ages, meant marriage. It did! What was an affinity? It meant to feel the border of something, that line between people, structurally similar, vibrating at the same frequency.

I felt an affinity for him, so strongly that it brought tears to my eyes. What could I do to remove his past? Nothing. Not a thing. Life only accumulates, it's never removed. Jenna was wrong. You can only learn to accept time's demons as they pile like silt into our souls.

I walked into the Washougal. That cold, green water, that blessing, antidote to sun, it numbed my feet, then my thighs. I moved forward until it brought its frozen bite into my gut, surrounding my ovaries and their endless abandoned machinery, and I kept going. I walked my whole metropolis of a micro biome into the river. The water chilled my heart. It washed the dust off my skin, and it fed my spirit or whatever I had that passed for a modern soul.

I'd lived a long time, to get to this place.

Jenna said demons seep in after soul loss. Who doesn't lose soul, every day? Only a good river can give soul back. If what Jenna said was true, every day the world's demons could make themselves more comfortable, like an unwelcome guest spreading out on the couch.

Under water, I held my eyes open. The world was blurry, rich in floating detritus. I tried to see water creatures, little lives surrounding ours, through that sunshine water haze. In my secret heart, all I wanted was to be one half of one of those couples famous for living to the same ripe old age, dying in unison like a suicide of some well-nourished, conjoined spirit. That was love! I forced myself to stay under the cold water in the world of other creatures until my lungs drove my body back to the surface, to sun and oxygen and doubt.

I came up and shook the water from my micro-life-laden eyelashes. Pilgrim reached for the Tupperware. "Brought a snack?"

He moved too fast, pulled the bowl toward himself. The egg slid against the edges of its Tupperware bed. He said, "An egg, or a jumping bean?"

The egg shook, side to side. I said, "Don't shake it." It'd break.

"I'm not moving it," Mr. Demon Lover claimed, but I could see how it shook in his hands. A crack came to the surface. He had broken it! The crack turned into more cracks as I came, dripping and goose-bumped, out of the water up to the sun-warmed towels.

A beak, or a claw, broke the egg from inside. We were witnessing something—birth? A chick.

"The sun is the best sun lamp for little hatchlings," Pilgrim whispered. Just like that, he was selling the idea of sunshine again. I was pale as a root.

I said, "I had no idea—"

He asked, "You were just carrying around an egg?"

That egg's yolk had been a single cell floating in albumen, balanced, decorated with its germinal disc, and then the dangling chalazae, those two strange strands of coarser white threads that held to the sides of the shell. I learned about eggs in eighth grade science, when I'd made a model out of paper mache—eggs are one of the few single-cells visible to the naked, human eye.

But that single cell had been fertilized, and now here it was, a chick, and I wanted to yell, *Jenna!* Damn her.

Satan's Pilgrim cradled the baby bird so tenderly, I could've bitten his bony shoulder out of love for his love, and for the world. I hadn't cured anyone on that river trip. I only sank into love a little deeper.

***

Back home, Pilgrim parkedin the driveway. He opened wide all the van's doors, airing it out. He opened it up like a tent or an open heart, open arms. The sun was still out, resting just over the tops of trees to the west. I headed to my barn, with my hands cupped around the chick. Jenna came from her garden shed. She intercepted my path. "How'd it go?" she whispered. "Could you feel it exit his body? You don't look any different."

"I have not felt anything *exit his body*. Yet," I said, in my ordinary, loud voice.

She cringed and held a finger to her lips, hissing for me to hush. He could hear me. The two of us knocked into each other as we made our way through the narrow door to my place.

"I don't think you candled the egg right," I said.

She danced along beside me, wild hair in my way, her face eager and close to mine. She asked, "Wasn't it fertilized?"

"It was definitely fertilized." I unfolded my top hand to show her the baby. As soon as the light reached its tiny eyes, it started its peep-peep-peep song like a wind-up toy. I'd gone into the wilderness and given birth, more or less. I loved that tiny bird already. The love was too much for me to contain. Life was too fragile. I hated it. This is why I never wanted kids! How could love for something so small feel so huge?

Love is bigger than all bodies.

"We ran into another one of Pilgrim's wives at the gas station on the way back," I said. We definitely had made zero progress on de-demonizing. His ex's were still tethered, all cords and entities intact, if you believed in that sort of thing, and maybe I was starting to.

This fourth ex was a determined blonde pound cake with a habit of cracking her knuckles. He'd been washing the van's windows when she came around the corner, restroom key chained to a dirty white bucket lid still in her hand. She called his name, across the lot. His voice quavered. He yelled, "The restraining order is still in effect!" He had trouble opening the van's door, because he moved so frantically. It was the first time I'd seen him scramble. I was inside, in the heat like an incubator, holding the delicate baby chick, letting it tap my calloused finger with its baby beak. Once we were driving again, when he could breathe, he said, "I think she followed me to Oregon on purpose."

I wouldn't argue with that.

She definitely followed us home. I could still see her car, even now, from the barn. It was parked down the street, a burgundy Buick with a dented front fender. She stayed what I'd guess was the legal distance from him, and watched through the twin dark circles of binoculars brought to her eyes. The whole time driving home, her car behind ours, he'd talked quickly about how he'd never been monogamous, never promised he would be, how it drove that woman crazy. He rambled as though he were still explaining to her, not to me.

"I'm in love with the world," he'd said, forlornly, though without apology. "You only get one time through, far as I can tell."

Earlier, at the river, in a calmer moment, we'd leaned into each other, all warm skin and cool water, surrounded by sun and the scent of hot blackberries, sweet and warm as fresh homemade jam. We watched that chick come damp and fragile into the world. An egg is a strange thing. A rooster leaves its semen, then only later the shell is formed around the fertilized egg, inside the chicken's body, so it looks immaculate, right? It's a magic trick.

After the gas station scare he drove too fast. We jostled along curving roads in his licorice-and-apple scented van, with his bedding tumbling in the back. "Is she the one who broke your nose?" I asked, softly.

He put a hand to his face, remembering. "They all did. Broke my bones, broke my heart. It always ends badly. I can't help it."

Now, in my barn house, looking out the window at that lurking Buick, I felt the slick, muscled tentacles of an octopus-like entity press jealously through my ribs, into my throat, creating pressure on my words. Satan's Pilgrim, he was practically Jesus—chicks were born in his hand, like tiny miracles. I wanted to protect him and the chick, both. My fragile family.

I wanted to claim him as mine.

Jenna said, "A demon is a disease. You'd never be the same. You can't cure it with acidophilus, if you're thinking it's that simple." She pushed her way between me and the window, to block my hyper-vigilant, longing gaze.

I saw past her shoulder and dark curls, when Pilgrim's anxious wife with the dog happened to swing by. *Oh, hello!* I could see the woman's mouth move, saying those words though pink lipstick-lips, and I repeated them out loud, in an extra-snotty way, I admit. "Hell-lo!"

Jenna said, "Forget about her—"

I was degrading myself by caring. "She's been waiting out there. Watching for him." Of course she had her own bug-eyed binoculars kept on a windowsill. Didn't everyone? The woman tucked one plump knee in close to the other, cocked a hip and coyly pulled single hairs out of her head, one after another, as she listened and smiled. That was her way of flirting—listening while silently picking herself apart.

Who goes for a self destructive woman? A predator. Or a bleeding heart, or a lover, a care-taker. Satan's Pilgrim was maybe all of those in one package.

My body made its own decision. My mind heard it loud and clear. Jenna could know, I wouldn't fight it. "I'm going to host his parasites," I said. I touched a careful fingertip to the chick's down. "What's a wedding if you don't share your life—your lives, those little lives that ride along in and on your skin? Bring it on."

It felt daring to jump in with both feet. It'd been a long time. I was old enough to think I'd already made all of life's mistakes.

Here was a new one, ready for me to go down another wrong path, and I was entirely interested.

I upturned a shoe box from under the bed, shaking out a dusty and worn pair of shoes, took out the tiny package of desiccant, and put the chick in the box instead.

Jenna said, "You don't mean it."

She had me confused with herself. I did mean it. Humans are barely human. We're only pretending, all the time. According to Jenna—and science!—we're mostly water and the rest is more bacteria than DNA, by count if not by weight. I said, "I'm ready to put a wing on that demon manse and make babies. I'll make more tailbones and spines. Why not?"

Even a human baby in the womb is a parasite. Maybe there are no entirely human babies? There are no entirely human adults. There are no entirely adult humans, either. "People give in to the heterosexual demon baby spawn agenda every day. Even gay couples are making babies. Why not me?"

I wouldn't be hemmed in by Jenna's fear. I said, "You love babies, I've seen you hold them."

She said, "Parasites elicit love. That's how they hang on. But still your body has to change to accommodate a baby. It gives up its nourishment. That can't be healthy."

The beauty of feeding even an imagined demon would be a chance to fuel your own built-in, second, shameless self. I could blame all my urges on a creature that wasn't me but was inside my skin. The chick peeped, happy to be alive. I wanted to protect it! I wanted to crush it now, because what was up ahead? Life only got harder. I touched it so very softly. "What will this birdy eat?"

Then I added, "This love is bigger than me. It's bigger than time, bigger than the universe."

Jenna said, "Thinking any love is bigger than time is delusional. It's like being high. It might feel good now, but you have your whole future to consider—"

I said, "You sound like those abstinence videos from seventh grade." I was not in seventh grade anymore. My future was decidedly less weighty. This was my future: a barn, a job cutting cake, the private project of writing *Moby Vagina,* alone with the mites on my eyelashes and the flora and fauna of my skin.

I noticed a man walking toward our lot. He was still far down the street, barely coming into view. He wore a baseball cap pulled down low against the sun. From the swing of his arms, the clip of his gait, he looked efficient and directed enough to be part of a SWAT team, except for the white lunch sack dangling in his hand. As he came closer, he started to take on a familiar shape. It was my Rose Festival date, my friend from the taqueria.

"Grilled chicken burrito," I said. "That's what he's got." I could tell by the heft and grease stains on that white bag where it jostled to the side of his thigh.

Jenna said, "You're always good at that."

It was one of my super powers—guessing a fast food order by estimating the weight. I said, "It comes from experience. But he makes it easy." Still making his way toward our house, he'd brought me dinner. He knew what I liked. I really did love a good chicken burrito. I was hungry. That was true. Or my demon was hungry, if you believed in demons and the demon paradigm. My demon was starving.

"Look," I said, and pressed my palm against the glass.

Jenna gasped quietly, a small intake of air, there where we stood at the window watching the theater of our world, the chicken burrito coming closer. "For you—?"

My baby chick was fragile and dear; I couldn't navigate that divide between a steamy chicken dinner and the sweetness of my darling. As hungry as I was, I sort of hoped he'd take a turn, head off to seduce somebody else with that fine wrap, all tender white meat, beans and avocado.

The Buick started its motor, crept forward a few feet, then stopped and shut off again. The motor made a sound like very loud crickets ticking in the heat.

I had one more day of running free. Then I'd go back to cutting cake for an endless stream of blind dates, grandparents, and teenagers who imagined romance as some untarnished thing. I didn't have those illusions. I'd cut cakes at wedding after wedding, sometimes seeing the same bride coming back for a second party, like a kid at the fair doubling back in line.

I could cut cake smaller, and smaller, and smaller until it verged on crumbs. With every slice I imagined the rewards of being legally tethered getting smaller over future years. Cheers, bride and groom!

Maybe I'd always been afraid of marriage.

The urge I felt now was real and valid even if it was impulsive. I said, "There aren't enough rocks in the river to contain our love." My voice came out low and determined, with a strange lilt and swing. "All the fertilized eggs of Easter can't compete with our dreams. If you want to try to stop me, you can just watch me—" Every inch of my body joined this song, down to the micro organisms making out on my eyelashes.

"Listen to yourself," Jenna said. "You're writing songs!"

"I am not." But she was right—my words were bad country music, the sappy kind. The possessed kind.

In desperation, she negotiated, "It's not my ideas, or insight. I'm a conduit telling you what I know to be true. You don't want to engage with this man, gorgeous as he is. Listen to the ancient wisdom."

"The ancient art of cock blocking," I said. My feet were damp against my tennis shoes from walking in the river, and I kicked them off in a small flurry of gravel. It might help to brush my hair? Pilgrim had seen me all day without makeup, dirty on riverbank, but still I reached for a hairbrush to comb out bits of debris. My clothes, scattered on the floor, all looked inadequate. I'd found them on street corners in free boxes. I was trying to be somebody new, now. I stood at the window and brushed.

She took my head in her hands, stopped my frantic brushing. I'd been basically slapping my head with the hairbrush. She said, "I am a healer. The food I ferment is medicinal. My booze is palliative. Shaman work is one path to a more restful soul. Don't close your mind. Don't give in to easy charms..."

"Don't give away the cow—?" I said, cynically. I found a bottle of coconut and sea salt natural hold hair spray, and started spraying. That hairspray was like insect repellent: she let go of my face. I felt that absence immediately, where her hands had contained me.

Jenna's face twitched with anxiety.

Darling witch. I knew her story. She'd been fighting off parasite infestations her entire life, in the guise of rape-y dates, narcissistic parents, bummer roommates, raw deals, and a general lifetime of making her way alone as a beautiful, fragile thing.

I asked, "Are you afraid I'd leave?" The world is always unstable.

She said, "Where would you go? He lives in his car, and there's nothing to rent in this city."

True.

"But I could leave the world of being single," I said. I could quit sitting by the fire at night, unattached. There's always a risk.

I think that was Jenna's biggest fear, since childhood, since she was left home alone with her lice and impetigo while everybody else went to school and her mother went to work: to be alone even when we're never alone, carrying three trillion invisible lives on our bodies as a walking miniature ecosystem as diverse as the Galapagos islands. She'd be alone, and I'd still be right there, only on the other side of a transparent border: in love.

What is that biological nature of connection? It's the brain and the gut, the terrain where parasites thrive, driving their hosts to a symbiotic goal.

There is no such thing as a truly single person, only a lonely one. Humans are porous in the borders of our skins, these walking micro cities. She quietly drew the brush through my hair.

"We share an affinity," I said.

She said, "We do."

The street outside was usually quiet but now it had grown increasingly jammed with cars and people like somebody on the block was throwing a party. Another man came from the other direction, walking quickly. It was the guy who'd been calling, who was heavily into making money. I said, "Remember him?" Jenna looked where I pointed.

There were others, men I barely remembered, getting out of cars in front of our house. I said, "I know all these guys..." it was dizzying. Some of them nodded to each other. Some were less friendly. They found their way to our sidewalk. I started looking for something else to put on, that wasn't marked with sand and water. Then I saw Mack, shuffling down the middle of the road. I couldn't breathe, at the sight of his familiar sloped shoulders and dark hair. He still had that hair, glossy and black, but cut shorter now. He came toward us in a wandering, meandering way, like he had no idea where he was headed. Mack, that old hockey player, survivor, he was still sexy even as he'd aged. How did he age faster than I did?

My burrito deliveryman had made it to the edge of our yard. The tall, slinky silhouette of one of Satan's wives, the woman who'd smashed my cake to destroy illusions, was now lurking near a tree at the edge of the yard. I said, "We should call the police, on that one."

Then the man we always called the Deposed Dictator drove up in a worn out Miata, honking his horn as he navigated the narrow street. I ducked, and tried to hide. Tino was there too. I recognized him right away, even though now he was a balding, weathered ex-junky with a briefcase. I wanted to cry for him! He was the sweetest man, once. Now he was worn down, first by drugs, then by work, and as far as I could tell the second looked like a harder gig. He paused to check his cell phone. Maybe he was Instagramming the moment.

"An infestation of exes," Jenna murmured.

Where was that fleeting Romeo, Ray Madrigal? He was nowhere around. Dead? Or just too immune to the dimensions of love.

Everything was out in our crowded lawn, really—love, anger and jealousy. History and intimacy. You could breathe it in, thick as fog. I wanted to yell, *Get out of our yard!*

Jenna said, "I've read about this phenomenon." She said, "You... may have a demon, too, already—?" She seemed nervous to say it out loud. "I don't want to deliver bad news."

I'd felt a demon climbing inside the cage of my bones, from the first night I met this Pilgrim. He'd woken up my sleeping creature.

She said, "The two of you. You're the Romeo and Juliet of the demon world. Now that you've found each other, you're calling your spawn back. Your electromagnetism is strong, the iron in your blood is overcharged. Those old dates? They're like iron filings."

My laugh came out with a sound more wicked than I meant it to, and it went on longer, and I could hardly bring myself back under control. "That's absurd! He's an angel." I was an angel. My voice was so low.

Angels and demons are one and the same. We carry pieces of each other with us forever, human collectors, land of thriving symbiotic and parasitic relations. Who you love changes you.

Jenna said, "Their demons are calling out to each other. This could be a nightmare. It might be an orgy, I don't know." She said, "There'll definitely be a few babies."

"Happy demons make happy humans!" I growled, low and quiet, in that voice that wasn't entirely mine.

There was a knock on the door. "Burrito delivery!"

I cringed with discomfort. What did I owe him? Civility, that was all.

The Buick rolled closer. Pilgrim slammed the doors on the van, closing himself inside.

"These people aren't happy," Jenna yipped.

I felt the truth of what she said, but part of me denied it. "Happy Customers Are Return Customers," the voice that was and wasn't mine said, from deep in my throat. It was a line from the taco shack, on the wall. My burrito date knocked again.

Pathogens coexist with other microbes on human skin, all the time, on all bodies. Jenna was the one to tell me that you can never wash them away or cleanse or fast. Trillions of tiny microorganisms are so entwined with what we imagine to be our own lives that they are us. We are them. When microbes don't sap our life force, they support it.

I opened the door. The man from the taco shack was freshly showered, smelling of cilantro and bay rum. He held up the white bag. Tempting!

"Hang on. Not now," and moved past him, into the crowd forming in our yard.

"It'll get cold!" he called out. He was always a practical man. The impulse made him a good restaurateur. He said, "I brought two green sauces, one red!"

That was love: kind and reliable. He knew me well. Maybe that should be enough?

Mack had started a conversation with Pilgrim's tall, angry beauty. The two gazed into each other's eyes, both leaning on one slim Asian Pear tree between them, a thing I'd planted only a year or so earlier in an effort to conjure up the orchards of my childhood home. Our demon spawn in their spines seemed to find each other compatible. Oh, Mack! Those demons of love would keep them busy for a while, in a hit of intergenerational possession. But I didn't want to be there if the two of them came to blows.

Tino saw me and squinted like I was some distant memory.

I ran for the van. Jenna ran to catch up, behind me. She closed in fast on her strong dancer's legs. The blond hair-plucking ex-wife was over in the grass with a plastic bag, picking up the poop dropped by her love-on-a-leash. I knocked on the door, under the blue moon. Jenna pulled on my shoulder to peel me away. I slapped a quiet palm against the windows. *Open up! Let me in! Let me bring my demons and sympathetic vibrations to mingle with your pelvic cage. Let out this octopus of longing.*

Pilgrim opened the sliding van door.

That was his choice. He opened it for me. He reached out a hand, invited me to make the big step up. We were making this decision together. I clawed away from Jenna and took his hand, then climbed inside. Jenna lay sprawled across the threshold of the van's sliding door.

"You will be my favorite ex," I whispered in his ear. "I'll be your fifth former wife. We'll mutter crazy dreams together then apart, but you will always be with me."

His breath was warm and so very human, not demonic at all. He said, "Don't break my nose."

I said, "I won't even break your heart."

We were writing our sappy songs together.

"That part is inevitable," he said. We were both old enough to know that all happy endings had longer dance versions that found their way to another place, not always so charmed.

Jenna said, "You'll never be the same—"

Pilgrim reached out a hand for her. "Join us?" he said.

I'd been jealous of every other woman in the yard. I was jealous of the past. This time? I whispered, "It's okay to write a few bad songs, for love." I held out a hand for her, too.

Jenna's eyes were big. Her hair was insane as her microbes. She hesitated, wavering. We're tiny creatures hosting tinier lives in a big universe. When you're that small, all decisions feel weighty. Our entities are complex. We're flora and fauna. We're not alone.

The door would close soon. She had a choice to make.

Love is a demon. It would take over, and it would kill us, but first it would keep us all alive.

NEIGHBORHOOD NOTES: LIGHT SLEEPERS

It'd been years since I'd seen Mack, Tino or Satan's Pilgrim. Even demonic possession-style love has a shelf life. Now he was gone, off in his primered van. If there was any blame, it was my fault as much as his. I walked my days raising our daughter, Pilgrim's child. She was my angel, my life. She was his gift to me. She was my darling demon-spawn, if you asked Jenna. Aren't we all demon spawn, though? Humans are a difficult species.

Jenna had moved to France. She married a male model with a cocaine habit. She said the coke kept parasites away, so for now it was all good.

I was still living in the barn-house. I'd built a standing screen as a wall to make a tiny bedroom for our daughter. Instead of a yard, we had a cluster of more tiny shed houses behind ours in a crowded compound. I'd bought the one we lived in. The owners called it a condo. They put all the sheds on the market individually. Instead of a driveway, we had a pod of food trucks taking up that slim space. I could order Pad Thai by just shouting out to the world.

This was the new Portland: crowded.

I'd worked all my life to get to this place: a tiny house on a side street, life as a single mom and a long-term pro cake cutter with frosting on my shoes, always freelancing on the side. At night I'd dream of wild land. I'd climb trees, feet bare against the rough bark, my hands gripping higher limbs. I'd eat apples covered in dark spots made by rain and bugs. In those dreams, kids would push their way through the forest out back to call my name. I'd find hallways branching off other hallways in a low, flat house with a half-basement full of ghosts. My father would be there to say, "Evidence is not intimidated." He'd ruffle a hand through his hair. I'd wake up to my tiny room, my child so close by.

Why do I say "my child," and not give her name? Her name is her own. The world is complicated. We need to allow for privacy.

She was still sleeping, early morning, when a neighbor texted from the next shed over to ask if I heard gunshots in the middle of the night.

"Eleven shots," the neighbor woman wrote.

I had woken up that night, when I heard something like shots. Then I'd lain awake, wondering if it was a gun or fireworks. "They sounded about a block away," I wrote back. "Didn't hear them enough to count."

"I'm a light sleeper," she texted.

It was late spring. The sun was climbing up to the east, high and hot. I took my girl to school. When I came back to the shed condo-compound later that morning, there was a red headed white woman in a Kelly green Gortex coat out in the middle of our street. She had a pair of binoculars and was looking around. In windows? My first thought was that she was one of Pilgrim's wives! That was a flash of old times. Those days were far behind us. What was she looking at? Birds? Electrical wires? She turned in slow circles like a lost urban hiker. The way she stood, with her shoulders brought forward, reminded me of my little sister.

The sound of distant hammers sang a song of somebody throwing up sheetrock or framing in a building off in the distance, turning a two-bedroom house into six apartments. The sun gleamed off the side of an Animal Control truck parked down the block. Two Animal Control employees were looking over a neighbor's fence in another compound of tiny houses.

I thought they were together, Animal Control and that lost urban birder in her unnecessary Gortex on that sunny day, until she turned and powerwalked off.

"What's going on?" I called, to Animal Control.

One of the men said, "A dog has its legs caught in that rope they've got it on. Got a call from a neighbor."

Our street is short but crowded with tiny mysteries. I said, "There's never been a dog at that house."

"There is now," one of the Animal Control officers said.

Had they planted a dog, like planting evidence, to set up the corner drug dealer? We stood near a Port-a-Potty not far from a construction site, where a house had been knocked down to make way for four more.

One of our local working ladies came out of the Port-a-Potty, shoving a few bills in her front pocket. Two men tumbled out behind her, all three pulling themselves together. One rubbed on hand sanitizer—what my daughter called "hanitizer,"—and so moved in a cloud of the strong bite of clean alcohol in the air. A portable toilet is the tiniest of tiny houses, smaller than our sheds, but big enough to crowd three people inside if you're smoking crack or doing other close-quartered human behaviors. I didn't judge.

The woman murmured, "That dog's only temporary."

I thought, *aren't we all?*

She wore jeans and rhinestone-silver-and-Lucite high heels. Her hair was a pile of curls and glittering pins. She looked like a party and a hangover and a good recipe for every occasion. She said, "I'll find the owner, get this sorted out." While the two men slunk off, she jogged with purpose in those pretty party heels to the other end of the block. She knocked on a car, woke up a neighbor who was sleeping there. She was running interference, doing her part to keep a neighbor from getting a fine, a dog from being impounded.

A seventy-nine year old junkie woke up and stretched, where he'd nodded off on the steps of a porch that wasn't his. I was still in the middle of the road. Ten years I'd been on this block. So had he. He used to walk around saying, "I'm sixty-nine years old!" when I first ran into him, so I'd always known his age. Now the junkie called out, "I ain't dead! I ain't dead!"

The Animal Control twins in their uniforms wiped sweat off their foreheads, waiting but ready to go.

The junkie said, "I'm talking about me." He yelled, "You ain't blossomed yet, that's all! You ain't blossomed."

I couldn't argue. Had I blossomed?

Hot sun poured down like a mother's hand smoothing our hair, even as it pushed us closer to the ground. Glossy black crows called back and forth overhead and one bird echoed my thoughts, shouting a command down at us all: Blossom! Blossom!

Back inside, I stood in the shower with hot water pouring down, my eyes closed. I opened my eyes and the water was reddish brown like drying blood. It ran in rivulets over my face, chest, and arms. It pooled at my feet against the white porcelain and our slow drain. Blood-red water climbed up my ankles. I screamed even as I reached to turn the shower off.

It was the reverse mortgages backing up, the backyard bones, the banks. This was blood coming up from the ground into my house. This was gentrification: bloody showers.

There's no way to clean blood off when all of your water carries in more of the same.

My mother had heard the voices of every child who had ever lived in our house. I was starting to understand. I could feel the lives of everyone around me, layered on history. I was now the mother in the house, and in the wind I heard my own mother's voice sing a soft *Happy Birthday* from the grave.

I threw on the baggiest of clothes, not wanting to touch anything and not wanting anything to touch me. I looked out the window. A tree had split and fallen, smashing a car out in the street. Its branches covered the sidewalk and reached into the yard. All the tiny sheds were still standing. The other half of the tree was still standing too though, a looming threat. It rustled, *I can kill you.* I picked up my phone and called for help. *Help!* I called the city about the water. I called a tree removal company.

It wasn't my tree. I'd have to get permission from the condominium complex's governing board, which is to say the former owners who sold the tiny houses to us.

But I'd grown up in the Arboretum, surrounded by fields where trees were slaughtered to make way for the suburbs and strip malls, and my heart was with the trees. Every time a tree was cut down, a good kid somewhere took up smoking. That's how it felt, in our ragged edge of a suburban Paradise Lost.

I was looking at the tree when the redhead in her unnecessary Gortex came traipsing back down the street. She was wearing brown loafers, almost a commercial kind of moccasins, and who wears shoes like that anymore? They were like something left over from the 80's, maybe even something I had. Something my sister and I had. My sister had worn a tiny pair, and I had mine that were bigger, and she loved that and I hated it.

I was slow to recognize—this was her, Lu, walking toward me, in those horrible moccasins, as though she'd been wearing them for thirty years. They'd grown with her feet.

My throat constricted, with tears or anxiety. Was that her? The last time I'd seen her had been our mother's funeral. My sister's hair wasn't red, so that was confusing. She was too thin. I made eye contact, and waited. Was it? She said, "Vanessa. I had the wrong address." She waved a scrap of torn, lined notebook paper.

She opened her arms. I stepped forward, let her hug me. Lu said, "I've missed you."

I said, "Little Carrion!"

She half-laughed, patient with me, but she said, "I don't really go by that anymore."

I invited her in to my tiny barn. Right away I felt awkward about how small my house was. What did she have, three bedrooms and two bathrooms, somewhere normal? She peeled off her Gortex. Underneath that coat she was a twig. My sister, she was the picture of lack.

"Stay for lunch," I begged her, really.

She said, "That's okay, I just ate." I didn't believe her. She pushed up her sleeves, showed a raft of tattoos. She touched a frame that hung on my wall. The frame was empty, but hung over the faint lines of old blood stains: Heathens. That word. History.

"Stay for dinner if you can," I said. Stay for all the meals. Forever. She perched on the arm of my short loveseat, the biggest couch I could fit in my designated couch-space. She was a bird on a branch and the shallow padding didn't even dimple under her complete lack of weight. I felt huge, being normal-sized.

I noticed then a familiarity about the blue of her oversized button-down men's shirt. I felt the cotton, rubbed it between two fingers. "It's a good shirt," I said. "It looks like a shirt I left in a free box."

She said, "It came from a free box, I think. It was a friend's. Sean. The first normal guy I ever dated. We're still friends."

And I squinted. Could that be the same shirt? Or only similar?

She said, "The blue is like dad's eyes."

And then it didn't matter if it was the same, or similar. We'd both been drawn to that shirt, to men in that color, to the memory of dad. "A man who can solve people's problems," I said.

She had a bruise on the side of her face, near her eye that almost looked like makeup. I said, "Are you okay?" I touched my own face, not hers, in the spot of that bruise.

She shrugged it off. "I just need a place to stay?"

"You're welcome here." I waved a hand around the tiny space of my barn and somehow in that gesture it grew even smaller, and more crowded around us.

Late that day, after my child was home from school, I put mac and cheese on the table for dinner. It's what Mom used to make for the dead kids back at the Arboretum.

We'd just sat down. Our postal carrier cut through the branches of the tree to bring a package to my door. When I opened the door, she said, "I've been looking for you." She held out a beat up old piece of cardboard. She said, "I delivered this yesterday, about three o'clock."

I took it, but was confused. She was delivering it now. And why deliver it? That box looked like garbage or close to it. My sister was waiting in the shadows, sitting on a spindly chair, drinking coffee, watching this interaction. The day had gotten away from me. I was not the center of my own world, not even close. I was orbiting somebody else's sun, falling behind. What was this life of details flooding in?

She said, "Neighbor of yours saw a man come up on your porch, take the delivery, open it, and throw the box in a yard."

I turned the cardboard over. There was our address on a sticker, on the front.

"You might see if it's insured," the postal carrier offered.

Inside, I called the post office. The box was insured! Except, the man who'd answered said, "Well, it's only insured until we leave it on your porch. Not after that." So...it wasn't exactly insured, in any meaningful way. What ever is insured, really?

I found my daughter in a corner of the barn, clicking away on the internet, on the desktop computer, speaking with strangers, playing games, trading virtual spike collars with kids who may or may not be kids in the virtual world, and I made her come out with me, into the street, to real world, IRL. Lu stayed inside, sacked out on the loveseat, getting rest she seemed to need. My child and I walked the neighborhood. We turned in circles, looking. "What are we looking for?" She asked.

"Clues," I said.

I planned to walk in the direction our package had supposedly gone. We could look for bits of ribbon, anything on top of a trash can.

The evening sky deepened into a heather blue. The arm of a tree was grey-black, and there on a branch was an owl, sitting so upright and ready. The owl was tan and white, with bits of grey, and the trees were bare, and it was all so beautiful I tried to breathe the world in. Seeing that owl? That was the gift that came in the empty box. It was wildlife, wilderness still alive in the city.

This was our reverse mortgage: for now, the world was ours. It wouldn't always be. This life was ours.

We cut around the block, up to a busy street, Martin Luther King Boulevard. Just as we got there, a small pickup rear-ended a larger truck. It was an accident. The broken plastic of taillights and headlights skittered onto the sidewalk. I pulled my child back, away from the street, glad we hadn't been closer.

Then the pickup truck revved and drove and hit the larger truck again, a second time. It wasn't an accident. It was a challenge. On purpose. Then a third time, like a small bird fighting a hawk. The big truck was taking it until it slammed on its brakes. This was a duel. The small truck pulled alongside the bigger one, and the large truck tore off its side mirror. They careened down the road like that, pieces of both of them falling off into the street, and then they were gone.

Back on our side road, we waved to the diabetic alcoholic out on his porch, who could only nod back. We looked for the old mothers who were never out anymore feeding their cats. Between thieves, road rage, Port-a-potties and rising cost of living, maybe it was time to leave this place we called home.

There's more than one way to live.

We came home to my sister's thin body stretched out like a corpse on the loveseat. Her arms were skinny and lifeless, marked with burns and tattoos, but her face was the kid I'd remembered her being. Seven years between us was a lot, back then. She'd been a kid when I was grown up. I heard my father's voice: *Lu, in particular, needs you…*

He'd been talking to mom, back then, when those words gave me permission to disappear. Now they roped me back in to family: I had to take care of us all.

The next morning, a Saturday, Lu to went to work. She went off early to make coffee or serve breakfast, I didn't recognize the name of the place. A little later my daughter and I got in the car and drove south. We went toward the suburbs, where a river cuts through town. I knew exactly what I was looking for—a big lot covered in trees, a place with apples, where a girl could climb a tree and read a book in the branches. I wanted the Arboretum back. I wanted my daughter, her aunt and me to live on a piece of land. We'd feel bark rough under the soles of our feet, and wander the yard naked when the weather was good, far enough away from immediate neighbors.

When I found that land, we'd start again. It would be healing. Life would take shape in new ways.

I drove to a place where the yards were big. The taxes were bigger though, higher, way out of my reach. This was what mom would've called Manicured Estates. It wasn't meant for us. She would've hated it. The roads curved left and right. We drove those needlessly winding streets, and I looked in the rearview mirror, asked over my shoulder, "Would you like to live in a place like this?"

Every house had a garage. Bark chips. Some had play structures.

From the back seat, my daughter said, "I'm not sure..."

"There are trade offs, I suppose." I was trying to read her mind. I don't pretend to know what happiness entails for other people, but how would she know? She'd only ever lived in our barn-house in the crowded corner of Portland's infill.

If we found a big enough place, maybe Mack could come live with us. He could rehabilitate, in the country. Maybe he could settle his angry, loving, lost mind.

Our car was warm inside from the sun. We sailed over smooth streets. There were no high, crackhead dancers on the corner out here, and I didn't see any stray cats. There were also no piles of free books or clothes. There weren't any tumbled, stolen, stripped bikes. There was no graffiti, those quiet missives, written voices dashed on the sides of buildings. We were used to reading the shout of graffiti on the walk to and from school. We liked passing people in the street, and flyers on phone poles advertising bands, lost animals, or sometimes just ideas and art.

I turned down a small side street. The street turned out to be a wide driveway. It took us to a school parking lot, in the back of the school. The school's drive curved around then opened up again on the other side of what passed for a block but wasn't remotely square, was amorphous as far as I could tell, and just like that I was lost. I tried to turn around, but saw then the drive had split.

The roads were all called Cherry, every last one. Cherry Avenue cut across Cherry lane, then ran into Cherry Avenue again until it found Cherry Way. We were in a vortex. I reached for my phone, for the safety of maps, but my phone was dead. We'd forgotten the charger. It was like we'd fallen back in time, cut off from technology. I drove Cherry lane Cherry Avenue Cherry Way Cherry Court Cherry Lane again and finally said, "I have no idea where we are."

Every Cherry street in all directions doubled back into another one, then turned to cul-de-sacs and dead ends. There wasn't a single cherry tree in sight. My daughter started wailing, all theatrics. She said, "We're lost in the suburbs! It's getting colder by the minute. I can barely blink my eyes..."

She fell over sideways against the car seat. "Go on without me!" she yelled. "One of us needs to keep going."

She was right, in a way. It was a cold place even there in the heat. In that neighborhood, there were no obvious problems, but there were no people either. There was nobody around except us.

I needed to smell the scent of decaying apples left to fall in a damp field. All the best parts of myself were strengthened by clinging close to the natural world. Living takes strength. My daughter needed to grow up with trees, to carry a connection with the land in her center, for whatever life brought up ahead.

I could see Mount Hood in the distance, tall and white with snow despite Oregon's drought years. That mountain is so elegant that it steals my breath every time. It watched over my shoulder, when I was a kid and ran wild.

Somewhere beyond the border of that neighborhood there had to be rough land. I wanted it. There'd be a yard big enough for a small farm. Wilderness. I headed toward the mountain. The road dead-ended again. I turned around in that funhouse maze, determined. I'd get us out of this. I was the mom. I wouldn't give up until I found a way back to raise my child on what was left of the earth's ragged Eden.

ACKNOWLEDGMENTS

The following stories have been previously published in the same or slightly different form: "Dearest Dear: Letter in a Culvert," *Menacing Hedge*; "See You Later, Fry-O-Lator," *Spork, Joyland,* and *The Lineup: 25 Provocative Women Writers*; "Help Wanted," under the title "Baby, I'm Here," in *Portland Noir*; "The Folly of Loving Life," *Three Penny Review* and as an independent chapbook by the author; "Models I Know" and "Honeymooning," *Alligator Juniper*.

THANK YOU

With all gratitude for the brilliance and kindness of so many, including the larger writing community, in all its intensity and love, and with particular appreciation for those who have supported my work along the way: Seth Fishman, Alexis Washam, Chuck Palahniuk, Lidia Yuknavitch, Rhonda Hughes, Suzy Vitello, Mary Wysong-Haeri, Erin Leonard, Chelsea Cain, Diana Page Jordan, Cheryl Strayed, Richard Thomas; Domi Shoemaker and the solid writing family at Burnt Tongue, who always make a place for me; Tom Spanbauer, Elizabeth Evans, Beth Alvarado; Cecily Crebbs and Storyland in Tucson; Jenny Forrester & the Unchaste reading series; Tom Manley for granting me time to complete the work and his words of wisdom in getting it done; Kevin Sampsell, Tina Morgan, Bryan Coffelt, Bianca Flores; Erin Ergenbright, Melanie Bishop; Wesley Stace and his Cabinet of Wonders; Lise Pacioretty, Mickey Lindsay, Sadie Lincoln, Cynthia Chimienti, Ann Duncan, Susan Musson, Kohel Haver; and always Barbara Drake, Albert Drake, and Mavis Drake-Alonso.

ABOUT THE AUTHOR

Monica Drake's debut indie novel, *Clown Girl,* (Hawthorne Books) won an Eric Hoffer Award, was a finalist for the Oregon Book Award, and spent time kicking around Hollywood optioned for film. She is the author of the novel *The Stud Book* (Hogarth/Crown). Her essays have appeared in *The New York Times, Paris Review Daily, Oregon Humanities Magazine, Northwest Review, Cut-throat, The Rumpus,* and other publications in print, on-line, and anthologized. She lives and works in Portland, Oregon, where she is a faculty member of the Pacific Northwest College of Art. (Photo by Chelsea Cain.)

CPSIA information can be obtained at www.ICGtesting.com
Printed in the USA
BVOW06s0925280216

438362BV00004B/8/P